Drybone
Hollow

Also by John Billheimer

Contrary Blues
Highway Robbery
Dismal Mountain

Drybone Hollow

John Billheimer

St. Martin's Minotaur ⚏ New York

www.minotaurbooks.com

Library of Congress Cataloging-in-Publication Data

Billheimer, John W.
    Drybone Hollow / John Billheimer.—1st ed.
    p. cm.
    ISBN 0-312-29121-3
    1. Allison, Owen (Fictitious character)—Fiction. 2. Government investigators—Fiction. 3. Coal mines and mining—Fiction. 4. West Virginia—Fiction. 5. Dam failures—Fiction. 6. Disasters—Fiction. I. Title.

PS3552.I452 D7 2003
813'.54—dc21

2002190755

First Edition: April 2003

10 9 8 7 6 5 4 3 2 1

For the Reverend Roy A. Lombard,
role model for the gods

Acknowledgments

This is a work of fiction. Names, characters, places, and incidents either are the product of the author's imagination or are used fictitiously. Any resemblance to actual persons (living or dead), events, or locales is entirely coincidental.

Every work of fiction reflects some matters of fact. As always, I am indebted to a number of people who helped me get a few facts straight. These include Mildred Billheimer, for a steady stream of clippings from my native state; Jim Billheimer, for construction particulars; Bruce Burgess for mine workings; Lisa, Denis, and Gail Boyer Hayes of the firm Hayes, Hayes, and Hayes, for legal and environmental details; April Holleman, for information on mall security; Bob Hubenette, for damage-assessment pointers; Dr. William Rogoway, for oncology procedures; and Don Steeples and others, for insights into the Martin County flood. Any blame for misstatements in these matters belongs to the author.

In the interests of spreading the blame, I once again wish to acknowledge the contributions of the Wednesday Night Pizza and Literary Society, whose members help to keep me on time, on track, and on my toes. Membership in this quasi-elite group includes:

Harriotte Aaron	Ann Hillesland
Sheila Scobba Banning	Melinda Kopecky
Bob Brownstein	Amy Mar
Anne Cheilek	Steve Skaar
Alison Derbenwick	Ellen Sussman
Scott Ennis	Anita Wahi

Finally, I wish to express my continued appreciation for the encouragement, support, and valued assistance of my agent, Ruth Cohen, my editor, Kelley Ragland, and her assistant, Ben Sevier.

The thoughts of others
  Were light and fleeting,
  Of lovers meeting
  Or luck or fame;
Mine were of trouble
  And mine were steady,
  So I was ready
  When trouble came.

—A. E. Housman, MORE POEMS

Drybone
Hollow

Prologue

The Black Flood

THE sheriff's office of Raleigh County, West Virginia, subsequently pieced together the movements of key individuals on the evening before what was to be called the greatest environmental disaster in the Southeastern United States.

At 9:30 p.m. on Saturday, March 12th, Riley Stokes missed the Trailways bus that would have taken him safely from Middleburg, Ohio, to Contrary, West Virginia, and his home in Drybone Hollow, to finish his junior year in high school.

At 10:30 p.m., Cable Stokes, Riley's father, heard his neighbor Maddie Tanner yelling at her husband Lyle as he left their trailer for his job as night watchman at the SpaceMart Mall in Contrary.

At 11:00 p.m., Purvis Jenkins, the mayor of Contrary, took two aspirin with a glass of tap water and went to bed. It was the last clear water that would come from his tap for more than a month.

At 11:15 p.m., Bill Muth, second-shift foreman at the Canaan II and Canaan III Mines above Drybone Hollow, shut down mining operations for the night.

At 3:30 a.m. Sunday morning, the impoundment dam holding coal waste on top of the Canaan II Mine failed, and three hundred million gallons of black coal slurry burst through the mine roof and poured out of the mouth of the main tunnel into Drybone Hollow.

The black ooze roared through the narrow hollow, tore the trailer homes of the Stokeses and the Tanners off their foundations, and carried them nearly a mile before they crashed into the piers at Crawley Creek Bridge.

The rampaging slurry collapsed the bridge and blackened the creek and the Little Muddy River on its way to the Big Sandy and the Ohio, leaving Maddie Tanner buried under twenty feet of muck, along with a couple from Tennessee who just happened to be crossing Crawley Creek Bridge when the black flood hit.

1

Going to Ground

Two men stood on the collapsed roadway leading to Crawley Creek Bridge the morning after the flood, looking down at the smooth black ribbon of slurry that flowed slowly between the surviving bridge piers. The black sheen stretched as far as the eye could see back up Drybone Hollow. An inky scum about six feet above the surface of the slurry recorded the high-water mark on either side of the hollow like the ring around a slow-draining bathtub.

Across the broken bridge, the aluminum underbelly of a half-submerged mobile home reflected sunlight at the two men from its boxed-in niche between the pier and the opposite bank.

The taller of the two, Lyle Tanner, a gaunt, hollow-eyed man wearing a slurry-splattered night watchman's uniform, sank down to sit on the roadway. "Maddie was so proud of that trailer. It would pain her to see it like this."

Cable Stokes, a heavy-set man whose protruding belly hid his belt buckle under a grimy T-shirt, squinted his tiny round eyes against the reflected light and put a puffy hand on Tanner's shoulder. "Don't pay to think on it, Lyle."

"The last words that passed between us were hateful, arguing words. About cigar smoke. Household smells. Spiteful words."

Stokes ran his free hand over his tight gray crew cut, which bristled in greasy spikes. "Like I said, best not to think on it."

"Seems silly now, arguing about such petty things."

"Try to think on the times you weren't arguing."

Tanner fell silent, then loosed a strangled half-sob, "Can't remember any." He blew his nose and peered out over the wrinkled handkerchief. "My God, who'd a thought it? To lose both our houses like that. Who'd a thought there was so much power in that goddamn sludge?"

Stokes eased himself down to the cracked asphalt beside his neighbor. "Sure seems like we must have made God's shitlist somehow."

Sightseers began to collect on the road behind the two men, pointing and gawking at the twisted concrete and the half-submerged trailer. Those who knew Lyle Tanner shook his hand or hugged him and told him how sorry they were about Maddie. By noon, cars were lined up on either side of the roadway and people crowded together in clumps on both banks of the broken bridge.

A short, sweaty man wearing a white linen suit used a battered leather briefcase to carve his way through the crowd and stand beside Lyle Tanner and Cable Stokes. He mopped the back of his neck with a handkerchief and announced to everyone within earshot, "Just come from downstream. The Big Sandy's black as a carload of coal. Contrary and Scobba have both turned off their water intakes. They'll have to start trucking in drinking water soon."

As his news percolated back through the crowd, the man stuffed his handkerchief into his pocket and held out his hand. "You'd be Lyle Tanner, I believe."

Tanner shook the hand and nodded.

"I'm Brady Jackson. I'm right sorry for your loss."

Tanner nodded again. " 'Preciate it."

Jackson handed Tanner a smudged business card. "I'm a lawyer by trade. Been talking to folks downstream. The muck spread out and ruined lots of homes, but nobody's as hard hit as you."

"Cable here was just saying we must have topped off God's shitlist."

4

"Sure seems like somebody ought to be made to pay," Jackson said.

Cable Stokes made a *tsk*ing noise with his tongue. "I figure the feds will come in, declare us a disaster, and start doling out some money."

"The feds." Jackson picked up a small chunk of broken concrete and tossed it over the twisted rebar spears into the black slime below. Instead of sinking, the chunk rode the top of the muck flowing slowly between the standing piers. "That hunk of concrete will be in the ocean before the feds even know your names. They're real quick to take your money, but slow as molasses in January when it comes to paying any out.

"When they do pay, they eke it out like the last gob from a toothpaste tube." Jackson pointed across the shiny black surface to the opposite bank. "See that upended mobile home?"

Tanner nodded. "That's mine."

"Oh. Sorry. But, hell's bells, you might as well know what's coming. If that home were brand new, the feds might replace it for you. But if it's not, they'll depreciate it like a totaled automobile. If it's more than fifteen years old, like as not you'll be lucky to get enough to replace the doormat."

Tanner's shoulders slumped. "Hell, we had it for at least twenty years."

"Sorry to be the bearer of bad news," Jackson said. "Look here, though. If you want to come out of this whole, you got to go after the bastards with the deep pockets. Hit the mining companies. They're the ones responsible. You got to haul their asses into court. Sue their hides off."

Tanners voice was tentative, uncertain. "You're saying we should sue Big Coal?"

"They're the ones made this mess. They're the ones who ought to clean it up." Jackson reached into his briefcase and pulled out a clipboard with a sheaf of typed forms. "What I been doing this morning is lining up some of the folks downstream for a class-action suit."

He held the clipboard out between Tanner and Stokes. "Now, you two have been hit hardest, so you'd stand to get the most from a lawsuit."

"How much could we get?" Stokes asked, barely a heartbeat before Tanner asked, "How much would it cost?"

"Won't cost you a thing, lessen I deliver the goods. Then I just take my cut out of Big Coal's payment." Jackson held a pen up beside the clipboard forms. "All you got to do is sign on the dotted line."

A snake slithered along the surface of the black slime, leaving a curving trail in its wake. When it reached the edge, it crooked around a dead fish and disappeared into the muck-encrusted grass.

"Nothing'll live in that sludge down there," Jackson said. "That's one reason the coal companies won't stand a chance in court. They've screwed up the environment. Believe me, they'll have to pay big time."

"How big?" Cable Stokes asked again. "How much could they have to pay?"

Jackson clicked the button on top of the pen in his hand over and over. "Well, Mr. Tanner here lost his wife. Now you surely can't put a price tag on a person's life, but my guess is, the coal companies will have to pay him a half million to a million just for that loss alone."

"A half million to a million?" Stokes repeated.

"They won't do it out of the goodness of their hearts, mind you," Jackson said. "We'll have to go after them in court."

Stokes eyed the pen in Jackson's hand. "But it could be as much as a million dollars?"

"Don't see why not," Jackson said. "Pittsfield Coal paid about a hundred grand apiece to Buffalo Creek survivors, and that was nigh onto thirty years ago. That'd work out to at least a half million today, allowing for inflation."

Tanner sucked in his breath. "My land."

"And that's not even considering what you might get for your home and your pain and suffering." Jackson shoved the pen and clipboard toward Tanner. "Just sign on the dotted line and I'll do my damnedest to get what's coming to you."

Tanner grabbed the pen and scribbled a signature on the top sheet.

Jackson put an unsigned form on top of Tanner's agreement and passed the clipboard to Stokes.

Stokes took the clipboard in both hands and shook his head slowly.

"What's the matter?" Tanner asked. "You worried about your brother the mine owner?"

"Hell, Anson never worried about me. Why'd I worry about him?"

"What is worrying you then?" Jackson asked.

Stokes half coughed to clear his throat, then said, "My boy Riley's missing."

Tanner put his arm around Stoke's shoulder. "Cable. Why didn't you say something?"

"Well, you was going on about Maddie." Stokes coughed again, bringing the back of his wrist up to cover his mouth. "And you know how teenagers are. I didn't see him before I left home last night. When he didn't show after the dam burst, I kept hoping I'd see him this morning."

Stokes raised the back of his wrist and wiped it slowly across his eyes. "But I didn't. I sure didn't."

He took the pen from Jackson and signed the top form. "I guess I better face up to it. Riley's missing for sure."

CABLE STOKES SAT alone in his battered blue pickup a half-block away from the diner that served as the Trailways bus station in Contrary. It was 3:25 on Monday morning, almost exactly twenty-four hours after the black flood came pouring out of the Canaan II Mine. The diner had been closed since midnight, and Cable had shot out the streetlight above him before settling in to wait for the bus. He fingered the butt of the revolver stuffed in the belt under his frayed denim jacket and stared down the deserted street, hoping there'd be no one else meeting the southbound Memphis run.

At 3:40, the bus pulled up alongside the darkened diner. The door hissed open and a rangy teenage boy swung down onto the sidewalk.

The boy dropped his backpack at his feet and lit a cigarette as the bus pulled away. Cable waited until the bus was out of sight before he turned on his headlights, flashed them once, and pulled slowly forward.

The boy opened the pickup door and flicked a spray of glowing ash onto the sidewalk. "Didn't see you back there."

"Get in, quick."

The boy flung his backpack into the pickup bed and swung his lean frame up into the passenger seat.

Cable pulled the truck into the alley behind the diner, parked, and turned off the headlights. "Anybody see you? Anybody you know on the bus?"

"No, why?" The boy's cigarette glowed as he squinted through the smoke at his father. "Why are we stopping?"

"Got no place to go, Riley."

"What happened? We heard on the news the dam broke, but we couldn't get through by phone."

"Black ooze come roaring down, took our trailer right off its foundations. Must be halfway to Ashland by now."

"My God."

"Was expecting you last night." Cable took his right hand off the wheel and shifted in his seat.

Riley ducked back reflexively, fearing he was about to be hit. "I'm sorry I missed the bus, Dad. Aunt Essie's car wouldn't start."

Cable reached out and patted his son's shoulder. "Hell's bells, don't apologize. If I hadn't been up here waiting for you, I'd be down there floating with our trailer right now, buried in black muck."

"Aunt Essie said you were pretty pissed on the phone last night."

"That was before I knew what had happened at the dam. By the time I got back to our hollow, it was a sea of slurry."

"What about the Tanners?"

"Their trailer's lodged against the Crawley Creek Bridge. Maddie Tanner's somewhere under the muck."

"Mrs. Tanner. Oh, Jesus."

A car's headlights swung into the alley and came slowly toward them. Cable hunched down below the steering wheel and tugged Riley down too. "Jesus had nothing to do with it. It was them damn careless mine owners. Your uncle included."

Riley Stokes peeked out over the dashboard. "Why we ducking down, Dad?"

"Brights blinded me, is all."

Riley stubbed his cigarette in the pickup's ash tray. "Anybody else dead? Anybody we know?"

Cable Stokes straightened and watched the car disappear in his rearview mirror. His protruding stomach chafed against the butt of the revolver. " 'Fraid so, son."

"Who?"

"You, son. You're about to go to ground."

2

The Returns of the Native

O WEN Allison started to steer their shopping cart toward the nearest checkout lane when his mother Ruth tugged at his sleeve.

"Let's go through Maude's lane," Ruth said. "She always enjoys seeing you."

Maude was the mother of one of Owen's classmates at Barkley Catholic High School. He'd been trying to avoid her checkout lane, because he knew he'd feel embarrassed when it came time to pay the bill. In deference to his mother, though, he loaded the cart's groceries onto the conveyor belt leading to Maude's register and watched as the plump, frizzy-haired woman dragged a box of Raisin Bran over the scanner.

"Talked to Ginny the other day," Maude said, bagging the box of cereal. "She was surprised to hear you were back in Barkley."

"He's just here till I can get around a little better," Ruth said.

"Ginny's oldest just got accepted at Pepperdine. That's out by where you used to live, isn't it?"

"No, Pepperdine's in Southern California. I'm from the Northern half, around San Francisco."

Maude examined a six-pack of Stroh's beer as if she were a temperance worker. "Still in the same state, though."

"California's a little bigger than West Virginia, Maude," Ruth said.

"Why, my goodness, Ruth, I know that. I was out there visiting my grandkids just last year." Maude started a second bag with the Stroh's. "You never had any children, did you, Owen?"

"No."

"Too bad. That's what life's all about." Maude finished bagging the groceries, rang up the total, and announced, "That'll be fifty dollars and forty-eight cents, Ruth."

Owen winced inwardly. The woman hadn't even bothered to pretend that he might be paying for the groceries.

Ruth laid three crisp twenty-dollar bills on the counter. "Let me pay for this, Owen. You got last night's dinner."

Owen appreciated his mother's white lie, but it was clear the clerk wasn't fooled by it. She'd seen Ruth pay for their groceries their last four trips to the store.

Owen had come home to Barkley five months ago to help his mother through surgery and chemotherapy treatments for ovarian cancer. At the time, he'd had three months' worth of back payments for consulting coming from the California Department of Transportation. He'd managed to stretch those payments over four months, but for the last month his mother had insisted on covering their bills with her savings and pension income.

Maude loaded the two bags of groceries into the shopping cart. "Don't expect you'll be needing help to the car?"

Ruth shook her head. "No, we're walking home."

Owen took one of the bags from the shopping cart and reached for the other, but his mother beat him to it, saying, "Let me take that."

Owen smiled. "You must be getting stronger, Mom. I remember when you couldn't lift twenty-five dollars' worth of groceries by yourself."

"Son, I remember when twenty-five dollars' worth of groceries would last a month."

"Ain't it the truth," Maude said.

Outside, Owen zipped up his Cincinnati Reds windbreaker and bent to untie the leash of a small black and white dog that stood on its hind legs, pawing at his knees.

Ruth set her bag of groceries on the ground, smoothed down the stray wisps of hair that poked out under her stocking cap, and tugged the cap down around her ears. Then she pulled on a pair of mittens, clapped twice, and said, "Good dog, Buster."

Buster danced back and forth between Owen and Ruth, tail wagging. When a young mother approached wheeling a stroller, the dog expanded its performance area to a triangle to take her in.

The mother knelt and scratched Buster behind both ears. "That tail's a perpetual motion machine. What kind of dog is it?"

"Poodle."

The woman stood. "Doesn't look like any poodle I've ever seen."

"Those fluffy cuts don't suit his name or personality." Because poodles with traditional powderpuff cuts had been the dog of choice of pampered rich dowagers in the movies he'd watched growing up, Owen insisted that Buster be trimmed without any frills, getting what the groomers called their "mutt cut."

Ruth ignored Buster and bent over the baby stroller. "How old's your little girl?"

"Fourteen months."

"She's lovely. That's what life's all about." Ruth straightened and turned to Owen. "Let's walk home by the creek."

The sun had cleared enough of the ridge above them to take the bite out of the clear February air and cause the gurgling water of Dogwood Run to sparkle as Owen and Ruth walked beside it. Buster strained against his leash, trying to go faster than Ruth's slow, measured pace would allow.

About halfway home, Ruth sat her groceries down beside a stone bench facing the creek and said, "Let's rest here for a spell."

Owen sat on one edge of the bench, unleashed Buster, and threw a tennis ball back up the winding footpath. The dog chased after the ball, retrieved it on the third bounce, and returned it to Owen's lap.

Ruth settled into the bench and crossed her arms. "Owen, honey, I sure appreciate having you around, but don't you think it's about time you headed back to California?"

Owen bounced the ball high off the dirt footpath and Buster scampered after it. "I'll go as soon as you can make the three-block walk home from the store without stopping to rest halfway."

"The groceries aren't going to spoil in the time it takes me to recharge my batteries. Besides, it's pleasant sitting here in the sun." She toed a pebble into the rippling creek. "It's hard to believe that just a few miles downstream the Little Muddy is black as pitch."

"They say the cleanup could take six months or more."

"There ought to be a law. Those mining dams are a sin against nature."

Owen was only ten when his father was killed fighting floodwaters from a failed mining dam. Thirty-eight years later, he could still remember watching his mother fix hot meals for the divers dragging the river for missing bodies.

Buster barked and Owen realized he'd been hanging onto the tennis ball, staring into the flowing waters. He threw the ball back up the path. "I hear at least four people died this time."

"One of them was just a teenager. A boy named Riley Stokes. Didn't you go to high school with two of the Stokes boys?"

"For a while. Neither of them graduated."

"I hear one of them's doing quite well."

"Which one? Anson or Cable?"

"Anson, I think."

"Was the dead boy his son?"

"Son or nephew, I'm not sure which. They're all related somehow."

Owen remembered the Stokes brothers in high school, finger-giving, hollow-dwelling outsiders in dirty overalls, quiet in the classroom but noisy outside it, regaling their classmates with tales of hot-wiring, shine-swilling, and gang-banging that were as far from Owen's experience as his passion for Buster Keaton, baseball, and Broadway musicals was from theirs. They vanished midway through their junior year, when the nuns shipped them both off to vocational school after one of their cousins turned up pregnant.

"Hard to imagine either of the Stokes boys turning out well," Owen said.

Buster returned with the tennis ball, rose up on his hind legs, and dropped it in Owen's lap. Owen stood and threw it as far as he could, then watched it bounce off the path into a patch of creekside weeds with Buster in hot pursuit.

"If you don't get back to California soon," Ruth said, "you may not have a business to get back to. You'll have to haul in your Failure Analysis shingle and analyze your own failure."

"I just need to write a few proposals. The business will come around." He wondered if that were true. Proposals were the bane of his business. And it would take at least two months with no contracts before bureaucrats could respond to anything he proposed now.

"You always said proposals are a crapshoot at best. And there's Judith. She won't wait forever. You need to get back together with her. Start a family."

Buster was rooting in the creekside weeds for the tennis ball. He returned to the path with no ball and stared, panting and empty-mouthed, at Owen.

I know how you feel, buddy, Owen thought. "Mom," he said. "Judith and I have a lot to settle before we start a family."

"Seemed like you got a lot of things settled the last time she was here."

"We did. But family planning wasn't one of those things. We'd have to remarry first. And it's not even clear she wants a family."

"I just don't understand why you're staying around here when your business and wife are in California."

"Ex-wife."

"That's one of the first things you need to fix." Ruth clapped her mittens together twice. Buster returned to the path, stared down at them, and then dove back into the weeds. "It's that senator, isn't it? That Dusty Rhodes. You've been staying around to dig up dirt on him."

"I told you. I've been staying around to help you through your chemo treatments."

"And don't think for a minute I don't appreciate it. But it's true, isn't it? You've been poking into the senator's business, hoping to bring him down."

"Just a little. In my spare time." Owen was convinced that the senator had ordered the death of a good friend and probably seduced Judith, his ex-wife, as well. How could he not try to bring him down?

"Owen, if there were evidence around to bring him down, don't you think his political enemies would have found it?"

"The political enemies I've seen couldn't find their ass with an anatomy textbook and both hands free. Besides, they have the disadvantage of being out while he's in."

"He's a dangerous man, Owen."

"Don't worry. I'm well under his radar."

Buster bounded out of the weeds, shook off a shower of water, and tore down the footpath toward them with his tail wagging and the ball clamped firmly in his mouth.

"Owen, whatever you think the senator did is blood under the bridge. You've got to get over it and get back to your life."

Buster skidded to a stop and nosed the tennis ball so it landed at Owen's feet.

"Back to California," Ruth repeated.

Owen laughed and picked up the wet tennis ball. "Give it a rest, Mom. You're as persistent as Buster."

"But not so cute." Ruth rose and retrieved her bag of groceries. "In my day, though, I could fetch tennis balls with the best of them."

As Owen, Ruth, and Buster turned into the cul-de-sac leading to Ruth's house, they saw a black widebody parked just beyond their driveway.

"My goodness, what's that?" Ruth asked.

"A Hummer. It's the latest status symbol for road hogs."

"Well, it's hogging our road for sure. I don't see how anything but a bicycle could get past it."

The words CANAAN THREE were painted inside a yellow circle on the driver's door of the parked Hummer. Buster sniffed at the vehicle's tires, then strained at his leash and began barking in the direction of Ruth's house.

"There's somebody sitting in our porch swing," Ruth said.

The swing moved, and a hulking man wearing a black baseball cap stood up. "Anybody you know?" Owen asked.

"I don't think so."

The man descended their porch steps to meet them, coming as close to a swagger as his short, stubby legs would allow. A black windbreaker with an insignia matching the one on the Hummer's door bloused out over a bull-like torso. His baseball cap had the monogram C3 stitched above its black brim.

There was something familiar about the near swagger, but Owen didn't make the connection until the man's strong, calloused hand was squeezing his.

"I can see you don't remember me. I'm Anson Stokes. From Barkley Catholic."

"Of course." Owen squeezed back, but it was a losing battle. Stokes stopped pumping his hand, but didn't release the pressure. "I recognized you right off, even with the beard. Of course, your picture was in the paper recent."

Seeking relief from the pressure, Owen said, "You remember my mom."

Stokes released Owen's hand and raised his black cap. "Don't believe I've had the pleasure."

"Oh, I remember you," Ruth said. "It's been quite a while, though. Won't you come back up on our porch?"

Stokes led the way back up the steps. "Your neighbors said you were out walking. I just made myself to home. I hope you don't mind."

Ruth paused at the doorway. "Goodness no. Can I get you something to drink? Coffee? Tea?"

Owen hefted his bag of groceries. "There's beer in the bottom of this sack."

"Beer sounds good."

Owen fished a six-pack of Stroh's out of the grocery bag, twisted the cap off a bottle, and handed it to Stokes.

17

Stokes took a swig and smacked his lips. "Nothing like a cold one." He stared hard at Owen and said, "Won't you be joining me?" in a tone that was more like a command than an invitation.

Owen was about to say, "It's a little early for me," when some inner monitor triggered by Stokes' tone clicked and he heard himself saying, "What the hell, why not?" and opened a beer for himself.

Ruth disappeared inside the house and returned with two tall glasses. Seeing that both men were drinking from their bottles, she excused herself and went back inside, taking Owen's grocery bag with her.

Stokes took another swig of beer. "Yessir, it's been quite a while." The good-ole-boy smile vanished and gave way to a hard, measuring stare. "Expect you've heard about the black flood downriver?"

"Hard not to."

"The muck came through one of my mines, the Canaan II."

Owen's face must have shown surprise, because Stokes smiled grimly and said, "Never would have figured me for a mine owner, huh?"

"Not at all. I heard you were doing well."

"Was until the flood let loose. Now I've got everyone from greenies to the governor on my ass. They're all over me, like vultures on roadkill." Stokes took another swig of beer and wiped his mouth with the back of his hand. "Well, I'm here to tell you I ain't roadkill."

"That can't be the only reason you're here."

"No, I come because I want to hire you. I want you to take a look at my mine, figure out what went wrong, and report on it."

"Why me?"

"Because that's what you do. Figure out why things fail. And because I know you to be smart and honest." Stokes pointed the mouth of his beer bottle at Owen. "What's more, the whole county knows you to be smart and honest. You nailed Amalgamated Coal for the dam burst that killed your dad."

"Fifteen years after he died. And it didn't make me real popular. Amalgamated pulled up stakes after that and took a thousand jobs out of state. There are still folks in this county that won't talk to me."

"Point is, that didn't stop you. You figured out the fault and went after them."

"All I did was figure out the fault. Lawyers went after them."

"That's all I want you to do here. Just figure out what went wrong."

Owen needed the money. But Anson Stokes was the last person in the world he thought he'd ever want to work for. He smiled and shook his head. "You're right. I never figured you for a mine owner."

"I started out in the coal hauling business. Cable and I had a truck together. Then we got ourselves a dog hole. Early seventies, though, everything went belly up around here. The spot market for coal went to hell. Everybody was bailing, including Cable. I bought him out and got myself a few mine leases dirt cheap."

Stokes toasted the air with his beer bottle. "Best lick I ever hit. Nineteen seventy-four brought the oil crisis and it was like coining money here in the hills. Spot market jumped from ten dollars a ton to thirty dollars a ton in two months. I mean, what the hell, up thirty percent in two months. That's not too shabby."

Owen laughed once, then stared at Stokes, who didn't seem to realize he'd just made a joke.

Stokes stopped in mid-sentence. "Why are you looking at me funny?"

"Ten dollars to thirty dollars is a two-hundred percent increase. Not thirty."

Stokes' brow wrinkled. "Don't be silly. How can you have more than a hundred percent of anything?"

Satisfied with his own analysis, Stokes continued, "I went from being dirt poor to clearing five grand a week. And it wasn't just me. High school dropouts with no more than a dump truck and a dog hole were making more than the president of the U.S."

"Well, 1974 was a bad year for President Nixon."

"I kept parlaying one mine into another and never looked back."

Owen sipped at his beer. "What became of Cable?"

"Got comfortable on welfare. Shiftless as a busted transmission. Wife run off and left him to raise four boys on the government tit."

Stokes set his empty bottle down on the stone porch railing. "Infected his boys with his own damn shiftlessness. You could have got them all jobs as pie-testers, chauffered them to and from work, and hired somebody to hold their mouths open. They would have bitched that there was too much chewing and quit. But not before they filed a complaint that their jaws had been weakened by repetitive workplace stress or some other damn foolishness."

Owen laughed.

"Tain't funny," Stokes said. "I tried to give Cable's oldest, Billy Joe, a start working at my mine. He hadn't been in the hole a week when he complained of a bad back and went on disability. I'm still paying out workman's comp."

"Was it one of Cable's boys that was lost in the flood?"

Stokes reacted as if he'd been stung by an invisible insect. "His youngest, Riley. Goddamn shame. He was the only one worth the powder to blow him up." He rubbed the back of his neck and shook his head slowly. "I run the safest mines in the county. Ask any of the inspectors. You got to look into it. Find out what went wrong. Will you do that for me?"

The more Owen listened, the less he wanted to work for Anson Stokes. He tried to figure out why. He didn't think he was jealous of Stokes' success. Owen's apartment complex in California had been filled with newly minted dot-com millionaires who boasted that they were "going to get the money thing out of the way by the time they were twenty-eight." He hadn't begrudged the Internet princes their success. Why would he begrudge Anson Stokes his?

"I don't know, Anson. I've been away from my work for five months. I was just saying to Mom that I've got to be getting back to California."

Stokes closed the distance between them. He was almost a foot shorter than Owen's six feet, but he thrust his face up within six inches of Owen's nose. "Goddamn it, haven't you been listening? It's work I'm offering you. Here and now. Did you think I wasn't going to pay you?"

Stokes' flushed face was so close to his that Owen could have leaned forward and bitten the bill of his baseball cap. The miner's chin and chest bulled forward, and his hands balled into fists that bore into his hips.

Owen recalled a scene from their high school days when Stokes had assumed a similar pose opposite him on a street corner in downtown Barkley. At the time, Stokes was just telling a bawdy story, but his stance was so pugnacious that a small crowd had collected just out of earshot, thinking they were about to see a fight. Stokes was oblivious to the crowd, but Owen was uncomfortably aware of their expectations. When Stokes finally delivered the punchline and laughed, breaking the tension, the onlookers drifted away, muttering their disappointment and leaving Owen embarrassed.

Stokes thrust his chin even farther forward. "I don't get it. It's what you do, isn't it? Figure out why things fail?"

Owen was aware that his mother was watching through the screen door, concern written on her face. He did what he should have done in high school and took a step backward, distancing himself from the bobbing baseball cap. "You don't really need me, Anson. The paper says the governor is going to appoint a blue-ribbon panel to investigate the cause of the flood."

"He'll appoint a bunch of shrub cuddlers and tree huggers. They've been looking to railroad me ever since the mine opened. Them as ain't greenies will side with Dusty Rhodes."

Now it was Owen's turn to close the distance between them. He brought himself back within range of the baseball cap and put his hand on Stokes' shoulder to keep from eating the cap's bill. "Wait a minute. What's Rhodes got to do with this?"

"He owns the dam. Or Mountain View Development does. Same difference."

"But the mine under it is yours?"

"That's what I've been telling you."

"Why build a dam on top of an underground mine?"

"Hell, the dam takes up at least a half-mile of hollow. Anything that takes up that much space in coal country is bound to be on top of a mine. Or right next to one."

"But Rhodes owns the dam?"

"And the processing plant. That make a difference? I can understand if you don't want to get on the wrong side of Dusty Rhodes."

"I'm already on the wrong side of Dusty Rhodes."

"Then you're on the right side of me."

"What if I look into this and find you're at fault?"

"No frigging chance."

"If I do, though, I've got to be free to go public with whatever I find."

"You mean our deal's not like with priests and lawyers?"

"I'm not a priest or a lawyer, Anson. If I find you're at fault, I won't forgive it or finagle it."

"I can live with that. Does that mean we got a deal?"

Owen extended his hand. "We've got a deal."

Stokes squeezed Owen's hand even harder than he had on their meeting. "I'll get you the mine layout and inspection records." He reached inside his windbreaker and pulled out a checkbook in a black leather holder. "Let me give you a retainer. How much do you charge?"

Owen decided to quote him the rate fully loaded with overhead. He still had his California office rent to pay. "I get a hundred dollars an hour."

Stokes frowned. Owen worried that he'd queered the deal by quoting California prices in a West Virginia economy.

Stokes scribbled something on a check. "That all? Hell, my lawyers charge me two hundred an hour just for shuffling papers."

Owen felt as foolish as he had when the crowd had collected around them in high school "Well, I've got to keep my prices low to compete for government jobs."

Stokes handed the check to Owen. It was made out for four thousand dollars. "Here's an advance to get you started. Let me know when you need more."

"This is a week's pay. I shouldn't need this much."

"Consider that a minimum. I'll call you as soon as we can get into the mine to look around." Stokes started down the porch steps, then turned and said, "Glad we could get together on this. Good seeing you again, Owen."

"Same here."

Ruth Allison joined her son on the porch as Stokes maneuvered his Hummer out of their cul-de-sac. "That's quite a vehicle."

"It would cost me a year's salary." Owen pocketed Stokes' check and reflected that, if he didn't get back to full-time work soon, a used Hyundai would cost him a year's salary.

3

Acts of God

T HE next morning, Owen drove to Drybone Hollow to assess the
flood damage and watch the cleanup operation. He wanted to
see firsthand the effects of the raging slurry before investigating its
causes. The hollow itself was completely devastated from the mouth
of the Canaan II Mine to the Crawley Creek Bridge. He photographed two razed foundations where sludge-covered cinderblocks
served as tombstones for homes swept away by the rampaging slurry.
The muck that remained in the creek bed had shrunk to a depth of
two feet, but the black netting on an abandoned basketball hoop and
the scum that rimmed the hollow like a dingy bathtub ring showed
that the river of slurry had been at least ten feet deep and two hundred
feet wide when it exploded out of the mouth of the mine.

At the Crawley Creek Bridge, the flood had left an upended mobile
home lodged between a pier and the far bank. Exposed rebar from the
broken bridge poked out of the crumpled concrete like the rigid ten-
tacles of a dead octopus. A dredge operating along the near bank
sucked sludge from the bottom of the creekbed and fed it into waiting
trucks.

Beyond the bridge, the channel widened, dissipating the force of the flood. The scummy residue showed that the slurry had spread to a width of four hundred feet in spots, but most houses had been set far enough back from the creekbed so that only garages and outbuildings were damaged.

Houses became more frequent and more upscale as Owen followed the frontage road that paralleled the winding creekbed beyond the bridge. He stopped when he recognized the name on a rural mailbox. Tharp. Dan and Mary Tharp had been friends of his parents, playing in penny-ante poker games on Friday evenings before his father died.

He had parked his car and started up the walk when he heard a loud humming noise coming from the rear of the orange brick house. Behind the house, a manicured lawn sloped down about a hundred yards to the creek bed. The last fifty yards, which included a garage and flower garden, were overlaid with a veneer of glistening sludge that reached to the windows of the garage and bent the branches of rose and rhododendron bushes. The garage door had been scrubbed down, and a coiled garden hose and two sudsy buckets sat in the driveway.

A thick umbilical cord led from the center of the creek to a tank truck parked beside the garage. The humming noise Owen had heard was the sound of a pump siphoning sludge from the bottom of the creekbed to the truck.

Two canvas director's chairs and a camp table had been set up on the lawn at the edge of the sludge line. A man and a woman sat in the chairs, facing the creekbed with their backs to Owen. Standing beside the camp table, a man wearing an orange jumpsuit and black goggles had taken off one work glove so that he could handle a tumbler full of lemonade.

The man in the orange jumpsuit watched as Owen approached, but the couple in the director's chairs kept their backs to him. Finally he said, loudly enough to be heard over the pump noise, "Dan? Mary?"

The couple turned to look at Owen. The man stood up, smiling. Small and wiry, with thinning blonde hair and lively blue eyes, he was wearing tan chinos, a navy blue windbreaker, and black boots with unfastened metal clasps that dangled around his ankles. Owen recognized him immediately, but realized as the man's smile faded uncertainly that Dan had no idea who had just called his name.

Owen extended his hand. "I'm sorry. It's been quite a while. I'm Owen Allison."

The man's smile returned.

His wife stood up beside him. "Of course," she said. "You're Ruth and Wayne's youngest. Dan, run to the garage and get a chair for Owen."

"The rest of the chairs are all gunked up."

"Well, bring one from the house then."

"That's all right," Owen said. "I don't mind standing."

Mary Tharp was taller and broader than her husband. She wore a pink sweater, beige slacks that disappeared into unfastened pink boots, and dark glasses that Owen remembered hid a right eye with a severe cast. "Isn't this a pleasant surprise," she said. "How's your mom?"

"Much better, thanks. She'll tell you she's in good shape for the shape she's in."

"That sounds like Ruth," Mary said. "We visited her at your Aunt Lizzie's hospice just after her operation."

"That's a pretty grim place, that hospice," Dan said. "Not many make it out of there alive."

"Mom's been lucky so far."

Suddenly remembering the man in the orange suit, Mary said, "Well, I'm forgetting my manners. This here's Mr. Hank Clanton, of Johnson, Crane, and Associates. He's helping the state clean up this mess. Mr. Clanton, this is Owen Allison, the son of old and dear friends."

Clanton raised his goggles, exposing black rings around both eyes, and lifted his lemonade glass in salute.

"My goodness, Owen," Mary said, "the last I remember of you is your little face poking through the banister over the poker table. Whatever brings you here?"

"I've been asked to investigate the cause of the flood. Thought I'd look things over, see how the cleanup is going. Saw your name on the mailbox."

"Aren't we glad you did," Mary said.

"How is the cleanup going?" Owen asked Clanton.

"Pretty slow. We've got four dredges going, along with maybe twenty-five of these trucks and three hundred workers. Not nearly enough, if you ask me."

"How long will it take?"

"They're saying six months, but I don't see how they can make good on that promise. It's like cleaning a stable with a wisk broom. You can get the job done, but it'll take a while, and you're a little too close to the crud for comfort."

"Where are you trucking the crud?" Owen asked.

"There's settling ponds the next hollow over, along with a whole batch of ditches we dug to dry it out."

"Environmentalists are trying to have it declared toxic waste," Dan said.

"There's some mercury and lead in it," Clanton said. "Sulphur too, of course. We're still getting a neutral pH on it, though."

"What nonsense," Mary said. "It's mostly coal dust, clay, and water. Only way it's harmful is if you get too much in one spot, like here, or are under ten feet of it, like that poor woman in Drybone Hollow. It's not bad in small doses. Dan and I used to sneak some out of the dam to use as fertilizer."

"It'll grow grass on doorknobs," Dan said.

"Not much call for that," Mary said. "Sure helped my roses, though. Till it came down from that dam in great galloping gobs."

Owen nodded at the tank truck. "Who's paying for all of this?"

Clanton put his empty glass down on the camp table. "Governor declared an emergency, ordered Mountain View to clean up its mess. We'll be billing them. If they don't pay, guess we'll bill the state."

"Heard the cleanup alone could cost twenty million," Dan said. "And that's not counting damages."

"Mountain View must be insured," Owen said.

"Got to be," Dan said. "They just opened a storefront in Contrary to handle folks' claims."

"George Sink wasn't too happy with their claim handling," Mary said.

"George lives just up the creek," Dan said. "He took his claims in. Turns out they wanted receipts for everything, then offered him thirty cents on the dollar. Wanted him to sign a paper saying he wouldn't sue."

"He walked right out on them," Mary said.

Dan shook his head. "May have to go back, though. His house is a lot closer to the creek than ours. He's got a lot more damage."

"What about suing?" Owen asked.

"There's more lawyers around than you can shake a stick at." Dan ran his hand through his thinning hair and stared at his black-rimmed garage. "Which is maybe what you ought to do to them."

"There's a couple of class-action suits in the works," Mary said. "But they'll take a while to settle. Mountain View will give you cash right now."

"Just not as much of it," Dan said. "Not near as much as you need."

"That's what Mountain View is counting on. People who need the money will settle quickly for much less than they could get if they waited." Owen ran the toe of his shoe along the manicured lawn just shy of the high-water line. "What'll you and Mary do?"

Dan shrugged. "Wait it out. We're not hurting. There's talk the president might declare us a disaster area, get FEMA involved. That'd be another source of funds."

"I can't imagine finding receipts for everything we lost." Mary waved her hand halfheartedly toward the bushes bending under their coal black burden. "Took me ten years to grow those rhodies. Don't know that I've got ten more to put into them."

Dan put his arm around his wife's shoulder. "Somebody ought to pay, that's for sure."

Clanton pulled on his work glove and adjusted his goggles. "They're calling it an Act of God."

"Try sending Him your bill," Owen said.

Mary frowned. "God didn't build that dam on top of a worked-out mine."

" 'Act of God' is just legal talk," Dan said. "It's a loophole Mountain View is trying to squeeze through."

"They'll find a way to do it, too, if the past is any guide," Mary said. "Big Coal's been screwing up these hollows for a hundred years without ever being called to account."

Dan tightened his grip on his wife's shoulder. "That's not true, Mary. Owen here nailed Amalgamated Coal for the flood that killed Wayne."

Mary shrugged free of Dan's hug. "Fifteen years too late." She adjusted her sunglasses and looked sideways at Owen. "People thank you for that, did they, Owen? As I recall, Ruth had to bring in groceries from Charleston to keep from facing people who'd lost their Amalgamated paychecks."

"We didn't exactly win the hearts and minds of the rest of the county," Owen said.

"I'd say not," Mary said. "Big Coal owns eighty percent of the land in this county and a hundred percent of what's under it. I can't put my hoe six inches deep in my own garden without trespassing on their mineral rights."

The steady thrum of the sump pump was suddenly drowned out by the noise of an engine in the driveway. They all turned to see a motorcyclist clad in black leathers brake a dusty black Harley between the two sudsy buckets in front of the garage door. The motorcyclist dismounted, took a sheaf of papers from a black briefcase, and started down the lawn toward them.

As the motorcyclist approached, he raised his visor to reveal a clerical collar, then took off his helmet to expose a totally bald head to the morning sunlight. His eyebrows and lashes were so pale there appeared to be no hair anywhere on his face. In place of hair, a half-inch blue band had been tattooed around his skull.

"Oh, for Christ's sake," Dan said under his breath.

The motorcyclist stopped at the edge of the high-water line, knelt, and uprooted a handful of slurry-stained grass. Standing, he raised the grass overhead and flung it to the earth, saying in a deep, sonorous voice, "It's an abomination unto the Lord."

He bowed his head briefly, then pierced each of them with his pale gray eyes and said, "Good morning. I'm the Reverend Moral Brody."

"We've heard you speak," Mary said. She introduced herself, Dan, Owen, and Hank Clanton.

Owen held out his hand while Clanton fumbled with his work glove. Dan made no move to acknowledge the introduction.

The Reverend held up his right hand, showing its sludge-blackened palm. "Sorry I'm not able to shake your hands." He handed each of them a gray sheet of paper and announced, "I'm here to invite you to a candlelight vigil for the deceased at the Drybone Hollow Dam this Saturday night."

Owen glanced at the sheet of paper, which was smudged with slurry stains from the Reverend's black handprint. It advertised the vigil, listed the names of the four flood victims, and displayed a hand-drawn map of the road leading to the dam site. He looked from the flyer to the Reverend, who he guessed must be at least fifty years old. Up close, he could see that the tattoo encircling the bald head was a series of interlocking vines.

"I see you staring at my halo," the Reverend said.

Owen smiled. "It looks more like a crown of thorns."

"Depends on the sermon of the day. Today it's a halo, and I'm an avenging angel ready to smite the coal-loving, land-defiling, God-challenged parasites responsible for this abomination to your land." The Reverend took a long breath and continued. "They have the nerve to call this an 'Act of God.' It's a celestial insult. It's not the King of Kings that did this, but King Coal. Not the Almighty, but the Almighty Dollar. Not the Light of the World, but the World of the Lightfingered."

The Reverend paused, chuckled, and shook his head. "Well, you get the idea. Come to the vigil and hear the rest of it."

He donned his black helmet, which had a white halo painted around it. "Tell your friends and neighbors. We need to shout loud enough to give these parasites God's answer."

The Reverend flipped down his visor, turned, and strode off to his motorcycle. The back of his black leather jacket was embossed with a bleached skull and a pair of wings under a halo with the inscription HEAVEN'S ANGELS in Old English lettering.

Owen watched the Reverend fire up his Harley and roar out of the driveway. Then he laughed and said, "Man's a real spellbinder."

"He's got quite a following," Dan said. "Couple of years ago, the state was trying to cut through a stand of trees to widen a roadway. Brody thought that was an abomination too. He held one of his rallies at the site. The next night, somebody spiked a few of the trees. One of the road workers lost an arm. Lucky he wasn't killed."

"I remember that. I was here then," Owen said.

"Surely you're not suggesting the Reverend had anything to do with the tree spiking?" Mary said.

"He may not have been out there with a hammer and spikes, but he gets people riled up. Things happen."

"What's his denomination?" Owen asked.

"Some sort of Baptist," Dan said. "Hardshell, softshell, I don't know. He's got a little church a couple of miles down the road."

"It's little, but he's fixed it up real nice," Mary said. "It fills up every Sunday."

"Word is, he was drummed out of a bigger church in the state capital," Dan said. "Too much Old Testament fire and brimstone for those Charleston sophisticates."

Mary held up her smudged flyer. "Well, I think it's a good thing somebody is reminding us that four people died in that muck. I intend to go to his little vigil."

Dan wadded up his flyer and stuffed it in Clayton's empty glass. "Just stand clear if he starts demanding an eye for an eye. You've only got one good one left."

4

Acts of Man

OWEN had already stayed longer than he had planned in West Virginia, so he called his ex-wife, Judith, at her law office in California to tell her he'd be extending his stay still further to look into the causes of the Drybone Hollow Dam failure.

"If the flood was such a big deal," she asked, "why hasn't it made the news here in Palo Alto?"

"I don't understand that myself. I checked on the Internet. The papers between here and Cincinnati are full of it. But beyond the immediate area, nobody's picked up the story."

"Think somebody's trying to cover it up?"

"There's three hundred million gallons of gunk out there, nearly thirty times as much as the Exxon Valdez spilled. That's pretty hard to cover up. For some reason the national news media doesn't seem to be interested. Maybe dead fish just aren't as photogenic as oily birds."

"But you said people died as well."

"At least four."

"Then I really don't understand why it's not bigger news."

"Maybe West Virginians aren't as photogenic as oily birds either."
Owen paused, weighing what he would say next. "Your friend Dusty
Rhodes is trying to get some national attention. He's pressuring the
President to declare us a disaster area."

"Then it will probably happen," she said. "Dusty usually gets what
he wants."

Not only did Judith fail to react to Owen's labeling Dusty Rhodes
as her friend, she was calling him by his first name. "I think he just
wants the feds to pick up some of his tab for damages," Owen said.

"Why is it his tab?"

"His company owns the dam and the processing plant that produced the slurry."

"I don't understand. I thought your high-school buddy owned the
dam."

"He wasn't a buddy, and he owns the mine under the dam. The
slurry broke through into his mine."

"Is he insured?"

Owen hadn't thought to ask Anson Stokes about insurance. "I
don't know. Wouldn't Rhodes' company have to pay? After all, it was
his slurry that broke through."

"Depends on why it broke through. Is that why you're staying
around? To pin the blame on Dusty?"

"I told you. My high school classmate hired me."

"But you just said he wasn't your buddy. And you said earlier you
didn't much care for him. In fact, you sounded a little jealous of him."

"Don't be silly. Why would I be jealous of Anson Stokes?"

"He's the same age as you, he's from the same background as you,
and he's rich enough to drive a Hummer and buy you and sell you
several times over."

"Lots of people younger than me are rich enough to buy and sell
me. My apartment complex is filled with dot-com millionaires who
haven't passed thirty. I'm not jealous of them."

"A lot of them aren't millionaires any longer."

"A lot of them won't be under thirty much longer. I wasn't jealous
of them when they were young or when they were rich."

"That's because they're bright people. You're snobbish about things like that. It's the rich people who aren't brainy that you resent. With you, it's the reverse of the old saw. It's not, 'if you're so smart, why aren't you rich?' What you want to know is, 'If you're so rich, why aren't you smart?' "

"That's not true. I don't resent Alex Rodriguez or Ken Griffey Jr. They're the best there is at what they do."

"Bad example. Those two are far from stupid. And you admire their skills. You may not resent the players, but you can't tell me you don't resent the baseball owners. I've heard you rant about them over and over. What is it you say? That they never met a bad idea they didn't like?"

"Actually, Roger Angell said that. But it's true for a lot of them."

"Ex-used-car salesmen, I believe you called them."

"That was when they shut down the '94 World Series. Even then, they weren't all bad. A few of them are pretty good guys. Why are we having this conversation?"

"I'm showing you there's a pattern to your distaste for this man Anson Stokes, and it goes to his having lots more money and much less education than you."

"Saying Anson lacks education is like saying Dracula lacks table manners. Stokes has the brains and social polish of a diarrhetic mule."

"Maybe you shouldn't underestimate him. He was smart enough to hire you."

"I'm just not sure I can trust him."

"Then don't work for him."

"It's a good job. And the money will come in handy."

Ruth Allison came into the living room and set a cup of tea on the telephone table next to Owen. She mouthed the question, "Judith?"

Owen nodded.

Ruth picked up that morning's paper and settled into the easy chair across from Owen. Before disappearing behind the newsprint, she mouthed the words, "Say hi for me."

"Mom says 'hi.' "

"How is she?"

"Much better. There's been no recurrence. And she's able to get out and walk."

Ruth raised her right hand over the newspaper and joined her thumb and forefinger in an "okay" signal.

"Give her my love. Then wrap up your work there and get back to your work here. Your ex-wife misses you."

He realized he missed her as well, but didn't say so. Was it just because his mother was listening?

When Owen didn't respond, Judith said, "It's Dusty Rhodes, isn't it? That's why you're staying. You're hoping to bring him down."

"The possibility has occurred to me."

"At the risk of repeating myself, I think you're all wrong about him. So here's another possibility you should consider: if you're wrong, you're just wasting your time staying there. And you're wasting my time as well. Our time."

"I don't think I'm wrong."

"Let me finish. Suppose you're right. Suppose Rhodes has not only milked the taxpayers for millions, but has gotten away with murder as well."

"That's what he's done. Literally. He's gotten away with murder. More than once."

"If that's the case, dear heart, you're overmatched. Start poking your stick into his hive and you're liable to wind up dead."

"You underestimate me."

"I know you better than anyone. God help me, I love you. But you're either operating under a woeful misapprehension about Rhodes or you're horribly overmatched. Either way, you ought to take a plane back to California right now."

"I'll do that as soon as I can wrap things up here."

"Have you heard any of the words I just said?"

"Every one. I miss you too."

"At least promise me you'll be careful. Don't underestimate Dusty. Or your buddy Stokes. If he's stayed rich this long, he's probably got smarts he's not showing. A fool and his money are soon parted."

"What I can't figure out is how they got together in the first place."

"I still haven't heard you say you'll be careful."

"I'll be careful."

"And call more often. If I have to settle for aural intercourse, let's do it at least twice a week."

ANSON STOKES CALLED Owen that afternoon to say that the sludge levels in the Canaan II Mine were low enough so that they could inspect the location of the leak. Owen found an old pair of surveyor's boots that had belonged to his father and learned that he could make them fit by wearing two pairs of sweat socks to keep his narrow feet from slipping around. He laced up the high-top boots, put new batteries in his tape recorder, and drove back to Drybone Hollow.

The Canaan II and Canaan III mines were at the end of a winding gravel road that split off from the paved ridge-top route above the hollow. A guard in a rickety wood outbuilding at the head of the access road checked a list on his clipboard, found Owen's name, and phoned ahead to announce his arrival.

The gravel road led to a cleared cul-de-sac that contained two mobile homes, a tool shed, a barn-like structure, and a conveyor belt that slanted upward from the mine entrance to feed a conical pile of coal at least two stories high. The nearer of the two mobile homes bore a sign saying OFFICE, and a worker at a desk just inside the door told Owen that Anson Stokes could be found in the barn.

A continuous mining machine dominated the interior of the barn, which was lit by two dangling strings of exposed light bulbs stretched diagonally between opposite corners. To Owen, the machine, which consisted of two monstrous jawbones on caterpillar treads, looked like something built by George Lucas to fight land battles in the Star Wars epic. The lip of the upper jaw was the ripperhead, a cylindrical drum with protruding steel teeth that spun into the mine face to gouge out coal. The lower jaw resembled a giant dustpan fitted with mechanical claws that swept the coal onto a conveyor belt leading to the monster's digestive tract. In the mine, conveyor belts at the rear of the beast would deliver its black load to waiting shuttlecars.

Anson Stokes knelt in the mouth of the monster, doing dental work with a spanner wrench while two workers with smudged faces and grimy overalls stood watching. Stokes glanced up when Owen entered, then returned to his task, saying, "With you in a minute."

When Stokes had finished, he duck-walked under the monster's steel molars to the edge of its lower lip, where he handed his tools out to one of the workmen. Kneeling there in the mouth of the Star Wars machine, with his bulky torso and the inscription C3 on the bill of his cap, Stokes reminded Owen of another George Lucas creation, the cylindrical droid R2D2, C3PO's clanking companion.

Owen smiled at the mental image of Stokes as a *Star Wars* droid.

"Something funny?" Stokes asked.

"No. I'm just amazed that you repair this monster yourself."

Stokes climbed out of the mouth of the machine. "Kind of hard to find a local service station that can handle it."

"What about the manufacturer?"

"Oh, they'll send somebody out, but they're never in any hurry about it, and I can't stand the downtime."

Stokes patted the machine's caterpillar tread. "This honey's usually pretty solid. Every now and then the wiring goes or the intake mechanism gets a little gunked up. Kind of like a beautiful woman with the clap."

"Hard to see her as a beautiful woman."

"She knocks ten men a week off my payroll and never complains about aches and pains. I'd take this baby over a woman any day." Stokes punched Owen's shoulder. "Not any *night,* though. Now that's another matter entirely."

One of the workers handed Stokes a sheaf of paper towels and he wiped his hands. "Ready to take a look inside the mine?"

Owen nodded.

Stokes turned to the worker who'd brought the paper towels. "This here's Bill Muth, my late-shift foreman. He'll be coming with us. I asked him to rig some equipment for you."

Muth shook Owen's hand, then left and returned with a miner's hat and a battery pack. Owen tried on the hat while Muth fitted the battery pack around his belt and plugged it into the lamp on the hat. Owen switched on the lamp and watched the beam slice through the dust motes in the barn.

They went outside and Owen waited by the mine entrance while Stokes and Muth outfitted themselves. Instead of joining him at the entrance, they motioned for him to follow them down a path along the side of the mountain.

"I thought we were going into the mine," Owen said.

"We are," Stokes said. "But that was the main entrance to the Canaan III. The slurry broke through Canaan II. It's an abandoned shaft we'd walled off over a year ago."

"Good thing, too," Muth said. "Otherwise the flood would have shut down our entire operation."

The path led downhill through a forest growth so thick it blocked out most of the afternoon sunlight. "Almost dark enough to use our lamps right here," Owen said.

Stokes held two low-hanging branches aside so Owen and Muth could pass. "Like Lorena Bobbitt said when she cut off her husband's johnson, 'It won't be long now.'"

The woods ended in a sloping clearing overlooking Drybone Hollow. A black stain spread as far as the eye could see from the mouth of a tunnel cut into the slope to the valley below. Behind the tunnel, a wall of shale nearly thirty feet high stretched across the hollow.

Stokes pointed to the tunnel's mouth. "That's where it all come out. Sprayed down the hollow like water out of a fire hose."

"How'd they stop it?" Owen asked.

"Mountain View's people bulldozed boulders and big clods of earth into the holding dam."

"Just like plugging a bathtub," Muth said.

"If the bathtub covers eighty acres and holds a billion gallons of water and coal slurry," Stokes said.

"The news said about three hundred million gallons poured down into the hollow," Owen said.

"They got on it pretty fast once the alarm went out," Stokes said. "Managed to stop it off right quick."

"Not quick enough to limit the damage," Owen said. "I took a look around yesterday. The cleanup crews were saying it would take twenty million just to mop it all up. And that's without paying for any damages."

Stokes stared down into the slurry-covered hollow. "I can believe it."

"Would Dusty Rhodes and Mountain View carry that much insurance?"

"He might. He's got Big Coal behind him."

"What about you?

"Me? I'm strictly Little Coal. I've got a two-million-dollar liability policy, but that only covers what happens here in the mine."

"Aren't you worried somebody might come after you for damages as well?" Owen asked.

"It wasn't my dam that leaked. And I've got damages here myself. I can tell you I'm going to be looking to Mountain View to clean up the mess in my mine shaft." Stokes led the way across the black stain to the mouth of the tunnel. Bent, empty hinges hung from steel beams on either side of the entrance. "Their slurry ripped the doors right off my mine."

"Found one panel all the way to the Crawley Creek Bridge," Muth said. "Other one's still missing."

"Might as well get to it." Stokes switched on his miner's lamp and turned toward Owen, shining the beam in his face. "Ever been inside one of these?"

"Several years ago. And then once recently. Almost didn't make it out."

Stokes looked speculatively at Owen. "Dark's like nothing you'll ever know this side of the grave." He started into the mine. "Just stick close and you'll be all right."

Muth followed Stokes into the dark tunnel, but Owen paused at the entrance. He never thought he'd follow Anson Stokes anywhere. Now he was about to trail him into a black hole where, he knew from experience, cave-ins could occur without warning and men could keel over dead from oxygen deprivation. He recalled Stokes' surprising expertise with the continuous miner, sucked in a lungful of the clear outside air, switched on his lamp, and followed the two men into the mine.

The flood had washed away the rock dust that had coated the tunnel walls, exposing shiny black seams of coal and shale. Slurry dripped slowly from a few roof bolts and covered the floor of the mine in a black slime that clung to the men's boots. Moving through the puddled slurry was like slogging through a molasses pond.

Stokes shined his light on a happy face carved into the wall at a blocked-off junction. The date carved under the face was more than two years old. "That's Steve Skaar's mark," Stokes said. "He's one of the state inspectors. Likes to dress up his visits with little pictures."

Owen ducked his helmet and aimed his lamp at the outline of a footprint under the scum at the edge of the wall. "Thought this tunnel was abandoned."

Stokes' lamp beam dipped up and down in what Owen took to be a shrug. "Print could be as old as the mark on the wall."

They slogged on in a silence broken only by sucking noises when their boots sunk into puddles. Owen could feel the blackness pressing in, devouring everything but the cones of light emanating from the three helmets.

Stokes broke the silence. "Should be coming to the end soon."

Muth stopped in his tracks. "Holy shit."

The three beams of light played on the end of the tunnel. A great gouge ran from the roof halfway down the wall, as if the mining machine had run amuck and taken an enormous bite out of the ceiling.

Stokes groaned. "Looks like somebody blasted hell out of it. From the inside."

5

Our American Cousin

OUTSIDE the mineshaft, Owen inhaled fresh air and scraped the slurry off the soles of his boots with a twig. "We need to call the sheriff."

Anson Stokes snapped off a thin branch, sat on a boulder, and went to work on his own boots. "The sheriff? Why the sheriff? Can't we keep this private for a while?"

Owen shook his head. "Not a chance. There'll be an investigation soon anyhow. It's best if you bring the law in yourself right now. You say nobody in your outfit blasted that hole. But somebody set off a charge at the end of the shaft, and whoever did it is responsible for at least four deaths and a hell of a lot of damage. It's a job for the sheriff."

"I guess you're right."

"Before we call him, though, there's something we've got to get straight."

"What's that?"

Owen pointed the slurry-coated twig at Anson. "Why didn't you tell me you'd checked the shaft out before I got here?"

"I didn't."

"Don't lie to me, Anson. That footprint in the mine fits that boot you're cleaning. And the flood that filled that shaft would have washed away any prints that were there before the blast."

Anson scraped his twig across the heel of his boot, then rubbed it against the boulder, leaving a dark smear. "I couldn't wait. I didn't think it would matter."

"Why lie about it?"

Anson shrugged. "I thought you'd want to be the first in. I know I did."

"Did you touch anything?"

"What do you think I'd do? You saw the size of that crater. Think I'd try to plaster over it?"

"That crater makes it look bad for you, Anson. Lawyers could argue you're complicit in the flooding."

"Lawyers can argue whatever they want. Nothing that happened in my mine would have hurt anybody if Mountain View hadn't built that dam right on top of my shaft."

Owen looked from the mouth of the mine to the black stain spread over the hollow below. "Yeah. And Pompeii would have been a great place to live if it weren't for that damn volcano."

Sheriff Thad Reader brought two deputies along with him. He introduced the tall, thin deputy as Bob Jeffreys, so it was inevitable that his short, chunky companion, Harold Stammers, would be nicknamed Mutt. Mutt and Jeff lounged on either side of the door of the mine office while the sheriff questioned Anson and Owen.

Sheriff Reader took off his mountie's hat and ran his hand through the few strands of graying hair left on his forehead. "So you say somebody blasted out the end of your mine shaft?"

"Clean through to the dam above," Anson said.

"But you got no idea who did it." The sheriff turned to Owen, fixing him with his one good eye. "You have a look at it?"

Owen nodded.

The sheriff smiled. "Surprised you'd ever go back inside a mine after what you and I went through."

Owen recalled the panic he felt being trapped underground. "Surprised me too."

The sheriff turned back to Anson. "You say you don't blast for coal any more?"

Anson nodded. "We use continuous mining machines to chew up the coal face."

"Use explosives for anything?"

"Sometimes with low seams we need to blast to make room for the conveyor belts."

"So you've got dynamite around?"

Stokes tilted his head toward the window. "Outside. In the tool shed."

"Keep records on it?"

"Have to sign your life away to get it in the first place. Government keeps tabs on anything that might be lethal except farts, and I hear they're going to start counting them next year."

"So you keep a record of what you buy. How about what you use?"

"There's a sign-out sheet in the shed, but we don't keep a good count until the inspector's due."

"So anybody could help themselves?"

"We generally keep the shed locked. But we don't pay much attention. Couple of years ago we caught a man taking sticks of 'mite home in his lunchbox."

"What did you do about it?"

"Fired his ass."

The sheriff took a thin spiral notebook from his pocket. "We'll need his name."

"Stokes."

The sheriff looked up from his notebook.

"It was my nephew. Cable's oldest boy, Billy Joe. He got back at us by hitting the mine up for disability."

"What about the shaft itself? You say it was abandoned?"

"That's right."

"Any security?"

"Hasp lock on the doors. About as strong as a length of wet spaghetti."

"Why not use something stronger?"

"Got nothing to protect. It's a hole in the hill."

"So somebody broke the lock?"

Anson shrugged. "Don't know. Can't find the doors, let alone the lock."

"Who'd want to do a thing like this?" the sheriff asked.

"Damned if I know."

"Got any enemies?"

"Got my share."

"Any of them who might try to get at you through your mine?"

"There's Ed Kaufman. He thought he was selling me a played-out mine. He's real pissed I made it pay off." Anson stared at his calloused hands as if he were mentally counting off names on his fingers. "There's my brother Cable. He thinks half of everything I own ought to be his because we started out together. But he bailed at the first bump in the road." He let his hands fall to his lap. "Neither of them would blow up a worked-out mine shaft. Especially one that was likely to flood Drybone Hollow. Hell, the flood carried away Cable's trailer and killed his youngest."

"What about labor troubles? Do you run a union operation?"

"I'm nonunion. But I treat my men fair. Ask anybody. You add up benefits, bonuses, and all, and my men make out better than union workers."

"Ever had any trouble over being nonunion?"

Stokes took a framed picture off the wall. It was a front-page article from the *Barkley Democrat* headlined CANAAN NO EDEN. The photo with the article showed a dark station wagon surrounded by a crowd of protestors carrying UMW signs and placards. One of the protestors had just shattered the station wagon's windshield with a baseball bat.

"Had plenty of trouble back when I was starting out." Stokes tapped the station wagon in the photo. "That's me in the driver's seat.

And that's Cable with the bat, casting the first stone. I carried a forty-five in the glove compartment. Came pretty close to using it that day.

"That was twenty-five years ago, though. Union was a lot stronger then. Now no more than one miner in four's a union man."

"Well, whoever did this must have a grudge against you, against mining, or both. Either way, they may not be done." The sheriff scratched his forehead. "Course, there's another possibility. How do we know you didn't do this yourself trying to reopen the abandoned shaft?"

Stokes sighed heavily. "We wouldn't have done it at three in the morning. We would have reopened it with a machine, not dynamite. And if we had used dynamite, whoever set the charge would have washed away."

"You don't use timers?"

"I told you, we don't use dynamite much at all any more. When we do though, we just set the charge and back off a safe distance."

"Which in this case would have been the next county," Owen said.

"How many of your current workers have experience blasting?" the sheriff asked.

Anson shrugged. "Five. Maybe six."

"We'll need a list of your employees."

"How far back?"

"Five years to start. Mark anybody who has handled dynamite."

Anson raised his voice. "Aaron, you listening?"

The sound of rolling desk chairs and opening file drawers came from the other side of the trailer partition.

"We'll take care of it," Anson said.

The sheriff put on his mountie's hat and cinched the chin strap. "Might as well go have a look at the mine."

"You'll have to trade in that hat for a miner's helmet," Anson said. He outfitted the sheriff and his deputies with battery packs, helmets, and caplights. Then Owen and Anson accompanied the three officers down the hill to the mineshaft.

"Reckon any real evidence will be washed away," the sheriff said as they approached the shaft."

"Not necessarily," Owen said.

47

"What do you mean, 'not necessarily'? 'Pears to me it's like looking for the remains of a flea who was sleeping inside a fire hose when the pressure got turned on."

"I saw a few things," Owen said.

The sheriff paused at the mine entrance. "Like what?"

"First thing is right here," Owen said. Just around the corner of the entrance, he pointed to a gray plastic shard lodged between the tunnel wall and the steel pillar that had once held the mine door.

"Get me a picture of that," the sheriff said to the shorter deputy. "What do you suppose it is?"

"Could be a piece of a timing device," Owen said. "Or just something knocked loose from a miner's lunch bucket. It's worth analyzing, though."

"All right, bag it and tag it," the sheriff said to Jeffreys, the taller deputy.

The deputy had started forward when the sheriff slapped his hand. "Son, don't you watch TV? Put on your rubber gloves before you pick up that piece of flotsam."

The sheriff waited and watched while Jeffreys donned rubber gloves and retrieved the plastic shard. Then he asked Owen, "You see anything else?"

"We were in and out pretty quick before we called you. I didn't get much of a look around. Wouldn't hurt to comb the place with a metal detector."

They began slogging through the ankle-deep slurry, sweeping cones of light off the shaft's black interior.

"Nothing here but gunk, goo, and more gunk," the sheriff said.

As they neared the end of the tunnel, Owen and Anson hung back, letting the sheriff and his deputies slog ahead. All three lawmen stopped in their tracks when their lamps picked up the enormous crater the blast had gouged out of the roof and walls.

"Holy shit," Jeffreys said as his partner began taking flash photos.

"I've already got some photos," Owen said. "But you ought to have your own. Then you ought to scrape samples off the wall all around the edge of the crater. That's where you're most likely to find traces of any explosives that haven't washed away."

"Don't see how anything useful could be left," the sheriff said.

Owen tilted his head back, aiming his caplight at the highest point of the crater rim. "Could be something up there around twelve o'clock. Depends on how high the slurry rose before it broke free and poured into the hollow."

"We'll need a stepladder to sample up there," the tall deputy said.

"I'll get you one," Anson said. He started back out of the shaft, motioning for Owen to join him.

"I want you to stay on this," Anson said when they were out of earshot.

"You hired me to find out how the mine failed," Owen said. "We know that. It's the sheriff's job to find out who made it happen."

"You get on with the sheriff. He won't mind your helping out. You've already found out more than him and his deputies are likely to for the rest of the day."

"I'd been there before them, Anson. I knew where to look."

"That's my point. I doubt that tall one could sniff out shit in a one-hole privy."

"What do you expect me to find out?"

"Who did this, for a start. Somebody killed four people, gunked up three creekbeds, and fouled water supplies all the way to the Ohio. My liability insurance won't cover any of that."

Owen stopped slogging through the muck and stood still, focusing his light beam on Anson. "You said yourself it's Mountain View's dam. What makes you think you might be held liable?"

"Flies light on as many shit piles as they can find. There's enough lawyers flitting around so that it's a damn cinch at least one of them is going to claim I'm liable."

Owen could feel his boots sinking into the mire. "It's not my kind of fight, Anson. You need lawyers, not an engineer."

"If it comes to a legal fight, Mountain View can outlawyer me with their third-string team. If some judge decides to split the difference between us, I can't afford any part of the damages."

"Suppose I work with the sheriff and we find whoever set the charge. How do you see that helping your liability?"

"Hell, it takes any possible blame off me. Nobody sues a store owner if somebody's killed in a holdup."

"You're making this up as you go along, aren't you?"

"Just stick with me a little while, okay? At least long enough to use up that advance I gave you. Hang out with the sheriff. I need somebody on my side. Let me find out where I stand with all this."

Owen lifted one boot out of the muck and edged sideways toward the tunnel wall where the footing was more secure. "All right, I'll use up your advance. But if it looks like we're getting nowhere, that's as far as I'll go."

"That's great. I really appreciate it. Now get back there with the sheriff and make sure Mutt and Jeff don't stomp on any evidence."

THE CANDLELIGHT VIGIL run by the Reverend Moral Brody was held in a large revival tent raised in the parking lot of a combination restaurant, grocery, and liquor store on the ridge road above the Drybone Hollow Dam. By the time Owen arrived, cars had filled the lot and were parked up and down the two-lane road. Owen drove past the rows of cars and finally pulled in behind an SUV just above the dam itself.

A slow drizzle dotted the surface of the water behind the dam with hundreds of interlocking circles. In the overcast twilight, the dark rippling surface might have been mistaken for a recreational lake, but the black scum that rimmed the surface and traced the pre-flood highwater mark gave it away.

Four bonfires had been lit on the other side of the dam, and four motorcyclists wearing black HEAVEN'S ANGELS jackets carried burning torches back and forth across the rim of the dam, cycling between the bonfires and the vigil site.

Owen watched the motorcyclists complete one loop of their torchlight parade and then walked through the drizzle back up the road to the revival tent.

Inside the tent, a black-robed teenager handed him a lit votive candle, which he carried to a seat in the last row of folding chairs. The rows ahead of him held at least three hundred people with candles that sent flickering shadows and twisting streams of smoke upward into the canvas overhead. Spotlights cut through the skinny smoke streams to illuminate four wreaths, two on either side of a raised pulpit draped with black crepe paper.

Inside each wreath was an enlarged photo of one of the victims. From the last row of seats, Owen could barely make out their features. Maddie Tanner appeared to have been a somewhat plump woman, while Riley Stokes had an unruly shock of black hair. The Tennessee couple was represented by a wedding photo which had been enlarged and cut in half so that the bride and groom could each occupy a separate wreath.

A choir of ten black-robed teenagers standing behind the raised pulpit sang "Here I am, Lord" as the Reverend Moral Brody made his way down the center aisle to the pulpit. The congregation of candle holders stood until the hymn ended and the Reverend had ascended the pulpit, and then sat down.

The Reverend Brody waited for the rustling of the folding chairs to subside, then fixed his audience with a righteous stare and intoned, "It's time to say NO TO COAL."

A strange beginning for a memorial sermon, Owen thought, but a quick check of the rapt faces around him suggested that he was alone in thinking the message out of place.

"Our land and our people have been too long exploited by this black plague," the Reverend continued. "In the last century, twenty thousand people died in our coal mines. That's two hundred a year, or nearly four every week.

"If that many people had died in a plane crash, the papers would be full of it. If a sniper had picked them off from a tower, it would be front-page news and spawn a series of symposiums on the disaffected. If they had died in an earthquake in California, we'd see each of their pictures in news magazines and the government would be handing out checks to survivors."

Brody drew himself up and swept his eyes over the crowd before delivering his punch line. "But because the dead were West Virginians, *already* laboring in their own tombs, nobody pays heed. The rest of the U.S. thinks of us as marginally literate hillbillies, so it's easy to write off this wrong. To them, we're a third-world country, except that nobody in Congress is busting to give us funds."

The word *hillbillies* drew a smattering of nervous laughter, and Owen scanned the audience once more. The faces around him were still rapt, but he caught sight of the back of Anson Stokes' head three rows ahead. Stokes' neck glowed red in the candlelight.

"It pleases the rest of the country to think of us as a national joke, barefoot and twanging, because then they don't have to attend to our misery. They don't have to pay us heed." The spotlight reflected the anger in the Reverend Brody's eyes. "But we're not a national joke when they need someone to crawl in dark, lung-fouling mines to heat this country. We're not a national joke when they need someone to crawl in the dark, life-threatening tunnels of Vietnam to defend this country. In terms of the numbers we had to give, West Virginia lost more of its sons in that war than any other state."

Brody took a handkerchief and patted away the sweat glistening around the tattooed band on his forehead. "Tonight we meet here to mourn four more deaths. Four more lives added to the toll our state has given up to the Lord. They call it an Act of God. What an abomination. This was an Act of Man. Look not to the King of Kings but to King Coal for the source of this tragedy.

"This was no Act of God. But it is a sign from God, a sign to the people of West Virginia that we need to rid ourselves of our dependence on the demon coal. This demon poisons us at every stage of its life. It pollutes our mountains when we take it from the ground, our streams when we process it, and our air when we burn it. And if that isn't enough, it takes the lives of our citizens."

The Reverend raised his right fist above his head. "I tell you, brothers and sisters, it's time to strike back. Let us all say NO TO COAL."

He raised both arms, palms outward. "Let me hear you say it."

The congregation responded, shouting, "NO TO COAL" in unison.

The Reverend lowered both arms to the pulpit and shot them back into the air. "Again."

"NO TO COAL," boomed from the audience.

Chairs scraped three rows in front of Owen, and a scowling Anson

Stokes strode down the aisle away from the pulpit and out through the tent flap.

Arms still upraised, the Reverend said, "Again."

Again the audience responded, "No to coal," increasing the volume.

The Reverend lowered his hands to the sides of the pulpit. "Lord, hear our prayers." He bowed his head and closed his eyes. "And let us also ask the Lord to hear our silent prayers for the four latest victims of the demon coal."

Owen bowed his head. In this revival meeting setting, the environmental sermon seemed less strange than it had at first. In his home in Northern California, environmentalism was closer to a common faith than most organized religions.

The Reverend Moral Brody raised his head, cleared his throat, and went on to say a little about each of the flood victims. Maddie Tanner had been the mother of three children. Riley Stokes had pitched for his high school baseball team. The Tennessee couple, the Tatums, had been returning from a honeymoon in Chicago.

Owen glanced over his shoulder during the eulogies. The tent flap was unfastened, and he could see Anson Stokes pacing in the light drizzle, trailed by a shower of cigarette sparks.

The Reverend stepped down and stood beside the pulpit. "We're going to pass the collection plate now. I urge you to give generously, because your donations will go to the families of the deceased." He nodded, and the black-robed teenage ushers started down each aisle with wicker collection baskets.

As the collection baskets were passed, the Reverend said, "I also invite each of you to stay a while after the closing hymn to share your condolences personally with the bereaved families. The ladies of my parish have prepared a buffet spread for those who remain."

When the last collection basket reached the last row, the Rever-end nodded to the choir leader, and the hymn "Nearer My God to Thee" signaled the end of the formal service. A few attendees filed out during the closing hymn, but most stayed in their seats as four individuals went to stand by the wreaths flanking the pulpit. At the same time, four aproned matrons began loading sandwich meat, bread, potato salad, and cookies onto two long tables at the rear of the tent.

Anson Stokes came back into the tent and buttonholed Owen across the last row of chairs. "That psalm-singing bastard's got a lot of nerve. This was supposed to be a memorial service. Instead, he turned it into a greenie revival meeting."

Stokes shoved aside two folding chairs so he could thrust his face closer to Owen's. "I mean, where's he get off with this 'No to coal' shit? Coal gives the U.S. better than half its electric power and keeps this state in the black. I didn't come here to listen to that line of crap."

Owen took two steps back from Anson, displacing another folding chair. "He did a little better with the memorial service after you left. He actually produced four eulogies."

"Yeah, well, I better go pay my respects to my son-of-a-bitch brother." Anson jerked his head toward the platform at the front of the tent, where Cable Stokes stood beside the photo of his son Riley. "Want to come?"

"I'll be along in a minute. There's someone I want to see first."

While Stokes joined the line of mourners waiting to talk to his brother, Owen made his way through the conversational clumps of two and three people to stand beside a tall, broad-shouldered teenager. "Jeb Stuart," he said. "I'm surprised to find you here."

Jeb Stuart Hobbs turned and smiled. "Riley Stokes pitched for our team."

"I'm sorry. I didn't know. I am glad to see you, though."

"Same here." The boy turned to the person standing beside him, a tanned and fit older man with a blond brush cut who towered over the two of them. "This here's Mr. Bill Anderson. He's a regional scout for the Reds. Mr. Anderson, I'd like you to meet Owen Allison. I spent the summer after my dad died visiting with Mr. Allison out in California."

Owen shook the hand the tall man offered. "Bullet Bill Anderson. You were a top Reds prospect back when I was starting high school."

Anderson rubbed his right shoulder. "Blew a rotator cuff halfway through my first year in Triple-A. Back then, there was nothing they could do about it. Nice of you to remember, though. I still keep my hand in by scouting prospects."

"You're scouting Jeb Stuart?" Owen asked.

"Jeb and his friend Riley. I came along to pay my respects."

"Jeb Stuart's quite a catcher," Owen said.

"I've heard real good things about him," Anderson said. "And I've seen him work out. Haven't seen any games yet, though."

"High school season doesn't start till next week," Jeb Stuart said.

"I know your dad wanted you to go to college," Owen said.

"Mostly, he just wanted me to stay out of the mines. The Reds would sure help me do that."

"We wouldn't want to stand in the way of a college education," Anderson said.

Jeb Stuart scuffed a shoe on the asphalt surface. "Guess I better go see Mr. Stokes. Don't hardly know what to say to him."

"Did you know him?" Owen asked.

Jeb Stuart looked as if the question pained him somehow. "He's a tough old man. Hard on Riley, I know that."

"Losing a son's about the roughest thing that can happen to a man," Owen said. "He'd probably appreciate hearing from you."

Jeb Stuart shook his head. "I just don't know what to say to him, is all."

"I'll go along to help," Owen said.

"Yeah, we'll both go with you," Anderson said.

They joined the line of people waiting to commiserate with Cable Stokes. The line leading to Lyle Tanner at Maddie Tanner's wreath was twice as long, stretching to the rear of the tent and bending around its perimeter. An older man and woman stood, stoic and alone, beside the wreaths dedicated to the Tennessee couple. Parents, Owen guessed. What could you say to someone who'd suffered such a loss? They'd come to a distant county to claim the remains of loved ones and stayed to listen to a preacher they didn't know harangue a tent full of strangers about environmental policy. While Owen watched, two of the aproned ladies who'd been stocking the buffet table approached the bereaved parents, each bearing a full plate of food. Their offering seemed woefully insubstantial, but Owen admired the ladies for making it.

"So, did you know Riley's father?" Jeb Stuart asked Owen.

"Went to high school with him."

"He play ball too?"

Owen formed a mental image of the hell-raising Stokes boys. Baseball had been the farthest thing from their minds. "No."

"What was he like then?"

"I didn't know him very well. He left school before we graduated."

"So you played high school ball?" Anderson asked.

"Mr. Allison pitched for Barkley the year they were state champs," Jeb Stuart said.

"No kidding," Anderson said. "What'd you throw?"

"Pretty good slider. Not much of a fastball. Enough control to keep me out of trouble in high school. Couldn't make it in college though."

"Where'd you go to college?"

"Marquette, undergrad."

"Wish I'd finished college," Anderson said. "You can be sure we'll let Jeb here go if that's what he wants."

"That's a long way off," Jeb Stuart said.

"Not so long," Owen said. "You're a junior now. Time to start thinking about it. If you like, we can visit some colleges together this summer. I'll talk to your mom."

A commotion broke out at the head of their line. Bodies surged around Riley Stokes' wreath, which wobbled and seemed about to topple before someone caught it. A voice shouted, "You fucking killed my boy!" Seconds later, a grim-faced Anson Stokes pulled free of the pack and strode toward the nearest exit, passing Owen without acknowledging him and disappearing through the tent flap.

The pack of bodies surrounding Riley's wreath backed away as if repelled by an electromagnetic force. All eyes went to the repelling agent at the center of the pack, Cable Stokes. The tent was dead silent for a moment. Then the noise of a hundred conversations rose to the level of a large generator and gradually subsided to a hushed rumble as mourners returned to the job of offering sympathy to the bereaved.

Through it all, Cable Stokes stared defiantly outward, his eyes focused on the exit Anson had used as if daring his brother to return. Except for the focused, feral eyes, there was little in Cable's countenance to remind Owen of the high-school hell-raiser he'd once known. A few thin strands of hair had been combed over his sweaty forehead and slicked down in a vain attempt to disguise his baldness. The middle button of his shiny serge suitcoat had stretched to the breaking point to cover his ample stomach. Even while receiving condolences, Cable's eyes danced nervously from the well-wisher to Anson's exit route.

When they finally worked their way to the front of the line, the spindly man in bib overalls ahead of them took Cable Stokes' right hand in his, put his left arm around Stokes' shoulder, and said, "Sorry for your loss, Cable."

"It's tough, that's for sure," Cable said.

"Toughest thing in the world, to lose a child. Lots worse than losing a parent or spouse."

"You'd think so." Cable nodded toward the line in front of Maddie Tanner's wreath. "But Lyle Tanner's line is twice as long as mine."

The spindly man smiled and patted Stokes' shoulder. "Why do you think I stood in your line?"

"Course, Lyle's wife, Maddie, was at least twice as big as my boy Riley, so maybe it all evens out." Stokes dug an elbow into the man's midsection. "Reckon they'll need a double-wide coffin for good old Maddie."

The man smiled. "Cemetery'll probably make Lyle buy adjacent lots just to fit her in."

"Could cremate her, I guess," Cable said. "But then, you'd need a five-gallon drum instead of an urn."

The man dropped Stokes' hand and patted his shoulder once more. "Same old Cable." He stepped back. "Well, take it easy."

Stokes raised his right hand, palm outward, and wiggled his fingers. "Take it any way I can get it."

As the man in overalls walked away, Owen stepped forward and introduced himself.

"You're working for my brother Anson," Cable said. "He jewed

57

me out of a shaft that was rightfully half mine, then blew hell out of it and killed my youngest boy, Riley. And then he had the nerve to show up here. And bring you with him."

"Anson didn't bring me, Cable," Owen said. "I came on my own to say I was sorry about Riley's death."

"What for? You never even knew him."

Jeb Stuart moved up to join Owen. "I did, though. I knew Riley pretty well, Mr. Stokes. I think this service is a good way to remember him."

"It's a good service, all right," Stokes said. "But you can bet the Reverend will take his cut offen the top."

"Well, anyhow, I'll sure miss Riley." Jeb Stuart stepped aside to bring Bill Anderson forward. "Mr. Stokes, this here's Mr. Bill Anderson. He's a scout for the Cincinnati Reds. He was going to scout me and Riley last weekend."

Stokes seemed to be staring at the EXIT sign over the tent flap. Then he squinted and focused on Anderson. "Scout? Riley?"

"That's right, Mr. Stokes," Anderson answered. "Everybody said your boy had a real talent. A good fastball, a sinker, and a lot of control. I came down to watch him pitch."

Stokes seemed unable to take in the information. He stared at the EXIT sign, blinked his eyes, and then asked, "You work for the Reds? The Cincinnati Reds?"

"I work for the Reds, yes."

"Lot of money in pitching now," Stokes said. "You think you might have signed Riley?"

"If everything I heard about him was true."

"But you never seen him pitch?"

"No, I'm sorry. I never did. I got here too late."

Stokes appeared to be hypnotized by the EXIT sign. He worked his lower lip almost up to his nose, scrunched his eyelids together, and jerked his head up and down repeatedly as if his neck hurt. "Know what?" he finally said. "You ought to check out Riley's cousin in Middleburg. He's every bit as good. Some say he's even better."

"Middleburg, Ohio?"

"That's the place."

"That's part of my territory," Anderson said. "I don't believe I've heard of your nephew, though. Is his name Stokes too?"

"No, Bricker. My sister married the oldest Bricker boy. I could set up something, I guess." Cable seemed suddenly to become aware of the line of people behind them. "Soon as this mourning's done, of course."

"Of course," Anderson said. "You can reach me through Jeb here."

"I'll do that. I surely will."

"Well, we just wanted to pay our respects," Owen said.

"Glad you did. Yessir, I'm surely glad you did." Stokes shook each of their hands. "Good luck there, Jeb boy."

On their way to the exit, Owen patted Jeb Stuart on the shoulder. "You did good. He's not an easy man to talk to."

"I'll say he's not," Anderson said. "He flip-flopped from hostile to friendly with no warning. Seemed confused and confusing sometimes. Other times he was right on top of things."

"More confusing than anything," Jeb Stuart said. "I didn't think Riley had any cousins in Ohio."

6

No Fraud Like an Old Fraud

THE morning edition of the *Barkley Democrat* reported that the six-county region affected by the slurry flood had been declared a national disaster area eligible for funding by the Federal Emergency Management Agency. State Senator Dusty Rhodes was credited with the successful lobbying effort that brought federal aid to the counties below the breached dam. Owen read the news with a mounting sense of frustration. The newspaper failed to mention that Rhodes was the majority stockholder in the Mountain View Development Company that owned the dam. Why in God's name had the newspaper failed to make the connection between Rhodes and the breached dam? Had they been bought off? Were they afraid of making an enemy in a high place? He shook his head, sighed, and shoved his section of the newspaper aside.

Without looking up from her section of the paper, Ruth announced from across the breakfast table, "Corbin's Outlet Store is having a sale. Could you use a new sportcoat?"

When Owen didn't respond, she lowered the newspaper. "Something wrong, dear?"

"Dusty Rhodes has got us declared a national disaster area. We're eligible for federal funding."

"Why are you looking so glum about it? Surely that's a good thing."

"It's good for anybody with flood damages. But it's better for Dusty Rhodes."

Ruth folded the newspaper and set it aside. "Why's that?"

"Mom, it was his dam that broke. Any taxpayer money that goes to the victims will lower his liabilities."

"As it should."

Owen lifted a corner of the paper and let it fall back to the table. "I just think the newspaper ought to be pointing that out, is all. They've only told half the story. The half that makes Dusty Rhodes look like a hero."

"It's not clear to me that the other half of the story adds much." Ruth took a sip of tea and returned her cup to its saucer. "Don't get me wrong. I understand all your objections to Dusty Rhodes. But it seems to me you may be letting your distaste for the man cloud your judgment here. Unless Rhodes dynamited that mine himself, he's as much a victim as Dan and Mary Tharp or anybody else living along the creekbed."

"Oh, come on. It was his dam that caused all the damage."

"Owen, I'm surprised at you. You analyze failures. It's not as if Rhodes' dam was substandard. Somebody sabotaged it. And a whole slew of lawyers are trying to saddle Rhodes with everyone else's bills."

"Mom, the man is a fraud and a scumbag."

"That may be true. I'm just saying that, in this case, it seems to me he's just as entitled as anyone else to look to the government for help. I doubt that the FEMA regulations say 'Frauds and scumbags need not apply.'"

Owen rose from the breakfast table. "I give up."

"Does the newspaper say what the flood victims have to do to apply for reimbursement?"

Owen slid the newspaper section across the table. "There's a toll-free number. It's listed right there next to Rhodes' picture."

"I think I'll call Mary Tharp and let her know. In case she didn't see the paper." Ruth gathered up the newspaper sections. "You know, Corbin's Outlet Store is having a sale. Could you use a new sportcoat?"

"You already asked me that."

Concern showed on Ruth's face. "I did?"

Owen mirrored Ruth's concern. She seemed to be repeating herself more and more often. "You did. Not two minutes ago."

"And what did you say?"

"I guess I was too busy damning Dusty Rhodes to answer."

The look of concern vanished from Ruth's face. "Well, then. No wonder I asked you again."

CABLE STOKES WAS one of the first to call the toll-free number advertising instant relief for flood damages. He made an appointment to meet an inspector at his former address at 8:30 the next morning.

From 8:30 to 9:00, Cable paced back and forth in front of the rectangle of scum-covered cinderblocks that had been the foundation of his mobile home in Drybone Hollow. It wasn't until 9:00 that a cream-colored Camaro trailing a mix of dust and exhaust kicked up gravel as it braked beside Cable's battered blue pickup.

A tall, balding man with a hint of a pot belly that bloused over the belt of his navy blue suit approached and held out his hand. "Sorry I'm late. I'm Hube Robinette."

Cable ignored the hand. "Guess you government types get paid whether you're working or not."

"I said I was sorry. It wasn't easy finding this place."

Cable waved one hand at the blackened cinderblock foundation. "There's no place left. That's why I called you."

Robinette took a clipboard from under his arm and a pen from his inside suit pocket. "This was your primary place of residence?"

"My primary and only place of residence."

"What type of mobile home was it?"

"Skyline double-wide. Top of the line." It was the model Cable had always coveted.

"How old?"

"Just got her about six months ago." About six months and ten years, he thought.

"Do you have a bill of sale?"

Cable frowned and shook his head. "Went downriver with the trailer."

The answer didn't seem to faze Robinette, who kept writing on the top sheet of his clipboard. Without looking up or lifting his pen, the FEMA representative asked, "Live here alone?"

"I'm alone now. My boy Riley lived with me before the flood. He got taken with the trailer."

Robinette looked up from the clipboard. "I'm sorry."

"No need. Wasn't your doing."

The FEMA man's eyes returned to his clipboard. "Your trailer. Was it fully furnished?"

"Oh yes. I lost me a brand-new dinner table and chairs, a bedroom set, a fine collection of shotguns . . ." When the man didn't stop writing, Cable added, "antique shotguns, they was." He figured he could keep fabricating as long as the man could keep writing.

At the end of a long list of imagined belongings, Robinette looked up again. "Don't suppose you've got receipts for any of these?"

Cable shrugged. "Somewhere downriver. Never expected to lose the whole shooting match."

"I'll need to see some sort of proof you lived here."

Cable pulled his wallet from his hip pocket and showed his driver's license with his Drybone Hollow address.

Robinette flipped over the top sheet and copied down the information. Then he handed the clipboard to Cable. "Fill in your social security number and current address and sign where I've indicated."

Cable took the clipboard. "Suppose I'd lost my driver's license too. What kind of proof would you have wanted?"

"A utility bill placing you at this address would do it. If everything's gone, sometimes we'll just interview the neighbors."

Cable signed the form and handed it back. "How much you figure I'm due?"

"Twenty-five thousand's the max. I'd say you qualify for that."

Cable frowned. "Twenty-five thousand. Hell, my double-wide alone was worth lots more than that."

"There must be some misunderstanding. We assume you have insurance for the double-wide. Our money is to help tide you over for the first few months following this tragedy."

"Well, twenty-five grand might do that." Cable sucked on his lower lip. "S'pose it'll take a while to get it, though."

Robinette tucked the clipboard under his arm. "We'll have a check in your hands within three days."

"Three days." Cable whistled silently. "You sure you're from the government? How long has this been going on?"

"It's the Individual and Family Grant Program. We call it the IFG. The first President Bush introduced it after Hurricane Andrew. It was part of his push to get reelected."

"I'll be damned. Sorry I never voted for the man." Cable put on what he hoped was an ingratiating smile. "Course, I never voted for the other guy, neither."

Robinette didn't seem to find any humor in Stokes' voting record. He turned to go, but stopped when Cable put a hand on his arm.

"Hold on a minute," Cable said. "Reckon the reason I got the max was because my boy died?"

Robinette shook his head. "Not really. We do count all family members, of course. Mostly, though, we count rooms and furnishings."

"Rooms?"

"Bedrooms. Living rooms." Robinette nodded toward the empty cinderblock foundation. "It's pretty clear you lost everything."

Cable released the man's arm. "Yessir, I surely did."

Robinette held out his hand. "Well, good luck. Glad we could be of service."

This time Cable shook the offered hand. "Pleasure doing business with you."

Cable watched the FEMA man disappear down the gravel road. Then he got in his truck, drove straight to the nearest phone booth, and called his oldest son. "Billy Joe, I want you to fill your pickup with cinderblocks and meet me in Drybone Hollow. I got me a way to turn them blocks into a shitload of money."

OWEN ALLISON CLIMBED the courthouse steps to the second-floor offices of the Contrary Comet bus company. Nearly two years earlier, his visits to these offices had repercussions that cost him his job at the Department of Transportation and sent him back into private consulting.

He paused at the door, running his hand over the yellow comet at the base of the company's logo. He wasn't looking forward to this visit, but there were promises that had to be kept.

He opened the door slowly and stepped inside. Mary Beth Hobbs was bent over the computer in the reception area, absorbed by the figures on the screen. It was the same place he'd first seen her. Her blonde hair was in a bun now, and, at a distance, there seemed to be a few crow's feet at the corners of her eyes. From the doorway he couldn't be sure. Maybe he just imagined they ought to be there. Or maybe his infatuation had caused him to miss them the first time around.

He waited quietly until Mary Beth looked up from the computer screen. When she saw him, she smiled and said, "Why Owen. My goodness, what a nice surprise." She glided out from behind the reception counter and offered him a cool cheek to kiss. "What brings you here?"

"I saw Jeb Stuart at the memorial service for Riley Stokes."

"He told me."

"I thought I'd stop by, let you know he's welcome to come to California and stay with me again this summer."

"That's awfully nice of you, but he's lined up with a summer league here."

"There was a Cincinnati Reds scout at the memorial service."

Mary Beth fingered the glasses on the gold chain around her neck. "Bill Anderson. Yes. He's been around for a while."

"He talked as if Jeb Stuart might be offered a contract out of high school."

"Wouldn't that be wonderful?"

Owen could see he'd be fighting an uphill battle. "I know Stony wanted Jeb Stuart to go to college."

"Stony wanted Jeb to stay out of the mines. So they wouldn't kill him too. A contract with the Reds would do that for him."

"Only if he eventually makes the Reds. Otherwise, he'll be left without any resources and a résumé that shows only catching and mine work." Owen leaned one elbow on the reception desk, affecting a nonchalance he didn't feel. The woman still had the power to unsettle him. "Jeb Stuart's a smart boy. It seems a shame to deprive him of the chance to go to college."

Mary Beth tilted her head and shrugged one shoulder. "If he takes the Reds' money, he can go to college any time."

"So the Reds would offer a significant signing bonus?"

"Bill Anderson thinks so."

"But he could be a lot more valuable with a college education and college coaching. Both to himself and to the Reds."

Mary Beth straightened a pile of pamphlets on the reception desk. "He can always get a degree later. After his big-league career is over."

"It doesn't usually work that way. I've seen what happens to kids who sign out of high school. Most of them don't make it to college or the major leagues. It's particularly true of young catchers."

"Jeb Stuart could be different."

"He could be. I hope he will be. But he'd be missing a lot. And the odds against making it to the majors are really long. Even with a signing bonus."

Mary Beth tightened the cord on her glasses, placed them on the tip of her nose, and peered over them. "Know what I think? I think you're jealous. Nobody offered you a contract out of high school, so you went to college. It doesn't have to be that way with everybody."

Owen fought to keep his voice level. "I'm not jealous. I promised Stony before he died I'd see that Jeb Stuart got a college education. Somewhere away from coal mines."

"Stony Hobbs had abandoned Jeb Stuart and me for alcohol long before you knew him."

"He only wanted what was best for Jeb Stuart. For both of you."

"He left us without a cent. Did you know that? His insurance was voided. That signing bonus would make up for a lot."

"If Jeb Stuart can get a signing bonus, he can get a college scholarship. Bill Anderson said the Reds wouldn't stand in the way of a college education."

"Well, it's not his decision. And it's certainly not yours." Mary Beth went back behind the reception counter, raised her glasses to the bridge of her nose, and sat down at her computer.

Owen didn't want to end the conversation on the unpleasant note she'd just sounded. He decided to ask about Mary Beth's brother, Contrary's mayor. "Is Purvis around?"

Mary Beth kept her eyes on the computer screen. "He's out mopping up flood damage. Probably find him at the purification plant or the bus barns. Both those places got hit pretty hard." She nodded toward the two bottles of water next to her computer. "We still don't have any tap water."

"What happened at the bus barns?"

"You know how close to the creek they are. Half our equipment's covered in gunk."

"How many buses do you have now?"

"Fifteen."

"And how many do you run?" It was a touchy subject, Owen knew. Mary Beth and her brother had narrowly skirted jail for billing the federal government for a twenty-bus system when they were running only two.

Mary Beth took off her glasses and fixed him with a steely stare. "We run exactly as many as we have to."

"But how many do you charge the government for?"

"Just as many as we run. They take odometer readings to make sure we're providing the service we bill the feds for."

"I can see where that might cramp your style."

If Mary Beth found any humor in Owen's remark, she hid it well. "If you really want to see Purvis, he's probably at the bus barns. You can count the equipment for yourself. I heard you'd graduated from the bus-counting business, though." She put her glasses on and turned back to her computer.

CONTRARY'S BUS BARNS consisted of two large Quonset huts wedged between a stream and a tree-covered slope. The stream overflow had left slimy puddles in a lower parking lot and a scum line halfway up the doors of the aluminum huts. A gravel parking lot higher up the slope had been untouched by the slime. Two buses sat on blocks in the upper lot, motors running and tires turning in the air. In the lower lot, a worker wearing hip-high waders was spraying black slime under the windows of a third bus.

The worker in waders shut off the spray as soon as he saw Owen and shouted into the nearest hut, "Purvis, we got company."

Purvis Jenkins burst through the door of the hut, buttoning a checkered vest. "Shitfire. They're not due until tomorrow." When he recognized Owen he smiled, left the bottom buttons undone, and held out his hand. "Good to see you, Owen. What brings you by?"

"Came up to see your sister. Thought I'd stop by and say hello."

"Glad you did. Yessir, glad you did." Purvis nodded to the man in waders, who resumed spraying slurry over the Contrary Comet logo on the parked bus.

Owen watched the slurry cover the bottom half of the bus and drip from the undercarriage. "What's going on?"

"Scum from the mining dam ruined everything in our lower lot. Didn't touch the upper lot, though. And that's where we kept our older buses."

Purvis undid the top buttons of his vest. "I figure, now we're an official federal disaster, if the old buses look damaged too, the feds will pay to replace them with new ones. Inspector's due tomorrow."

"What are you running on your routes in the meantime?"

Purvis jerked his thumb in the direction of the two buses with their motors running in the upper lot. Both were covered in slime from their tires to their windows. "Spray don't hurt the runnin' of them none."

Owen counted thirteen buses on the upper and lower lots. All but one looked as if they had been dipped in a sludge bath. "You've got fifteen buses."

Purvis squinted. "Thereabouts."

"So there are two out on the road."

"Well, hell. It's midday. Not peak commute time."

"You're still just running two buses, aren't you?"

"We mined this seam before, Owen. It's a waste to run more than two buses in a town the size of Contrary."

"For Christ's sake, Purvis. You and Mary Beth nearly landed in jail last time. Didn't you learn anything from that?"

"Learned to keep better records."

"Mary Beth says they're checking your odometers now. To make sure you're putting in the miles."

Purvis smiled. "So they are."

Owen looked at the two buses up on blocks with their motors running. "That's what's going on with those two buses? You're running up the odometers?"

"Hell, Owen. You know eighty percent of the cost of a bus is operating it, not owning it. It's a sight cheaper to run without drivers and passengers. Look at the money we're saving the taxpayer."

"But you're not saving it. You're claiming it from the feds."

"And putting it to better uses. When Big Coal pulled out of Contrary, they took our tax base. But they didn't take away the need to keep our town running."

Owen sighed. "I've heard all this before, Purvis. No matter how you spend it, it's still fraud." He shook his head. "I can't protect you this time. I'm not with the feds anymore."

"Don't worry your head about me." Purvis took a handkerchief from his vest pocket and mopped his brow. "Why'd you want to see Mary Beth?"

"Wanted to talk to her about Jeb Stuart."

"Boy's got quite a future ahead of him."

"I wanted to make sure it included college. I promised his dad I'd see he got there."

"Stony didn't know the Reds would be after his son."

Owen was tired of arguing. "Maybe I'm wrong to butt in. It just seems to me Jeb Stuart would be better off going to college first."

"Could be you're right."

"You know Jeb Stuart. You know your sister. What do you think? Should I push harder on the college option?"

"Hell, Owen. Asking me for help with Mary Beth is like asking a moonshiner for help with the twelve-step program." Purvis took out the handkerchief and mopped his brow again. "Tell you what, though. If you're really interested in Jeb Stuart, I'm surprised you're not at his game."

"Game?"

"First game's today. Against Logan."

"Mary Beth didn't mention it."

"With you pushing college, she probably didn't want you there. If I know my sister, she's got that bonus money about half spent."

"The game home or away?"

"Away. But Logan's not far." Purvis squinted up at the sun. "Ought to be starting about now."

"Can't think of any place I'd rather be." Owen started to leave, then waited while the man in waders dragged his spray gun past him over to the last clean bus on the lot. "Purvis, tell me something. If you're not running more than two buses, why bother to replace them all with new ones?"

Purvis looked as if the question should answer itself. "Man's gotta take some pride in the system."

7

Blockbusted

OWEN arrived at Jeb Stuart's baseball game in the bottom of the third inning. The stands were lightly populated, with clumps of students and a few parents scattered along the wooden bleachers that paralleled both foul lines and ended well short of the chain-link outfield fence. He saw Bill Anderson sitting behind the home-plate backstop and joined him. While Anderson filled him in on the scoring, Owen took off his sportcoat and leaned back, stretching his arms along the plank seat behind him and drinking in the sunlight and the infield chatter. There was no place he'd rather be than a ballpark, and the smells of fresh-cut grass, wooden bleachers, and oiled leather brought his own playing days back to him.

Contrary was trailing three to two and Jeb Stuart's broad back was right in front of them as he squatted behind home plate to signal the pitcher, then reached high to corral a pitch well over the batter's head. The Logan hitter walked, and Anderson made an entry in the spiral-bound scorebook on his lap. "Contrary misses the Stokes boy," he said. "For all the control this pitcher's got, he might as well be throwing blindfolded."

As if to illustrate Anderson's point, Contrary's pitcher threw two balls well wide of the plate. On the third pitch, Jeb Stuart moved quickly to his right to block a ball in the dirt and, still on his knees, rifled a throw to first to pick off the runner.

Owen and Anderson joined in the clapping. "He's like a grown man playing with little boys," Anderson said.

"He's still just a boy, though," Owen said. "He's not even sixteen, and he needs a college education."

"I told you, we won't stand in the way of that."

"But you might stack enough money in front of him to cause him to lose sight of that goal."

"We're not the bad guys here. Jeb Stuart's getting to be a hot commodity. Good young catchers are rare as rocking-horse turds." Anderson nodded toward a man in a yellow polo shirt sitting alone along the first-base line. "That's Dale Lewis from the Indians. They're watching him too."

"He's just a junior."

"We're watching other players as well. If Jeb keeps going the way he has been, though, he could draw top dollar in next year's draft."

"Unless he decides to go to college."

"He'll have until the fall semester starts to make up his mind."

"Wouldn't he be worth more as a seasoned college graduate with four years of good coaching?"

"Could be. Jeb has all the tools now, though. If he were to be injured in college, or for some reason couldn't hack the competition . . ." Anderson spread his hands, palms upward, as if he'd just dropped an easy pop-up. "He'd miss his chance and the bonus."

"So you'd advise him to take the money right out of high school?"

"If it's offered, yes."

"And his mother would, too."

Anderson looked up from his scorebook and pointed his pen at Owen. "You talked to his mother?"

Owen nodded. "Earlier today."

On the field, the Contrary pitcher walked another batter but got out of the inning with a double play. Jeb Stuart was the second batter to hit for Contrary in the bottom of the third. Kneeling in the on-deck circle and taking off his shin guards, he spotted Owen in the stands, smiled, and waved.

The Logan pitcher hit the first batter and Jeb Stuart stepped into the batter's box. "He tripled and scored the first time up," Anderson said. The scout hunched forward, watching Jeb Stuart take a high pitch for a ball. Jeb ripped the second pitch into the left-center field gap for a double, scoring the runner and tying the game. Anderson led the applause. "He just outclasses everybody on the field."

"It does a mother's heart good to hear you say that." Mary Beth stood at the end of their row. She'd let her blonde hair down from the bun she'd worn at work and changed into a yellow sundress that accented her cleavage. A light blue cardigan hung loosely over her shoulders. She nodded to Owen and climbed over the bench behind the two men to sit beside Bill Anderson. "Owen was telling me the majors are a long shot, Bill. What do you think Jeb's chances are of making it all the way?"

"Hard to say," Anderson answered. "Pretty good if he goes high in the draft and commands a bonus."

"But he'll do that, won't he?" Mary Beth asked.

Anderson shrugged. Owen saw him reach out to cover Mary Beth's hand with his and watched her pull her hand away to shield her eyes from the sun. He looked on Anderson's left hand for a wedding ring, saw none, and wondered who was recruiting whom.

The half-inning ended with Jeb Stuart stranded on second base and the teams still tied. After that, the lead changed hands regularly, with Contrary's pitcher unable to hold a lead and Logan's pitcher unable to contain Jeb Stuart's bat.

The joy of an afternoon at the ballpark slowly leaked away as Owen watched the interplay between Anderson and Mary Beth. Was Anderson scouting Jeb Stuart just to get close to Mary Beth, or was Mary Beth luring Anderson to get a contract for her son? Either way, Jeb Stuart's interests were likely to come in second- or third-best.

As the game on the field seesawed back and forth, Owen contemplated another option. Maybe the attraction he was watching out of the corner of his eye was mutual and genuine. He hadn't been able to read Mary Beth's motives when he'd been her prey. How could he hope to now? He leaned forward, rested his forearms on his knees, and tried to concentrate on the game.

Contrary came to bat in the last inning down by one run. The Logan pitcher alternated walks and strikeouts until Jeb Stuart stepped up with two outs and runners on first and second. He took a ball and a strike and hit the third pitch squarely on the nose, but lined it straight into the shortstop's glove. The game was over before he dropped his bat.

As the stands emptied, Owen led the way down into the Contrary dugout. Jeb Stuart sat alone in the far corner, stuffing his catching gear into a dusty dufflebag. "Couldn't have hit it any harder," Owen said.

"Just a tough break," Anderson added over Owen's shoulder.

Jeb Stuart tightened the drawstring on the bag and stood up.

"You did your best, hon," Mary Beth said.

"We're going out for pizza," Anderson said to Owen. "Want to join us?"

"Yeah, come on," Jeb Stuart said.

Owen glanced at Mary Beth. Her hazel eyes were hard and uninviting.

"No thanks. I've got to get home to help Mom." Owen patted Jeb Stuart's shoulder. "I picked up a schedule, though. I'll catch your next home game. Maybe we can do the pizza thing then."

On his way home, Owen took the ridge road above Drybone Hollow. He noticed that there were now four empty foundations on the far side of the hollow above the creekbed. He was sure there had only been one there the last time he'd looked.

CABLE STOKES PACED in front of the pickup truck his son Billy Joe had pulled onto the slurry-blackened grass that had once been Lyle Tanner's front yard. The bed of the rusted-out truck was filled with gray cinderblocks.

"I tell you Lyle, it's foolproof," Cable said. "Billy Joe here will do all the work. Just let us lay a foundation or two down your road."

Lyle stood with his arms folded, his right foot resting on the raised foundation that had once held his mobile home. "If it's so foolproof, add 'em to your own damn road."

"We've been doing that, as you can see," Cable said. "But we've just about run out of room on our side of the hollow. Besides which, the last inspector who come out was the same one who interviewed me when there weren't no foundations down but mine."

"So he caught you?" Lyle asked.

"Not quite. He come out, saw four foundations, scratched his head, and must have assumed he'd just missed them first time around. They was all covered with slurry, after all. He interviewed Billy Joe here. The check should be in the works already."

"I don't know," Lyle said. "I don't want to risk doing anything that might endanger our lawsuit. You shouldn't neither."

"These FEMA checks don't affect our lawsuit. It's just walking-around money. We can still sue for loss and damages. I checked."

"It's just too risky, Cable. What if they put us on the stand, under oath, and ask us whether we lied about these claims?"

"You've been watching too much TV, Lyle. This is real life. It's the government. How they gonna know?"

"You said yourself one of them was looking goggle-eyed at all those foundations on your side of the hollow."

"I also said the man approved my claims."

Tanner shook his head. "Trouble with you, Cable, nothing's ever enough. You're not happy with your rightful share, so you take more."

"Money's there for the public. I'm the public."

"You're not happy with your wife, so you take somebody else's."

"Women all had a choice. Never forced nobody against their will." Cable flashed the grin of a cat with a mouthful of feathers. "Never had to."

Tanner nodded toward the load of cinderblocks. "Wouldn't surprise me if those cinderblocks belonged to somebody else."

"Well, now, one cinderblock looks pretty much like another. Nobody put a brand on 'em."

"I was right, then. They're stolen." Tanner spat on his slurry-blackened lawn. "It's all gonna catch up with you one of these days, Cable."

Cable raised his right hand high and shook it as if he were playing an invisible tambourine. "All right, all right. If you're going to be a candy-ass about all this, we'll fix it so's you won't have to lie. We'll let Billy Joe here do it for you. Course, that means he gets cut in for a full share."

"Damn straight," Billy Joe said.

"Thought you said they already interviewed Billy Joe," Lyle said.

"Hell, that's no worry. We'll cut off his pigtail, get him a pair of dark glasses and a fresh shirt."

Billy Joe ran his right hand through his hair. The back of the hand was discolored, and it was missing three fingers. "You'll play hob cutting off my pigtail."

"We just need to change his looks a little," Cable said. "The government folks'll never know. We all look alike to them."

"It's just not right," Lyle said.

"It's money the government wants you to have. They're giving it away. What'd I always say to do in that case?" Cable asked Billy Joe.

Billy Joe gave Cable a blank look.

"If somebody's giving something away," Cable prompted. "What'd I always say to do?"

"I don't know, Pa. What?"

Cable could barely hide his disgust. "Take two and run. That's what I always say."

"You've already taken two, Cable," Lyle said. "You've taken four, counting your claim on your own trailer. Ain't that enough?"

"What's enough?" Cable asked. "We're victims here. The flood took our homes and our loved ones. Carried them right away. Who's to say what's enough?"

Cable paused and blew his nose loudly into a wrinkled handkerchief. "I tell you, Lyle, this system's slicker than greased snot. I've already got my first check. And there's three more in the pipeline."

Lyle uncrossed his arms and scratched his head. "Lemme see the check."

"Hell, I cashed it already. Ain't you been listening? After you take two, you got to run. I run straight to the bank."

"It just can't be that easy."

"Tell you what. You want to know how easy it is, just call their 800 number. Set up an interview. You're entitled to claim the loss of your trailer. Nothing illegal about that. Tell them about Maddie, too. Let them count your bedrooms. See for yourself how easy it is."

"I can do that, I guess," Tanner said.

"You do that. Meantime, Billy Joe here will lay out a new foundation just down the road a piece."

Billy Joe started for the cab of the truck, then stopped and stood still when he heard a car coming down the gravel road. The oncoming vehicle rounded a bend and they could make out the light bar on top of the sheriff's patrol car.

Billy Joe looked to his father for guidance.

"Go on, git," Cable said.

Billy Joe reached the pickup, but stopped again with his fingers around the door handle when Thad Reader pulled his patrol car up behind the truck. The sheriff and Owen Allison got out of the car.

Billy Joe climbed into the cab of the pickup. "I was just leaving."

"Stick around a while," the sheriff said. "Got some questions I want to ask you."

"Can't it wait?" Cable asked. "Billy Joe's got a delivery to make."

The sheriff looked in the bed of the pickup. "Cinderblocks? Where you fixing to deliver cinderblocks?"

When Billy Joe didn't answer, Cable said, "Across the hollow. I'm shoring up my foundation."

"Little late for that, isn't it?" Thad Reader said. "Thought you might be delivering them to DPR Construction. They've been missing big batches of their stock lately."

"That so?" Cable said.

Reader walked around the bed of the pickup and hefted a cinderblock. "Guess you've got a receipt for all these?"

"All my receipts went downriver with my house," Cable said.

"DPR was missing so many cinderblocks, they took to marking

them." The sheriff reached into the pickup bed and pulled out a cinderblock with a slash of red paint in the center cavity.

Billy Joe slumped down behind the steering wheel.

"That must be one of the blocks you was saying you found by the side of the road, huh, Billy Joe?" Cable said.

"That's right, by the side of the road," Billy Joe said.

The sheriff tilted up several cinderblocks and examined them. "Must have found quite a few by that roadside. Maybe you ought to take these back to DPR. Could be there's a reward."

Billy Joe started the pickup's engine, but the sheriff reached through the cab window and turned off the ignition. "Don't go just yet. You still haven't answered my questions."

"You haven't asked any."

"We're talking to people who used to work for Anson Stokes in his Canaan mines. You ever do that, Billy Joe?"

Billy Joe grimaced, then nodded yes.

"What about the two of you?" Reader asked Stokes and Tanner.

"Nope," Stokes said.

"Never did," Tanner answered.

Reader turned his attention back to Billy Joe. "When did you work there?"

"'Bout a year ago."

"Why'd you quit?"

"Hurt my back."

"Hurt it smuggling out dynamite in your lunch bucket?"

"Who told you that?"

"Never mind. I'm more interested in what you did with the dynamite."

"Used it to blow out a dog hole in the hill behind my house."

"So your back was so bad hurt that you could draw disability from Anson Stokes' mine, but not so bad hurt that you couldn't mine your own dog hole?" Owen asked.

"Or unload a truckload of cinderblocks," the sheriff added.

"That's about the size of it."

"An interesting medical phenomenon," Owen said. "Maybe you

ought to contact WVU, see if somebody there can't get a journal article out of it."

"Let them get their own damn articles without my help."

"Any of that dynamite left?"

"Nah. They made me quit taking it."

While Reader was questioning Billy Joe, Cable Stokes worked his way around the bed of the pickup, examining cinderblocks. "Only one of these here blocks has any red paint. You trying to bluff us, sheriff?"

"We both know where you got those blocks, Cable. I think you better return them."

"And if I don't?"

"You're looking at jail time."

"For a load of cinderblocks? You can't prove these are DPR's."

"Maybe not. But if I were you I wouldn't be willing to risk it."

Something in Reader's tone stopped Cable cold. "Why not?"

Reader reached into the pocket of his uniform blouse. "Let me show you a couple of pictures." He held out two snapshots. "This top one is a picture Owen Allison here took of your side of the hollow from the ridge road about a week after the dam burst." Reader held up the second photo. "This bottom one's a picture we took this morning from the same place. See the difference?"

Cable glared at the photos, then at Owen.

"I'll help you out," the sheriff said. "There's three new trailer foundations in the picture we took today. That makes four in all."

"So what?" Cable asked, still glaring at Owen.

"So FEMA's fielded four reimbursement claims for trailers missing from those sites. Two are signed by you, one's signed by Billy Joe here, and one's purportedly signed by your sister."

Cable's face turned red and veins bulged in his neck. "You suck-ass pussy," he shouted at Owen. "This was your doing!" He hefted a cinderblock overhead with both hands and hurled it at Owen. It barely cleared the bed of the truck and plopped onto the black grass well short of its target.

Seeing how far he missed, Cable recalibrated, hefted another cinderblock overhead, and charged at Owen. "Just like high school. I'll get you this time, you ass-kissing brown-nose."

The sheriff stepped forward and stuck his boot in Stokes' path. Stokes stumbled, sprawling face down on the grass and thrusting the cinderblock forward like a running back lunging for extra yardage.

"You're not going to get anybody, Cable," the sheriff said. "What you are going to get is up off your flabby stomach. Then you and your boy here are going to take that load of cinderblocks back where you got them."

Cable pulled himself to his knees and shook a muddy fist at Owen.

"Then, if you're smart," the sheriff continued, "you'll go to FEMA and withdraw those extra claims you filed. Otherwise, you'll be facing felony fraud charges."

Still glaring, Cable joined Billy Joe in the cab of the pickup.

The sheriff leaned on the hood of his patrol car. "We'll just follow you a ways, make sure you don't get lost."

Cable slammed the pickup door so hard the springs squealed. "That Owen Allison's a dead man."

Billy Joe waited while the sheriff backed his patrol car out of the pickup's path. "I ask you something, Pa?"

When Cable didn't answer, Billy Joe said, "Why'd y'all lie when the sheriff asked whether you'd worked in Uncle Anson's mine?"

THE SHERIFF FOLLOWED the pickup filled with cinderblocks down the winding gravel road that led out of Drybone Hollow. When Billy Joe Stokes pulled the truck up to a stop sign and signaled for a right turn on the paved road leading to DPR Construction, the sheriff said, "Might as well follow them all the way to DPR."

"I notice they didn't need to ask directions," Owen said.

"Oh, they've been there before all right." The sheriff turned to follow the truck. "I'm amazed they thought they could get away with scamming FEMA. You caught on to their fake claims right away."

"I knew there'd never been any trailers on those foundations. FEMA didn't. Besides, I'd seen that kind of thing before."

The sheriff fixed Owen with his good eye. "No kidding?"

"I did some structural studies on failed buildings after the Loma Prieta quake in the Bay Area. FEMA got a lot of bogus claims back then. There was one fellow in Oakland, a transvestite, who filed eighty claims for a fish tank and a glass coffee table that never existed."

The sheriff whistled soundlessly. "Eighty claims."

"He lived in a run-down apartment. Changed his appearance each time an inspector showed up. Filed forty-six claims as a male and thirty-four as a female."

"What tripped him up?"

"He used the same social security number on all his claims."

The sheriff smiled. "Even Cable was smarter than that. Got his relatives to donate theirs."

The patrol car slowed as the road snaked downward into a hollow bounded by winding railroad tracks that paralleled a dry creekbed. A few loose-shingled homes had been shoehorned between the road and the creekbed. Out-of-work miners sat in their undershirts on the porches of these homes, tending a hodgepodge of yard sale goods hung on sagging clotheslines and laid out on swaybacked card tables.

"Can't get used to week-long yard sales," Owen said.

"Week-long, hell. They're year-long. There's just not enough work to go around."

"You know Cable lied when he said he never worked for his brother."

The sheriff smiled and nodded.

"Why would he do that?" Owen asked.

"Cable lies just to keep in practice. You can always tell when he's lying, though."

"How? With your little eye detector?" Owen had once seen the sheriff convince a suspect that his glass eye had polygraph capabilities.

"No. It's simpler than that. You just watch his lips. If they move, he's lying. It's a dead giveaway."

Ahead of them, the rusting pickup bounced over a railroad crossing and pulled into a narrow storage yard wedged between the rail tracks and the dry creekbed. Sorted piles of lumber, PVC pipe, bricks, and cinderblocks were laid out next to the tracks. The stacks of cinderblocks were noticeably lower than the stacks of other building materials.

The sheriff pulled his patrol car in behind the pickup so it couldn't back out and gave a quick blast on his siren. A shed door opened at the end of the stacks and a short man wearing bib overalls and smoking a stubby cigar emerged. He reached into the bed of the pickup, pulled out a cinderblock, and approached the patrol car. "Afternoon, Sheriff."

"Afternoon, Dickey." The sheriff left his patrol car and walked over to the cab of the pickup. "These two gentlemen found your cinderblocks and want to return them."

Dickey hefted the cinderblock in his hands. "Found our cinderblocks?"

"We knowed they was yours because of the markings," Billy Joe said from the cab of the pickup.

Dickey squinted at his cinderblock through a cloud of cigar smoke. "Markings?"

"The sheriff was just bluffing about markings, numbnuts," Cable said.

"Then how'd he know where the blocks come from?"

Cable closed his eyes as if the question were too painful to consider.

The sheriff rapped on the side of the truck bed. "I'm sure Cable and his boy here will be happy to help you unload their find."

"Nobody said nothing about us unloading," Billy Joe said.

Dickey set the block he was carrying on the stack in the yard. "Sure could use some help."

Neither Cable nor Billy Joe moved from the cab of the truck.

"When you see Peter and Ron, Dickey, ask them if they want to press charges," the sheriff said.

Cable climbed down from the truck cab. "All right. All right. We'll help unload. Come on, Billy Joe."

"We're missing more than one truckload," Dickey said.

The sheriff returned to his patrol car. "These boys know where to get more. They've got no use for them now."

Cable carried a cinderblock from the bed of the truck to the stack in the storage yard without acknowledging the sheriff's statement.

"Hear that, Cable?" the sheriff raised his voice. "You want to stay free of jail, you'll come back with another truckload."

Cable still gave no sign that he heard.

The sheriff backed his patrol car past the stacks of lumber and was about to cross the railroad tracks on the perimeter of the storage yard when Cable's truck exploded.

The cab of the pickup burst into flames. Billy Joe lay stunned beside the truck's rear wheel, while Dickey scrambled on his hands and knees to join Cable, who was cowering behind a stack of cinderblocks.

Reader leapt from his patrol car, retrieved a fire extinguisher from his trunk, and hurried to the burning cab. As the sheriff sprayed foam into the flames, Cable ran crouching from the cover of the stacked cinderblocks to reach his groggy son.

Cable grabbed Billy Joe's arm, jerked him to his feet, flung him back against the stacked cinderblocks, and began beating him. "I've told you and told you about handling dynamite," he shouted as he rained blows down on his son.

Billy Joe crouched and covered his head with both hands. "It wasn't me, Pa. It wasn't me."

Seeing that his blows were glancing off Billy Joe's raised elbows, Cable started kicking the boy in the shins. "It wasn't you, no. It wasn't you who blew up our henhouse and the Nelson's outhouse."

Billy Joe sank to his knees, curling into a ball to protect himself. "It wasn't me."

Cable continued to kick the boy's thighs. "It wasn't you who lost three fingers blast-fishing the Big Muddy with dynamite."

Owen ran up behind Cable, circled his waist, and pulled him away from Billy Joe.

Cable's legs cycled in mid-air as he tried to keep on kicking his target. "Lemme go. Lemme go. I'll kill him."

Owen dug in his heels and held fast to Cable's waist. "That's what I'm afraid of."

Billy Joe whimpered, rolled onto his side, and curled into a fetal position.

While Cable strained against Owen's grip, Dickey hooked up a hose and sprayed water into the truck cab, helping the sheriff bring the flames under control.

Steam sizzled and rose from the hood of the truck as the fire was extinguished. When the flames had disappeared, Cable turned his attention from his son to his truck, pulled free of Owen's grasp, and hurried to the gutted cab.

The truck's windows had exploded outward and the hood and top rows of the cinderblock load were singed with soot and dotted with foam. Inside, the blackened springs of the ruined seat thrust upward like a medieval torture instrument and the acrid smell of burnt plastic filled the cab. The blast had torn a jagged hole in the undercarriage.

Repelled by the odor, Cable reeled backward, coughed, and yelled, "It could have been us in there, numbnuts."

Billy Joe didn't move from his fetal position. "It wasn't me, Pa."

"Well, who the hell was it, then?"

Reader retreated to his patrol car and returned with two pairs of rubber gloves and several clear plastic bags. He handed Owen one pair of gloves and motioned him toward the pickup's passenger door, which had been blown open by the blast.

As Owen squatted by the passenger door, Reader opened the driver's door with a pair of pliers to avoid touching the hot metal. Then the sheriff took a knife and scraped some of the black crust surrounding the undercarriage hole into an evidence bag. "We'll run this through the lab, check it against the explosion residue at Anson's mine."

The sheriff used his pliers to pull out a jagged shard of red tin that had embedded itself in the door frame. "Looks like the explosive was in some kind of red container behind the driver's seat. A lunch box, maybe. Maybe a tackle box."

"Hear that?" Cable shouted at Billy Joe. "The dynamite was in your red tackle box."

Billy Joe had raised himself up on his hands and knees, but seemed unable or unwilling to stand upright. "Well, I didn't put it there."

"Cable, why don't you and your boy finish unloading those cinderblocks," Reader said. "I'm going to have your truck towed to the county yard where we can take a better look at it."

Cable walked over to Billy Joe to help him to his feet. The boy cringed and scuttled backward.

"Get on up, there," Cable said. "I ain't a-gonna hurt you."

Billy Joe rose unsteadily to his feet, taking care to keep his father at arm's length. "I wasn't carrying no dynamite."

"Well, I'm sorry I flew off the handle," Cable said. "It wouldn't have been the first time you've had dynamite misfire, though."

"Don't see that it matters much," Billy Joe said. "You've hit me for the last time, old man."

Cable took a singed cinderblock from the truck bed and carried it to the storage stack. "Sheriff wants us to go on with the unloading."

Billy Joe lumbered over to the truck bed, giving his father a wide berth.

Owen pointed out a small hunk of gray plastic on the ground beneath the jagged hole in the pickup's undercarriage. "Looks like the same kind of chunk we found at the mine site."

The sheriff recovered the piece with his pliers and dropped it into an evidence bag. "Could be part of a timing device. I'll get it checked out."

Reader went on collecting samples until Cable and Billy Joe were finished unloading cinderblocks from the truck bed. By that time the tow truck had arrived. The sheriff stood and gave instructions to the tow truck driver. Then he walked back to his patrol car and opened the door. "Cable, why don't you and Billy Joe ride on down to my office. I'll take your statement and then find you a ride home."

"We got to?" Cable asked.

Reader smiled. "Well, that burnt-out pickup isn't going to carry you very far. You can either ride with me now or walk home and I'll send a deputy to pick you up later. Whichever you prefer."

Billy Joe slid into the back seat of Reader's car. Cable stood halfway between his ruined pickup and the patrol car as if he were considering options he didn't have. Finally, he slouched into the back seat beside his son, saying, "By God, it's police brutality."

In the passenger seat, Owen laughed out loud.

"You may be sitting in the shitbird seat now," Cable said to Owen, "but you and my brother are in for a few surprises. Just wait until the court hearing."

8

Lean to Green

THE night before the judicial hearing into the cause of the Dry-bone Hollow flood, the Reverend Moral Brody staged an overnight vigil and an anti-coal demonstration on the courthouse steps in the hope that the hearing might turn the temporary restraining order against Mountain View Development's coal processing plant into a longer-lasting injunction. Brody's demonstration attracted enough of a crowd that Owen had to park five blocks away from the courthouse to attend the hearing. Even at that distance, he could hear the thumping of a bass drum and the staccato clamor of the crowd chanting, "NO TO COAL."

Owen's walk to the courthouse was slowed by a small group of men that had spilled over onto the sidewalk to admire a shiny brown and yellow Cadillac parked at the curb. Cable Stokes stood at the center of the group, one hand resting on the Cadillac's front fender. His voice carried easily over the chanting of the Brody demonstration.

" 'Pre-owned,' that's what they call it. None of that 'used' shit with a car this cherry."

The tall, hollow-eyed figure of Lyle Tanner shouted from the edge of the crowd, "You know what eight out of ten Cadillac owners say, don't you, Cable?"

Without waiting for a response, Tanner answered his own question. "Eight out of ten owners say . . ." he pitched his voice higher and adopted an Amos-and-Andy accent, ". . . Cadillac's the best mutha-fuckin' car I *evah* own, man."

Tanner laughed and slapped his thigh like a minstrel sideman, and the crowd of white males laughed with him.

Cable's eyes flashed. "What the hell do you know about cars, Tanner? You're just a glorified parking lot attendant."

The men stopped laughing.

"It's just an old joke, Cable," Tanner said.

"By God, it better be," Cable said.

Both Tanner and Stokes seemed to be handling their grief remarkably well, Owen thought. Maybe Elizabeth Kubler-Ross should include a section on the healing effects of automobile purchases in her next edition of *On Death and Dying*. He had stepped off the sidewalk to skirt the crowd when Cable caught sight of him.

"Hey there, sweetness," Cable shouted. "You tell my brother to watch his ass, 'cause this judge is likely to nail it to the wall."

The eyes of Cable's audience turned to Owen, expecting a response. He felt confused and uncertain, like a loner set upon by a high school gang. He stopped and said in a voice just loud enough for the group to hear, "Ass-watching's more your kind of thing, Cable. Tell him yourself."

A few of the men laughed, causing Cable to give Owen the finger and shout, "Up yours, ass kisser." When Owen shrugged and walked on, Cable reclaimed the crowd by saying, "So Tanner, tell me again what you think of my new car."

A block farther along, Owen spotted Sheriff Thad Reader on the opposite sidewalk and crossed the street to join him. By now, the din from the "NO TO COAL" chanters was deafening.

"You here under subpoena?" the sheriff shouted over the demonstration noise.

Owen opened his jacket to show the summons in his inside pocket.

"Me too. That'll get us in the back door." Reader nodded toward the hearing attendees lined up on the courthouse steps, splitting the group of chanting demonstrators in half. "No need to wait in that line."

They crossed the courthouse lawn, moving toward the back of the building. "I see Cable Stokes spent a good share of his FEMA money on a two-tone Cadillac," Owen said.

"Man never was one to hide his light under a bushel."

"Cable seems to think this hearing will do in his brother."

They rounded the rear corner of the courthouse and the sheriff squinted against the morning sunlight. "Don't see how. The temporary restraining order shut down Mountain View's operation, not Anson's. Unless he lit the fuse, he shouldn't have anything to worry about."

"I'd worry about any hearing where Cable Stokes claims to have inside knowledge."

"Cable always claims to know a lot more than he's telling. Usually, though, he tells a lot more than he knows."

"He seemed certain the judge would lay Anson low."

Reader sucked on his lower lip. "Well, the judge is a wild card. They drew Carter Vereen. The courthouse crowd calls him 'Lean to Green' Vereen. He tied up a good share of the state's timber industry when it threatened the habitat of some rare furry critter."

"So he's likely to be tough on miners."

"Already has been. He shut down strip mining in the state for two years by treating every dump site as a potential stream bed." Reader nodded several times in succession. "He could make it tough on Anson, all right. His rulings scatter like shrapnel from a grenade. Anybody within range is at risk."

Owen and the sheriff showed their subpoenas to a guard at the back door, who led them into an oak-paneled courtroom and ushered them to seats in the jury box, where three other potential witnesses already sat. The sheriff introduced Owen to the other witnesses. Brady Jackson, a lawyer for several of the flood victims, wore a white suit and clasped a bulging leather briefcase on his lap; Gail Meyers Connor, head of STAMP, the Society To Achieve Mountaintop

Preservation, was an attractive woman with gray-streaked brown hair who picked absently at a loose thread in her knitted sweater dress; and Stan Davenport, of the state's Division of Environmental Protection, wore a tweed jacket and fidgeted with a necktie that looked tight enough to strangle him.

Just before the hearing was scheduled to start, Cable Stokes strode up the center aisle of the courtroom, smirked at Owen and the sheriff, and joined the group waiting to testify. Owen raised his eyebrows, giving Thad Reader a "What the hell?" look. A shrug was the only response Reader could muster.

Cable had barely taken his seat when the court clerk asked all those in attendance to rise in recognition of the honorable Carter Vereen. Vereen swept into the courtroom as if he heard an invisible band playing "Hail to the Chief." A short, white-haired man with prominent cheekbones and a hawk nose, he wore an emerald green necktie with a bulbous knot that poked out over the collar of his judicial robes. Owen wondered if the tie were a random choice, or if Vereen knew about his "Lean to Green" nickname and chose to accent it.

"Think he means to make a statement with that necktie?" Owen whispered to Reader.

"Think the sun will rise in the east tomorrow?"

Judge Vereen explained that the purpose of the hearing was to explore the cause of the Mountain View dam failure with the aim of ruling on the Division of Environmental Protection's request for a permanent injunction shutting down the dam and the attendant coal processing operations. He began by asking if the opposing counsels were ready.

The lawyer for the state, Harrison Marks, was in constant motion, shuffling papers, conferring with assistants, loosening his tie, mopping his brow, and waving his arms to make a point. By way of contrast, Webb Clifton, the lawyer for Mountain View Development, sat quietly with his fingers forming a steeple, his eyes half-closed, and his lips curved in a faint smile that suggested he was enjoying a private joke with God.

Owen was the first witness called by the state's lawyer. The lawyer established Owen's credentials as a failure analyst, then paced in front of the witness stand as he questioned Owen about his first trip into the Canaan II Mine, the appearance of the ceiling crater, his opinion that the crater was caused by an explosion, and his subsequent discovery of a piece of Bakelite lodged next to the door frame.

The Mountain View lawyer, Clifton, seemed almost bored by Owen's testimony and waived his right to cross-examine. As Owen stepped down from the witness stand, he caught sight of Anson Stokes in the rear of the courtroom. Anson nodded without smiling.

Thad Reader was the next witness. The sheriff testified that his deputies had taken samples from several surfaces within the mine and that the FBI laboratory had found traces of sodium carbonate, sodium nitrate, and sulphur-bearing compounds on the topmost edge of the overhead crater and the piece of Bakelite found by Owen Allison.

"And what do these chemicals indicate?" Harrison Marks asked.

"They're the residue of a dynamite explosion."

A murmur ran through the courtroom. The appearance of the man-made crater had been described in the press, but this was the first time the use of dynamite had been confirmed.

The state's lawyer consulted a sheaf of papers, then asked Reader, "So it would appear that the flood was caused by a charge of dynamite?"

"That's right."

"And have you been able to apprehend the person or persons who set the charge?"

"Not yet."

"So that person or persons is still at large and could presumably strike again?" Marks paused. "Isn't it true that they've threatened to do so?"

The rumble in the courtroom grew so loud that the judge had to gavel it down.

Reader was clearly annoyed by the question. "We don't know that."

"Let me rephrase the question. Isn't it true that Mountain View officials have received overt threats against the Drybone Hollow Dam?"

Reader grimaced as the courtroom buzz picked up again. "Yes it is."

The state's attorney rummaged through the papers on his desk and came up with one encased in a glassine folder. He handed the folder to Reader. "I call your attention to State Exhibit B. Is this one of the letters?"

Reader nodded. "Yes, it is."

"Would you read it, please?"

Reader glanced at the letter, then looked out at the courtroom and recited from memory, "Keep Operating And Next Time The Whole Dam Goes."

"And how is it signed?"

"Friend of the Environment."

The attorney took the letter back and said, "I understand you have others like this."

"That's correct."

"How many?"

"Two others."

"In view of those letters, wouldn't you say that continued operation of the coal processing plant represents a threat to the community?"

Reader frowned. "The letters could be a prank."

"But they could be real. Couldn't they come from the same people who dynamited the Canaan II mine?"

"Unfortunately, they didn't give a return address. So we don't really know."

"But you have taken steps to guard against another explosion?"

"We have. Yes."

"So you must feel another attempt on the dam is likely."

"We don't know how likely it is. It's our job to keep it from happening."

The state's attorney tried several times to get Thad Reader to state under oath that reopening the processing plant might well lead to another explosion and flood. When Reader failed to rise to the bait, the attorney turned the witness over to the defense lawyer.

In cross-examining Reader, the Mountain View attorney first asked, "Sheriff Reader, would you tell the court why you did not make the threats against the Drybone Hollow Dam public knowledge?"

"Making the threats public would serve no useful purpose. And it could spawn a rash of copycat threats from people who want the see the operation shut down. That would just complicate our investigation."

"So the state's attorney has done your office a disservice by revealing the existence of the letters."

Harrison Marks rose in a flurry of papers. "Objection. Immaterial."

"Sustained."

Webb Clifton smiled and continued. "You've stated that you have no way of knowing whether the dam is at risk from another explosion. In your position, however, you must assume that the threat is legitimate and guard the dam."

"That's right."

"So the fact that you're guarding the dam and the mine doesn't reflect any judgment regarding the real legitimacy of the threats?"

"No. It doesn't."

"And I assume your office is taking steps to trace the origin of the letters."

"We are, yes."

The Mountain View attorney tilted his head back and let his eyes return to half-mast. "Thank you. No further questions."

The next witness called by the state was Gail Meyers Connor, president of the Society To Achieve Mountaintop Preservation. In between several overruled objections from the Mountain View attorney, she testified that there were at least forty-two other mining dams in the state located over subterranean shafts. She submitted the names of forty-two dams for the record and asked that they be investigated with the aim of shutting down any whose safety was questionable.

On cross-examination, Webb Clifton asked, "Ms. Connor, if a 7-Eleven convenience store in Charleston were held up and the owner killed, would you advocate closing every convenience store in the state?"

"Of course not."

"Then why advocate the closing of every dam that resembles the Mountain View dam in Drybone Hollow?"

The witness picked at a loose thread in her sweater dress. "It's not the same thing."

"I submit it is exactly the same thing. We have an act of violence against a single mine. And you want to shut down all mines like it." The Mountain View attorney peered over his steepled fingers. "No further questions."

The state's attorney rushed his redirect examination to counter the point made by Clifton before it had a chance to sink in. He began by saying, "Ms. Connor, let me pose another hypothetical question: Suppose a container of pain-relief medicine in a convenience store was found to be laced with arsenic. Wouldn't you advocate removing all containers of that pain reliever from the store's shelves?"

"I certainly would."

"And might that quarantine not extend to every convenience store in the state?"

"It certainly might."

"And why would that action be justified?"

The witness smiled like a bright student who knows she has the right answer. "It's a matter of safeguarding the public."

The state's attorney returned her smile. "Exactly. It's a matter of safeguarding the public." He held his smile as he returned to his table, passing the Mountain View attorney, whose eyes were still half-closed, but whose mouth was no longer smiling.

The next witness called by the state was the white-suited lawyer, Brady Jackson. The state's attorney started to lead Jackson through a litany of the losses and damages suffered by the members of his class-action suit when Webb Clifton interrupted. "I object, Your Honor. My client is willing to stipulate that the breaching of the Drybone Hollow Dam caused untold loss and damage. That is not the question before this hearing. The question we are here to address is, 'Why did this dam failure happen, and is it likely to happen again?' "

When the judge upheld the objection, the state's attorney asked, "Do I understand that the Mountain View attorney is willing to stipulate that all the damage cited by the witness is the responsibility of Mountain View Development?"

A few courtroom observers tittered.

The Mountain View attorney made a show of sighing heavily. "That's a matter for another trial."

Judge Vereen said, "I agree. Unless the state has some other line of questioning to pursue with this witness, shut it down."

Brady Jackson frowned. He opened his mouth as if he wanted to say more.

The state's attorney silenced Jackson with a look. "Very well, Your Honor. I have no more questions for this witness."

While Brady Jackson lugged his bulging briefcase back to the jury box where Owen and Thad Reader sat, the state called Cable Stokes as its next witness.

As Stokes put his right hand on the Bible and repeated the oath, "To tell the truth, the whole truth, and nothing but the truth," Owen nudged Thad Reader. "Forcing Cable Stokes to tell the truth is like forcing Babe Ruth to bat right-handed. This ought to be quite a show."

The judge directed Cable to state his name and address for the record.

"Name's Cable Stokes. Address used to be Drybone Hollow, but I got flooded out."

The state's attorney took over the questioning. "What is your relation to Anson Stokes, the owner of the Canaan II and III Mines?"

"He's my brother."

"Have you ever worked in his mines?"

"For a little while when they first opened."

Owen nudged Thad Reader. "The oath must be taking hold. He lied to us about working there."

The state's attorney continued. "Please tell the court about your brother's attitude toward the mine."

"At first?"

"When you worked there."

"At first he was really angry about it. He'd poured his life savings into it and the main shaft was pretty much played out."

"That's the shaft under Mountain View's Drybone Hollow Dam? The shaft that flooded?"

"That's right."

"You say your brother was angry about it?"

Without rising from his chair, the Mountain View lawyer objected. "Calls for a conclusion."

"It's pretty easy to conclude," Cable said. "My brother's got a real short fuse."

The judge rapped his gavel once. "Objection sustained. Mr. Stokes, kindly wait for my ruling before responding."

"Right sorry, Your Honor."

The state's attorney tried again. "Let me put it this way. Did your brother ever say anything to you expressing his feelings about the mine?"

"He said once he'd like to blow the shaft to hell and gone just to show . . ."

In the rear of the courtroom, Anson Stokes was on his feet. "You lying whorehopper. I never said no such thing."

The judge gaveled down Anson. "Mr. Stokes. Please control yourself."

"See what I mean, Judge?" Cable said. "A real short fuse."

The judge rapped his gavel again. "Please continue, Mr. Stokes."

"Well, Anson said he'd like to blow the shaft deeper and wider just to show Ed Kaufman—that's the fellow sold him the mine—there was still coal there."

"So your brother told you he'd like to blow the main shaft to hell and gone?" the state's attorney repeated.

"Yessir."

"Do you think he might have done that?"

For the first time in the hearing the Mountain View lawyer left his chair. "Objection. Really, Your Honor. That calls for speculation on the part of the witness."

"It certainly does," the judge said. "Please refrain from answering, Mr. Stokes."

"You mean I shouldn't tell you I think he done it?"

"Objection."

"Let it rest, Mr. Stokes." The judge addressed the state's attorney. "I expect you to do a better job of controlling your witness."

"Let's change the line of questioning," the state's attorney said. "Tell me about security procedures at the Canaan mines. How would you characterize them?"

The Mountain View lawyer was still on his feet. "Objection. The witness is not an expert."

"The witness has worked in several mines, Your Honor," the state's lawyer said. "I'm asking for a comparison."

"I'll allow it," the judge said. "Answer the question, Mr. Stokes."

"Security was lax. Real lax. Anybody could wander in and out of the main shaft."

Owen watched Anson Stokes. His face was flaming, and his cheeks were puffed out as if he were about to explode.

"And were critical supplies like explosives carefully controlled and monitored?" the lawyer asked.

"Not at all," Cable said. "The supply shed was always open. You worked there, you could take whatever you wanted. You were supposed to log stuff in and out, but nobody did it. I hear tell several sticks of dynamite went missing just last year."

Anson shot to his feet. "It was your shiftless son took that dynamite. And you well know it, pukemouth."

The judge's gavel hammered faster than a nailing machine. "Mr. Stokes. One more outburst and I'll have you removed from this courtroom."

Cable Stokes sat smirking in the witness box. The state's attorney caught a mild strain of the smirk from his witness. "No more questions, Your Honor."

The Mountain View attorney settled back into his chair to cross-examine Cable. "Mr. Stokes, how long ago did your brother purchase the Canaan mine site?"

Cable shrugged. "Ten, maybe twelve years ago."

"So it was at least that long ago that he allegedly threatened to dynamite the main shaft in order to find more coal and make good on his investment?"

Cable shrugged again. "Guess so."

"Now, in that time, your brother has opened at least two other shafts on that property, which must have repaid his investment several times over, wouldn't you say?"

"I don't know nothing about no profits."

"So your brother would have no reason to dynamite the main shaft simply to make good on an investment he'd long since amortized."

"I told you, I don't see none of the profits. You'll have to ask my brother about that."

"But, Mr. Stokes, you're the one that raised this issue." The Mountain View attorney spoke slowly, as if dealing with a child. "Let me try again. Does it seem likely to you that your brother would dynamite a played-out seam in an abandoned shaft when coal is still plentiful in at least two working shafts?"

Cable shifted back and forth in the witness box as if he couldn't find a comfortable position. "There's just no telling what my brother might or might not do."

"I see. One of the things we're trying to decide at this hearing is whether the Drybone Hollow Dam is likely to break loose again. Just for the sake of argument, let's assume that your brother did dynamite his own shaft to reclaim a hidden seam of coal. Unlikely as I think that is, it's got to be even more unlikely that he'd do it again. Wouldn't you agree?"

Cable slumped in the witness chair.

"Objection." Harrison Marks tried to rescue Cable. "Calls for speculation on the part of the witness."

"Your Honor," the Mountain View attorney responded, "this witness has been doing nothing but speculate all afternoon."

"Objection sustained. You've made your point, counselor. Please proceed."

The Mountain View attorney shook his head just enough to show his distaste for the witness without bringing a reprimand from the judge. "No further questions."

The judge raised his eyebrows at the state's attorney, who looked away from Cable Stokes and waved his hand in dismissal. "Nothing on redirect, Your Honor. The state rests its case."

THE FIRST WITNESS called by the Mountain View lawyer was Stan Davenport, the fidgeting representative of the state's Division of Environmental Protection. The lawyer led Davenport through a series of questions designed to establish that Mountain View's dam conformed to all state criteria and had passed all required inspections.

In cross-examining the witness, Harrison Marks made the point that Davenport's office had weakened state mining regulations so that certain rules for the construction of dams and sediment ponds would not apply to coal waste impoundments like Mountain View's dam. The state had then ignored several federal orders to strengthen those regulations.

The state's attorney concluded his series of questions by asking, "So even though Mountain View's dam met state regulations, those regulations were watered down considerably?"

Davenport adjusted his necktie knot, which still appeared to be strangling him. "That's not the way we see it."

"I didn't ask how you see it. Isn't it true that the actions of your office have left the state regulations less effective than the federal regulations?"

Davenport fidgeted. "You could say that."

"I just did. No further questions, Your Honor."

Webb Clifton excused the DEP representative without attempting to take him off the hook implanted by the state's attorney. The Mountain View attorney then rested his case.

Judge Vereen made no attempt to conceal his surprise at Clifton's action and ordered the two attorneys to deliver their closing arguments.

The closing arguments held few surprises. Harrison Marks argued that the slurry behind the dam was a public hazard. It had already broken through once, security in the mine below the dam was lax, and the impoundment had become a target for ecoterrorists. Webb Clifton argued that the Drybone Hollow flood had been caused by unprecedented sabotage. The dam above the hollow met or exceeded all state safety requirements and deserved to remain in operation.

After hearing the arguments, Judge Vereen adjourned the court, announcing that he would return with his decision within an hour.

"Within an hour," Owen said. "Sounds like he doesn't expect to give it much thought."

"His mind's been made up for some time," Reader said. "Man's about as flexible as a tombstone. He'd rather make a political statement than worry over the legalities of his decision."

"So Mountain View won't reopen its operation any time soon."

"You can make book on that."

Judge Vereen returned to the bench after only forty minutes. Rapping his gavel once, he announced, "I have heard nothing that would cause me to vacate the restraining order shutting down Mountain View Development's processing plant and dam. Therefore I am issuing an injunction stipulating that the plant remain closed."

There was a smattering of applause, and a group of Moral Brody's followers began chanting, "NO TO COAL, NO TO COAL."

The judge smiled at the chant and waited a short time before he gaveled it down, saying, "These demonstrations may have their place outside, but I will not allow them in my courtroom."

The judge adjusted his green necktie. "The court further suggests that the state undertake a thorough investigation of all impoundment dams within its boundaries to ensure that the tragedy of Drybone Hollow is not repeated elsewhere."

To Owen's left, Gail Meyers Connor raised her fist in a victory signal.

"Finally," the judge said, "this court is issuing a temporary restraining order halting all operations at the Canaan III Mine."

Anson Stokes leapt to his feet. "Your Honor, that's my livelihood."

"From what this court has heard today, Mr. Stokes, the laxness of your security measures may have contributed to the flood that fouled Drybone Hollow and cost four lives."

"That's bullshit. My brother . . ."

The judge hammered his gavel. "Mr. Stokes, the court has thus far ignored your outbursts and intemperate language. Be advised that the restraining order is, as designated, temporary. You will be given ample opportunity to present arguments in this court as to why the order should be lifted, just as Mountain View did today."

"A shitload of good it did them. All they got was a lawyer's fat bill."

"Notify this court as soon as your lawyers are ready, Mr. Stokes. We'll be happy to hear their arguments."

"What kind of put-up job is this?"

The judge raised his gavel as if he wanted any excuse to pound Anson into submission. "Careful with that short fuse of yours, Mr. Stokes. If I jail you for contempt, it will take all that much longer for you to ready your case."

Anson's eyes flared. His face reddened from his hairline to his neck, but he sat down.

Judge Vereen rapped his gavel twice. "The business of this court is concluded."

OUTSIDE THE COURTHOUSE, Owen and Sheriff Reader picked their way through a group of leather-jacketed followers of Moral Brody chanting, "NO TO COAL." Just beyond the chanting crowd, they watched Cable Stokes exchanging high-fives with a group of men clustered around his newly purchased Cadillac.

"Jesus," Owen said. "What kind of a system gives credence to the testimony of an asshole like that?"

"I believe it's called democracy," Reader said. "One man, one vote."

"One pack of lies. Where does the judge get the right to shut down Anson's mine?"

"If he feels the mine represents a threat to public safety, Vereen has the right to issue a temporary restraining order. Anson will get his day in court."

"Does he stand any chance of reopening his mine?"

"Depends on the judge. If he draws Judge Vereen, I'd say he has all the chance of a quadruple amputee in a kicking contest with a colicky mule."

Horns honked across the street. Owen looked up to see Anson

Stokes blocking traffic with his black Hummer, sitting in mid-block with his left-turn signal blinking. When the oncoming traffic cleared, Anson made an abrupt left, crossed two lanes, and rammed Cable's Cadillac broadside.

The Cadillac's alarm wailed, and the crowd scattered like billiard balls after a break.

Anson backed up, blocking traffic in both directions, and rammed Cable's new car again.

The Cadillac's alarm sputtered and died.

Cable rushed into the street and pounded on the Hummer's hood with both fists, punctuating his blows with cries of "Motherfucker!"

Anson reached out of the Hummer's window and flipped a white business card at Cable's feet. "See my insurance agent, asshole. Next time you cross me, I won't stop with your car."

Cable kicked at the card and kept on pounding. "You're a dead man, motherfucker."

"Don't threaten me, Cable. I've got a short fuse. Remember?" Anson backed away and drove off, leaving Cable pounding the empty air.

9

Pennies off the Table

OWEN was freeing Buster from his leash at the end of their walk the next morning when his mother brought him a copy of the *Barkley Democrat* folded to a headline featuring Dusty Rhodes' name. "Your friend the senator is in the news again," she said.

"He's not my friend, Mom." Owen unfolded the newspaper. "What'd he do now?"

"He's promoted a federal grant. Going to turn the Drybone Hollow Dam into a recreation area. There'll be fishing and swimming, and I suppose those noisy ski boats."

The news article gave more particulars. The grant, which could amount to twenty million dollars, was the first of five to be awarded by the federal Mine Safety and Health Administration in a pilot study to reclaim coal slurry impoundments in Appalachia. The article recounted the recent failure of the Drybone Hollow Dam but failed to mention Rhodes' ownership interest in the operation.

Owen folded the paper to hide the picture of Rhodes' smiling face. No wonder the Mountain View lawyer hadn't worked too hard to keep the dam and its processing plant operating. "Some story. Rhodes covers the county with slurry and comes away with twenty million for his troubles."

"You're being too hard on him, Owen. He had nothing to do with that dam failure."

"He owns most of Mountain View Enterprises, Mom. The paper won't tell you that, but it's his damn dam."

"There's no need to be redundant."

Buster had raised his head from the patch of morning sunlight he'd co-opted and was staring at Owen, who realized he must have been close to shouting and lowered his voice. "Sorry. It pisses me off, is all."

The news of Rhodes' grant had squeezed the paper's reporting of Judge Vereen's findings into the lower right-hand corner of the front page. Owen had just started to read the *Democrat*'s account of the hearing when the phone rang.

Ruth answered the phone and covered the mouthpiece with her hand. "It's for you. Somebody named Marks. From Charleston."

"He's the guy who just prosecuted the state's case against Mountain View," Owen took the phone from his mother, who stood watching him.

The voice on the phone was brusque, with a faint twang that Owen recalled from the courtroom. "The attorney general would like to talk to you about contracting for your services."

"To do what?"

"He'd like to tell you that in person. Can you be here around 1:30?"

Owen agreed, wrote the address in the margin of the newspaper, and hung up the phone. He looked up to see his mother watching him and told her he'd just received a tentative job offer from the state.

"To do what?" Ruth asked.

"Man didn't say."

"For how long?"

"Didn't say that, either."

"Well, it's nice that someone wants to hire you, but shouldn't you be getting back to California?"

"To Judith, you mean?"

Ruth handed Owen the phone. "Why don't you call her? Right now."

"Mom, it's six in the morning in California. Let's at least wait until she gets to her office."

Ruth returned the phone to its cradle. "All right. But you be sure and call her then."

OWEN CALLED HIS ex-wife as soon as her law office in California opened. He recounted the previous day's hearing and asked, "How can the judge get away with shutting down Anson's operation?"

"Legally, all he needs is the threat of irreparable public harm and the likelihood that the subsequent hearing will uphold his order. Mr. Stokes will get a chance to make his case. And he can always appeal to a higher court."

"But that takes time. The shutdown has tied up his assets. He can't earn anything while his mine is shut down. It doesn't seem fair. All on the strength of some anonymous threats."

"I thought you said there was some negligence involved as well."

The call was starting to feel like an adversarial hearing. "Whose side are you on, anyhow?" Owen asked.

"I didn't think I was taking sides. I'm just responding to the case you're presenting. Didn't you say there was some negligence?"

"Anson didn't watch his empty mineshaft. He's watching it now, though. So is the sheriff. We're renting surveillance cameras to record comings and goings."

"If you're installing cameras, you must take the threat seriously."

"The cameras are more for the judge's benefit. To convince him things are under control. A watched plot never roils."

"If you want my legal advice, I wouldn't try that pun on the judge. Or anyone over the age of twelve." Judith paused. "I'm surprised the judge even has to issue an order to shut Stokes down. How can the man get anyone to work in a mine someone has threatened to blow up?"

"They're not working in the threatened shaft. And the sheriff was trying to keep the threat quiet."

"Was that wise? Or even honest? The people living below the dam are at risk."

"How much credence can you give to an anonymous threat? If all it takes is a letter or two to shut down a mine, the tree huggers would shut down every mine, dam, sawmill, and power plant in the state."

"Careful now," Judith said. "You're talking to a tree hugger. And making a threat against public safety is serious business. The writer can do jail time."

"You should have heard the demonstrators outside the courtroom. They were pretty ugly. I bet quite a few of them would be willing to risk jail time to get their way."

"There's a big difference between chanting 'NO TO COAL' and threatening to blow up a mine."

"I'll grant you that," Owen said. "And there's a still bigger difference between making the threat and carrying it out. But in the last month, we've seen chanting, threats, and dynamitings. It's not impossible that we're dealing with an ecoterrorist."

"Dynamitings? More than one?"

"Cable Stokes' truck blew up. Nobody was hurt. Most likely it was an accident."

Judith's voice registered incredulity. "How can a truck blow up accidentally?"

"Cable's oldest boy was given to hauling dynamite. He claims he wasn't hauling it this time, but he's not too reliable. An accident seems to be the most likely explanation. The sheriff is looking into it."

"For heaven's sake, Owen. You've had two unexplained explosions in the space of a month and you think posting a few surveillance cameras is excessive? I'd say it's not nearly enough."

"In any case, the judge shut down both Anson Stokes' mine and Dusty Rhodes' dam. They seemed to be the target of the first bombing."

"How did Dusty take the verdict?"

"He wasn't there. Your friend Dusty landed on his feet, though. He's promoted a federal grant to turn his dam into a recreation area."

"You sound displeased. If the verdict had gone the other way and they'd let him keep operating, you'd have claimed the fix was in. They shut him down and you're still complaining. There's no way he can win with you."

"He's milking the taxpayer to save his investment."

"Sounds to me like he's just finding a way to reclaim the land."

The conversation reminded Owen of their pre-divorce long-distance calls. Any topic would lead to an argument. "I don't want to fight about it."

"Sure could have fooled me."

To change the subject, Owen asked, "You remember Jeb Stuart Hobbs?"

"Of course. You and he had such good times together here the summer before last."

"I ran into him at a memorial service. I've been going to some of his baseball games."

"I remember his mother, too. You got well past third base with her. You sure it's your paternal instinct and not your mating instinct that's taking you to these games?"

"She's seeing a scout from the Cincinnati Reds. We're barely on speaking terms."

"It's not speaking I'm worried about. I just hope you're not grunting and groaning."

"Oh for Christ's sake. Can't we find a subject that doesn't leave us at odds with each other?"

"How's your mom? Is that a safe enough subject?"

"She's lots better, thanks. I'll let you talk to her." He tracked down Ruth and put her on the kitchen phone so that they could have a three-way conversation.

Owen returned to the phone in the living room in time to hear his mother ask, "Did Owen tell you he got a job offer from the state?"

"What kind of offer?" Judith asked with a chill in her voice that lowered the temperature of Owen's receiver at least ten degrees.

"I don't know yet."

"Why didn't you tell me?" Judith asked.

"I don't know any of the details. We've got a meeting this afternoon to discuss it."

"Does that mean you won't be coming back to California any time soon?"

"He doesn't have to take their offer," Ruth said. "I can manage on my own now."

"I'd like to hear what Owen has to say."

"I don't know what to say. How can I when I don't know what they have in mind? My only client just lost his income. It would be nice to have a solid client and a contract bringing in some money. I wouldn't have that right away in California."

"You won't ever have contracts here unless you come back and start writing some proposals," Judith said. "There are a couple of promising proposal requests on your desk right now."

"Send them to me. I'll take a look at them."

"Airfares are low now, Owen," Ruth said. "You belong back in California."

"Mom, I got you on the line to help smooth things over. Not so the two of you could gang up on me."

"I wouldn't need to smooth things over if you were back in California."

"Your mother's a bright woman, Owen," Judith said. "Didn't you inherit any of her genes?"

"My mother's still in chemotherapy. She needs more help than she's willing to admit."

"Your mother is tired of being referred to in the third person by her son and daughter-in-law," Ruth said.

"Ex-daughter-in-law," Owen and Judith said in unison.

"See. I knew I could get the two of you to agree on something," Ruth said. "Now if you'd only agree to make that title 'ex-ex-daughter-in-law,' I'd be the happiest bald woman in West Virginia."

THE ROAD FROM Barkley to Charleston had changed considerably since Owen left home to go to college. The winding asphalt road with switchbacks that conformed to the mountains' curves had been replaced by a four-lane interstate that gouged out the sides of mountains and crossed and recrossed creeks to straighten the route and cut forty-five minutes off the travel time.

Owen spent the forty-five minutes he saved cooling his heels in the reception area of the state attorney general's office. When he was finally admitted to the office, he found the attorney general standing at one end of an oak desk long enough to need a control tower. Harrison Marks stood in the flight path at the other end of the desk.

The attorney general, Hayes Boyer, a slim man with wavy white hair, stepped forward and stretched out his hand, displaying a cufflink in the shape of West Virginia. "Marks here said you handled yourself pretty well on the stand in the Mountain View hearing."

"My testimony was pretty straightforward."

"It went unchallenged, though," Marks said. "You didn't leave any openings."

"You're a West Virginia native with a Ph.D. from Cal Tech," Boyer said. Owen nodded.

"And you run a firm in California. What is it? Failure and Risk Evaluation?"

"That's right."

"How many people work at your firm?" Boyer asked.

"About half." It was an old joke, but Boyer was enough of a politician to laugh as if he'd never heard it. Marks frowned as if he didn't get it.

"Let me restate the question. How *large* is your firm?"

"A little over six feet." Owen explained for Marks' benefit. "It's just me. With a little part-time help."

Boyer raised his right hand as if he were trying to quiet applause. "At the hearing, Judge Vereen suggested the state undertake an investigation of all the impoundment dams within our borders."

"All those located over underground shafts," Owen said.

"That's right," Boyer said. "My office takes a suggestion from the judge to be marching orders. We're looking for someone to lead the investigation. Would you be interested?"

"Why me?"

"You have the credentials. You're a native. And as far as we've been able to determine, you've got no axe to grind."

Owen recalled the chill of Judith's voice when she heard he might extend his stay. "I don't think so. I've got to get back to California soon."

"Take some time to think about it." Boyer rubbed his fingers together as if he were polishing the tips. "The job needn't last long, but it's an important one. We need to flag any risky structures. At the same time, though, the state isn't in the business of shutting down mining operations."

"You just bottled up Anson Stokes' mine and shut down Mountain View's processing operation," Owen said.

Boyer nodded. "That was a special case. Mountain View's impoundment had already flooded the countryside, four people had died, and the slurry was polluting water all the way to Cincinnati. We were under considerable pressure to take action."

"And besides," Marks added, "Dusty Rhodes was behind the Mountain View operation."

Boyer smiled with his lips, but not with his eyes. "There was that too, yes."

His candid admission took Owen by surprise. "You don't care for Rhodes?"

The smile left Boyer's lips. "The man gives politicians a bad name. And it's no secret he wants my job."

"Word is, you don't much care for Rhodes yourself," Marks said.

"So I understand, then, that we have a common enemy?" Boyer asked.

Owen looked from one man to the other without speaking.

"Come, come, Owen. Ours is a small state."

"Evidently a lot smaller than I thought."

"That has its good and bad points." Boyer extended his hand. "Tell me you'll consider our offer. Judge Vereen personally asked for you. He was quite impressed."

Owen stared at the cufflink. A small diamond glittered in the ceramic map at the location of the state capitol. He shook the offered hand. "I'll consider it."

"That's wonderful. I'm very pleased. Harrison, take this good man back to your office and work out the details."

MARKS' OFFICE WAS half the size of Boyer's and twice as cluttered. He motioned for Owen to sit in a leather chair wedged between two stacks of law books, then perched on the only clear corner of his desk and crossed his arms. "How long you figure it'll take you to do this job?"

"If I decide to do it, it'll probably take two days at each site, with another two weeks to write a report."

"At forty sites, that's eighty, ninety working days. Can you get some help to speed it along?"

"I'd rather do it myself. That way I know it'll be done right. If I have to take time to find and train somebody, it won't be much quicker. Besides, your boss seemed to want me."

"Can you do it quicker than two days a site? Legally, all you really need to do is make sure the previous inspectors were doing their job and that the mine owners followed the inspectors' advice."

Owen tried not to show his annoyance. "Look. If I'm going to do this job I'll want to do more than follow in some other inspectors' footsteps. I'll do that, all right. But I'll also want to inspect the site, take soil and depth readings, and measure the amount of membrane between the bottom of the dam and the top of the underground shaft."

Marks found a pipe in the clutter of his desk and tapped it against his palm. "Legally, that's not necessary."

"It's the right way to do the job."

Marks pointed the well-chewed pipestem at Owen. "Doing the job your way, taking all that time, you'll be like a miner peeing in his overalls in midshift. You might get a warm feeling, but nobody else will know about it. And believe me, nobody would give a damn if they did know."

Owen rose from his chair. "I'd know about it. And I'd give a damn. You better get somebody else. Somebody who can keep their overalls clean."

Marks pushed the pipestem within an inch of Owen's chest. "No need to get so excited. You say it'll take ninety days, we'll give you ninety days. Understand, though, we're under pressure to convince the public Drybone Hollow Dam was a freak accident. Not something that's going to happen again."

"That's a public relations problem. That's not my business."

"You give us a good report, we'll handle the rest of it." Marks clamped the unlit pipe between his teeth. "We'll need a written proposal. With a budget. What kind of money are we talking about?"

"I get a hundred dollars an hour." Owen did the arithmetic in his head. "Ninety days would be seventy-two thousand dollars. Plus expenses."

The figure didn't seem to faze Marks, who nodded. "All right. Let's get the pennies off the table."

Owen sat down again. "Excuse me?"

"My boss told you, next election we're expecting a challenge from Dusty Rhodes. We'll be needing campaign contributions."

Owen froze in his seat. He struggled to keep his voice level. "How much?"

"Most state contractors give twenty percent. You're new, and you're a one-man operation without a lot of overhead. Let's say fifteen percent."

"Are you saying that without a campaign contribution I won't get the job?"

Marks took his pipe out of his mouth, shook his head, and smiled. "I didn't say that. You never heard me say that."

"But that's what you mean by 'pennies off the table?'"

Marks shrugged. "It's just an expression."

"An expression that'll cost me fifteen percent of my contract."

Marks fished around his desk for a book of matches. "Bump your fee to cover it."

Owen sighed. "Fifteen percent. Like the tip at a restaurant."

Marks lit his pipe and squinted through the smoke. "If you want to think of it that way."

Owen rose from the chair. "Tell your boss I don't like the menu and the service sucks."

"You're saying you won't contribute?"

"Loudly. Are you saying I won't get the job?"

Marks exhaled a stream of smoke. "Naturally, we'll have to interview other firms. It's a public contract."

"Naturally."

Marks pointed the pipe stem at Owen's chest. "I don't think you understand how we do business here."

Owen deflected the pipestem and started for the door. "I think I understand perfectly."

"Ours is a small state. You could find it difficult to get any job here."

"Lucky for me there are forty-nine other states." Owen stopped, fished in his pocket for change, and stacked four copper coins on the clear corner of Marks' desk. "Tell your boss I left the pennies on the table."

"Why are you so surprised?" Sheriff Thad Reader asked Owen in Reader's office the next morning. "You know campaign contributions grease the wheels of commerce in this state."

"I know people are mugged in Central Park. It's different when it happens to you."

"Don't tell me nobody ever solicited a bribe from you before?"

"No. Never."

"No wonder your business has never taken off."

"You think this is funny?"

"I think your reaction is funny."

"I told you. It never happened to me in California."

"You're small potatoes in California. In West Virginia, no potatoes are too small."

"Can't we nail them? What if I went back wearing a wire?"

The sheriff smiled. "You could have been wearing a wire yesterday without getting anything incriminating. The man asked you for a campaign contribution. Nothing wrong with that."

"The implication was clear. No contribution, no contract."

Reader shrugged. "Nothing we can do about it. Marks is a smart lawyer. He never would have said it outright."

Owen shook his head. "The job was tailor-made for me. They said Judge Vereen suggested me. And I could have used the money. The state just shut down my only client."

Reader leaned back and propped his boots on the corner of his desk. "You say they asked you for a proposal?"

Owen nodded.

"Give them one. Put it in writing."

"What good will that do?"

"Could make it difficult for them to give the job to somebody less qualified for more money."

"Now you're the one being naive. That happens all the time in my world."

"Why am I not surprised?"

"They called it 'getting the pennies off the table.' Ever heard that expression?"

Reader scratched his shin under his boottop. "No. But I don't deal in such rarefied air. My bribe offers usually come through a car window wrapped around a driver's license."

"Christ. It's like a third-world country. With kickbacks and petty corruption."

"Well, it's nothing new, it's not always petty, and it's not limited to West Virginia. Buying favors with campaign contributions happens all the time. Trial lawyers give money to the Democrats so we can sue over trivia. Oil interests give money to the Republicans so we can drill offshore. They deal in billions, not pennies."

Owen shook his head. "Steal a little, go to jail. Steal a lot, go to Congress."

A female deputy appeared in the open doorway of Reader's office. "Somebody here to see you."

Reader took his boots off his desk. "Show them in."

"Not you." The deputy nodded at Owen. "Him."

"Either way," Reader said.

The deputy disappeared and returned with Jeb Stuart Hobbs.

Owen stood. "Jeb Stuart. Is something wrong?"

The boy looked uncertainly at the sheriff. "I'm sorry to butt in." He turned to Owen. "Your mom told me where to find you."

"That's all right," Owen said. "How can I help you?"

Jeb Stuart stared at the floor and said, "This is going to sound a little crazy, but I think Riley Stokes is still alive."

10

Spring Cleaning

JEB Stuart Hobbs took a deep breath. "Riley's dad's been pestering the Reds' Mr. Anderson to go scout Riley's cousin in Middleburg. I mean, he just won't quit. He comes to our practices, even phones Mr. Anderson at our house."

The fact that Anderson visited the Hobbs' house often enough to take calls there disturbed Owen, but he focused his attention on Jeb Stuart's story. "What's that got to do with Riley Stokes?"

"Thing is, I know that Riley didn't have no cousin in Middleburg. The weekend of the flood, his dad sent him there to help his aunt with spring cleaning, because she didn't have no man around the house."

"No son?" Thad Reader asked.

"No husband. No son. No man. Riley didn't want to go. Mr. Anderson was going to scout our Saturday practice. He agreed to watch Riley and me work out on Sunday if Riley could come back early."

"And did he come back early?"

"He made arrangements to. He groused so much about going his dad said he could take the last Saturday bus back."

"Did he tell his dad why he wanted to come back early?" Owen asked.

"I doubt it. They didn't get on too good."

"So Riley would have been back when the dam broke early Sunday morning," Owen said.

Jeb Stuart shook his head. "No. No. That's the thing, see. The only bus he could catch late Saturday night got him in at 3:35 Sunday morning."

"That was just after the flood hit," the sheriff said. "The first 911 call came in at 3:30 that morning."

Owen frowned. "So you think this Ohio nephew Cable's been touting . . ."

"Is really Riley," Jeb Stuart said.

"What kind of a man would send his own son away like that?" Owen asked.

"Same kind that would build fake foundations to bilk FEMA out of recovery money," the sheriff said.

Owen looked from Jeb Stuart to the sheriff. "Middleburg's what? Three hours from here? Want to drive up and take a look?"

"Do we have an address?" the sheriff asked.

"Cable used his sister's social security number and address on one of his FEMA claims," Owen said.

"That's all we need, then." The sheriff turned to Jeb Stuart. "You know what Riley looks like. Want to come along?"

"I don't want to get Riley in any trouble," Jeb Stuart said.

"Cable's the one that'll be in trouble," the sheriff said. "And he deserves whatever trouble comes his way."

"Well, it's Saturday," Jeb Stuart said. "I guess I could go. I'll have to tell my mom first, though."

"We'll follow you to your house," the sheriff said. "If you've got any pictures of Riley, bring them. We may have to ask around to find him."

"There's last year's team picture. And the school yearbook."

Owen rode with Jeb Stuart while Thad Reader followed in his squad car. When they reached Jeb's home, Owen offered to go inside to explain the trip to Jeb's mother, but the boy shook his head quickly and asked him to wait outside.

Owen wondered whether the quick refusal reflected Jeb Stuart's fear that the house might contain traces of Bill Anderson, or Anderson himself. But he remembered that Mary Beth was careful not to let men stay over and decided that Jeb's failure to invite him in was just a teenager's shyness.

While Jeb Stuart was in the house, Owen joined Thad Reader in the front seat of the patrol car. "What do you make of all this?"

Reader shrugged. "Boy's bright and likable. He could be onto something. It's worth a trip to Middleburg."

Jeb Stuart returned with a yearbook and team picture under his arm. "Mom's not home. I left a note."

"Will that be all right?" Owen asked.

"Oh sure. She won't mind if I'm with you."

As THAD READER drove north out of coal country, the jagged limestone cuts that walled in the freeway gave way to rolling, tree-covered hillsides. After they crossed into Ohio above Parkersburg, the hills flattened and the land stretched out into furrowed fields and pastures dotted with grazing cattle. A roadside produce stand, two antique stores, and a block-long strip mall marked the entrance to Middleburg.

The frame house that belonged to Cable Stokes' sister sagged under some unseen weight. Paint flaked off the wood siding, and the floorboards on the porch creaked under a covering of worn AstroTurf. Thad Reader rang the bell three times before a gaunt woman whose rubber curlers were half covered by a sweat-rimmed bandanna opened the door just as far as the safety chain would allow. The hand clutching the door was encased in a rubber glove, and a strong smell of ammonia came from inside the house.

The woman didn't seem particularly surprised to see the law on her porch. "Whatcha want?"

"We're looking for a boy named Rusty Bricker," the sheriff said.

"Nobody here by that name."

"This is the Bricker residence, right? And you're Essie Bricker?"

"Right. But there's nobody else that lives here by the name you just said."

"Mind if we come in and look around."

"Not without you got a warrant."

"You're the sister of Cable Stokes?" Owen asked.

The woman nodded.

"Then you were the claimant on a lost trailer next to Cable's mobile home?" Thad Reader said.

"Don't know nothing about that."

"You signed a claim sheet," Reader said.

"Never did no such thing. Never had no trailer. Lived right here for the past twelve years. You can check it out."

"So you're saying the claim sheet was fraudulent?" Reader asked.

"Told you, I don't know nothing about no claim sheet."

"Your brother submitted it," Reader said.

"Then you'd best talk to my brother about it. Now I got to get back to my cleaning."

The sheriff tipped his hat. "We'll be back."

"Be still my heart." Essie Bricker dropped her hand to the doorknob and shut the door.

Back at the sheriff's patrol car, Jeb Stuart said, "Sorry, guess I was wrong."

"You weren't wrong," Owen said. "That woman was lying. It runs in the family."

"Then we're not going back home now?" Jeb Stuart asked.

"Not just yet," Reader said. "Let's try the high school."

"But it's Saturday," Jeb Stuart said.

"That just means there won't be many students," Reader said. "But there's always somebody around a school."

A SIGN IN front of the orange brick Middleburg High School announced it was the HOME OF THE COUGARS. Rangy boys in tank tops and baggy shorts played two-on-two at either end of an asphalt basketball court beside the parking lot. Owen and Thad had started for the concrete steps in front of the school when Jeb Stuart said, "Wait. Listen." Between the slapping of tennis shoes and clanking of playground backboards, they heard the faint sound of infield chatter and the far-off *thock* of bat meeting ball.

Behind the school, beyond a vast stretch of black asphalt, a wire mesh backstop and green bleachers marked the boundaries of a baseball diamond. In the infield, gray-shirted boys were fielding grounders hit by a stocky man whose beefy arms bulged out of a tattered red sweatshirt. Down the right-field line, a tall boy in gray sweats hit looping fungos to outfielders.

The infielders saw the sheriff first. Each in turn would field a grounder, throw it to first, take the return throw, and watch the approaching uniform until the ball was hit to them again. The coach in the red sweatshirt sensed that he was no longer the center of his team's attention, turned at home plate, and rested his bat against his hip until the sheriff, Owen, and Jeb Stuart were within hailing distance.

"Got a minute?" Reader asked.

The coach nodded. He handed his bat to the catcher, telling him to keep the drill going, and joined the visitors on the other side of the backstop.

After exchanging introductions, Reader showed Jeb Stuart's high school yearbook to the coach and pointed to the picture of Riley Stokes. "Ever seen this boy?"

The concern on the coach's ruddy face answered the question. "Why? What's he done?"

"He's done nothing," the sheriff said. "But he may have knowledge that could help solve a serious crime."

The coach chewed his lower lip, weighing the information.

"Well?" The sheriff took the baseball team's group picture from the yearbook. "Here's a photo of the boy in a uniform that might be more familiar."

The coach shrugged. "Yeah. Name's not Stokes, though. Calls himself Rusty Bricker."

"He here today?"

"No. First practice he's cut. Too bad you missed him. You know how they say Walter Johnson could throw a lamb chop past a hungry wolf? Well, this boy could get it by the wolf and put it on a dish sixty feet away without disturbing the vegetables."

"That'd be Riley, all right," Jeb Stuart said.

"You say this knowledge he's got concerns something serious?" the coach asked.

"Could well be." The sheriff handed the coach a business card. "If you see him or learn of his whereabouts, call me right away."

"His whereabouts? Has he gone missing?"

"Nobody at his home seems to know where he is."

"He'll be back, though, won't he?" the coach asked. "I mean, we open next week."

"Can't tell. Think any of your boys might know where he is?"

The coach turned and yelled, "Bring it in," through the wire backstop.

The catcher laid the bat down carefully, as if it might break, picked up his glove, and rolled a slow grounder to the third baseman, who rushed in, rifled it back to the catcher, and trotted over to the first row of bleacher seats.

Owen watched as the catcher went through the same drill with each of the infielders, then brought the outfielders in by taking throws to home plate after they'd chase down fly balls. The first two throws from outfielders blooped in, bounced short of the pitcher's mound and dribbled up the first-base line. Then a skinny, freckle-faced boy in deep center field cut loose a throw that carried all the way to home plate on a straight line and short-hopped the catcher.

"Nice," Jeb Stuart said, and Owen realized they'd both been scouting the team as if they might have to play against them.

When the whole team had assembled in the bleachers, the coach said, "All right, listen up. Anyone here seen Rusty Bricker today?"

The players looked from the coach to the sheriff, exchanged glances with each other, and then shrugged and shook their heads in unison.

"Apparently he's not at his home," the coach said. "Anybody know where he might be?"

The question brought on another round of shrugs and shaking heads.

"He hasn't done nothing wrong," the coach said, "but these gentlemen want to talk to him. Anybody sees him, let me know, okay?"

The players nodded. A boy with an unruly shock of reddish-brown hair asked from halfway up the bleachers, "Coach? What if Rusty's not back by Wednesday?"

"Then you'll start, Kerrane. Be ready."

The sheriff thanked the team and the coach, who walked with them a short distance beyond the backstop. "You let me know if he turns up, hear? That boy's our ticket to the state championship."

The sheriff squinted over the coach's shoulder at the players, who hadn't budged from their bleacher seats. "If we find him, I'll convey your concern."

On the way back to the sheriff's patrol car, Jeb Stuart said, "I was right, then. Riley's alive."

Owen put his hand on the boy's shoulder. "Sure looks that way." To the sheriff, he said, "Shouldn't we go back to see Essie Bricker?"

The sheriff shook his head. "I doubt she'll be any more forthcoming with us. Time we picked up some local reinforcements."

OWEN AND JEB Stuart waited in the patrol car while Thad Reader visited the local sheriff's office. After five minutes inside, he emerged with a tall, broad-shouldered officer whose Sam Browne belt and polished holster glistened in the afternoon sun. They spoke briefly on the courthouse steps before the local sheriff pointed down the street and made a turning motion with his right hand.

Thad Reader returned to his patrol car. "Local law offered to lead the way out. Name's Cook. Seems like a good man. He didn't need directions to Bricker's house. Turns out their place was a regular stop back when Essie's husband was living with her. Domestic fights. Flying dishes. Even a couple of shots one Saturday night."

"I take it they're divorced," Owen said.

The local sheriff pulled alongside Reader's squad car and motioned for him to follow. Reader waved and pulled out into the sparse afternoon traffic. "Never got a legal divorce. Nobody's seen Frank Bricker for over two years. Left his missus with the house, the gun, and whatever crockery survived their fights."

"Any signs he didn't leave under his own power?" Owen asked.

"None that Sheriff Cook could find. I got the impression he didn't look too hard, though. Evidently Frank Bricker was no great loss to society."

The local sheriff pulled up in front of the Bricker house, and Thad, Owen, and Jeb Stuart joined him on the AstroTurf-covered porch.

Essie Bricker cracked the front door open in response to their knocking. She was still wearing a sweat-rimmed bandanna and her sleeves were rolled up around her elbows. "Whatcha want now?"

Sheriff Cook said, "We just want to come in and talk a little."

"I told this bunch earlier. Not without you got a warrant."

"Now, Essie," Sheriff Cook said, "we could go get a warrant. If you make us do that, though, I'm going to come back with a whole crew and turn this house upside down. No telling what we might find. You could save us both a lot of trouble if you just invite us in."

Essie jerked the chain lock free from its slot. "All right. Come on in."

The living room smelled of stale cigarette smoke. A cluster of butts swam in an ash-filled saucer on the arm of a sofa polka-dotted with cigarette burns. A scattering of newspapers in the far corner of the room bore urine stains and leavings from a pet that was nowhere to be seen but was evidently well fed.

The local sheriff appeared to be unfazed by the clutter. "Essie, the high school tells us they've got a boy registered that calls himself Rusty Bricker and lives at this address."

"Not anymore, he don't. He left me flat. Took off yesterday with a hundred and twenty dollars of my stash and my mama's emerald brooch."

"A relative, was he?" Sheriff Cook asked.

"No, not really. He showed up about a month ago looking for work. I let him help out around the house. Ain't had much help since Frank left. There was lots to be done."

Sheriff Cook lifted the saucer full of cigarette butts off the arm of the sofa. "Helped out with the cleaning, did he?"

Essie either didn't catch the sheriff's ironic tone or chose to ignore it. "Helped some. Turned out he had no kinfolk. I gave him a room, let him use my name, got him into the high school. Lot of thanks I get."

Thad Reader joined the questioning. "Folks at the high school say that this Rusty Bricker looked a lot like your nephew, Riley Stokes."

"In the dark with the light behind him, maybe. He didn't favor no relative of mine. Besides, Riley died just recent when that dam broke in West Virginia."

"Which was just about the time this visitor of yours showed up," Reader said.

Essie stared at Reader. "You getting at something, Sheriff?"

"We think maybe Riley didn't die," Reader said. "We think maybe Cable sent him up here to hide out and reported him drowned to collect death benefits."

Essie sneered. "Cable ain't near smart enough for that."

"This Rusty Bricker," Sheriff Cook said. "He have a room here?"

"Upstairs."

"Mind if we take a look?"

"Go right ahead."

The two lawmen let Essie Bricker lead the way up the stairs, which were an obstacle course of stacked magazines, withered plants, and piles of laundry. A mop and soapy bucket stood in a doorway to the right of the stairwell. Essie moved the mop and bucket aside and nodded toward the doorway.

The doorway opened into a bedroom which, in sharp contrast to the rest of the house, was sparkling clean. The floor was bare, the bed had been stripped to its mattress, and the only other piece of furniture in the room, a white particle-board dresser, gleamed in the rectangle of sunlight that flowed through the curtainless window.

Sheriff Cook opened the closet door to expose a crossbar empty of hangars. He raised an eyebrow at Essie.

Essie shrugged. "Spring cleaning."

"And you started here," Sheriff Cook said.

"Had to start somewhere."

"There's no sign anybody ever lived here," Thad Reader said.

"Didn't want nothing to remind me of that ungrateful scamp."

Thad Reader fixed his good eye on Essie. "Don't suppose you have any idea where he might be headed?"

"None at all. You find him, though, he's got six twenties that belong to me."

"We'll keep that in mind," Sheriff Cook said. "I'll send a fingerprint crew around tomorrow, see if they can't pick up a lead."

"Reckon I may have ruined any chance of that with my cleaning," Essie said. "I had no idea you'd be coming."

Thad Reader ran two fingers along the top of the closet door sill. The tips were so black they might have been dipped in fingerprint ink. "It's hard to clean everywhere. Like as not you missed something."

"If you did, my boys'll find it tomorrow," Sheriff Cook said. He exchanged glances with Reader. "Not a lot we can do here now. Might as well leave."

Essie picked up the mop and bucket. "I'll just get on with my cleaning then."

Outside, Owen asked Sheriff Cook, "What good will it do to get fingerprints? Even if you find Riley's prints, she can always claim he left them there before the dam broke."

"Hell, I'm not going to bother sending a crew tomorrow. I just said that to give her more mopping time. The thought of that lying harpy spending the night scrubbing to get ready for a visit does my heart good."

"Maybe you ought to send somebody anyhow, just to keep the pressure on," Thad Reader said.

Sheriff Cook shrugged. "Even if we catch her in more lies, she'll just change her story."

"Get her to tell enough lies, though, we might be able to triangulate the truth," Reader said.

"You think something bad's happened to Riley?" Jeb Stuart asked.

"I don't think even Cable Stokes would harm his own son," Owen said. "They've probably just found another place to stash him." He looked to the lawmen for confirmation.

Thad Reader was slow to respond. "Most likely. Something spooked them into yanking him away, though." He turned to Jeb Stuart. "You tell anybody else what you suspected about Riley?"

"Just my mom."

"She likely to gossip?"

"Don't think so."

Reader turned back to Owen. "What do you think?"

Owen just shrugged. He had an uneasy feeling about Mary Beth Hobbs, but it was nothing he wanted to discuss in front of her son.

CABLE STOKES CROSSED the Ohio River into West Virginia just above Parkersburg and turned off the main highway onto a winding creekside road.

"This isn't the way home," Riley Stokes said from the Cadillac's passenger seat.

"Ain't going home."

"Where are we going then?"

"We just need to lay low for a while."

"Why? What's happened?"

Cable didn't answer. The bumpy gravel road caused the Cadillac's damaged side to rattle and squeal.

"Jesus, Dad. This car sounds like it's not going to make it."

"Your uncle stove in the doors pretty good. But it don't hurt the running of it none."

The Cadillac's left rear door had been lashed to the car's centerpost with clothesline rope, and it rattled with every rut in the road.

"Can't you get that fixed?" Riley asked.

"I'm working on it. Insurance company's going to give me ten grand to take it to one of their high-priced body shops in Charleston. But I got me a guy in Logan who'll pound out the dents and put it right for two grand. I just need to wait until he's free to get to it."

The door grated and clattered.

"You need more than dent pounding. You need a whole new door."

"My guy says he can make this one work."

The door scraped again, and Riley heard two thumps from the rear of the car. "Did Uncle Anson hit you in the rear as well?"

"No. Just the sides. Twice."

"Then what's that thumping?"

Cable frowned and shook his head. "Didn't hear nothing."

The next rut in the road brought more scraping and another thump.

"There it goes again," Riley said.

"It's the muffler, most likely. Anson dislodged it and I had to wire it up so it wouldn't drag. It still bumps the undercarriage though."

A straight, level stretch of asphalt quieted the car's creaks. Riley looked over his shoulder at the duffel bag he'd packed that morning. "You going to tell me why we had to leave in such an all-fired hurry?"

"Somebody got suspicious."

"Who?"

"Never you mind. I got it covered like a blanket on a blister."

"Jesus, Dad. I don't want to have to start another school."

"You won't have to. We just need to make sure nobody's on our tail."

"But you said somebody was already on to us."

"I said somebody suspicions us. I also said I got it covered."

"Who was it?"

"If you must know, it was your good buddy, Jeb Stuart Hobbs. His mama tried to blackmail me."

"Jesus. What made Jeb suspect anything?"

"Never you mind. He won't be telling anyone."

"How do you know?"

"I left him a note. Told him bad things would happen to his mama if he don't keep his mouth shut."

"Jesus, Dad."

"I told you, I got it covered."

"Like hell you do. That tapes it. I'm through. Take me home."

"Afraid it's too late for that."

"No it's not." Riley turned in the passenger seat. "I been thinking on it. I'll just show up, let on like I ran away. I didn't tell nobody 'cause I was afraid of you. That's why you thought I was lost in the flood."

"That'd kill the death benefits."

"Dad, it's not working out. If Jeb Stuart and his mother know, it won't be long before others catch on."

"Jeb Stuart don't know for sure. He only suspicions. I told you, I got it covered."

"How? With threats?"

"Son, I know we're stomping all over your life right now. I'm sorry, but it can't be helped. Once the money starts rolling in, you'll see it was all worth it."

The Cadillac rounded a curve and hit a pothole. The rear door grated and squealed, and a loud scraping noise rose through the undercarriage.

Cable pulled off to the side of the road, braked the car, and pounded on the steering wheel. "Shit. Shit. Shit."

"What happened?"

"Muffler let go. It's dragging underneath."

Cable got out of the car, checked the tailpipe, and climbed back behind the wheel. "Wire come loose. Don't see it nowhere. How about you go back down the road a piece and look for it?"

Riley nodded toward the long length of clothesline wound around the centerpost to hold the read door shut. "Why not just use some of that rope?"

"It'll burn right through."

"Maybe there's some wire in the trunk."

"Ain't nothing in the trunk."

"Let's look at least."

"What the hell. I'll go back and find the wire myself." Cable leaned past his son to take a pair of pliers from the glove compartment. As he did so, Riley saw the butt of a gun peek through the buttons of his father's shirt.

Cable pocketed the pliers and took the keys from the ignition. "Just wait here. I'll be right back." He slammed the car door shut and disappeared around the curve behind them.

Riley climbed down from the passenger seat, squatted on his haunches, and examined the dragging muffler. It was red hot to the touch, so he found a thick branch by the side of the road and tried to use it to manipulate the muffler into position. The branch broke and the muffler clanked against the asphalt.

An answering thump came from the rear of the car.

Riley checked back over his shoulder. Cable was nowhere to be seen. The boy climbed into the driver's seat and looked for the lever that would pop the trunk open. The first lever he found popped the hood, but the second unlocked the Cadillac's trunk.

Riley ran to the rear of the car and threw open the trunk. Jeb Stuart Hobbs' mother lay trussed up like a mummy with gray duct tape that strapped her wrists to her ankles and pinned her arms to her sides.

Her forehead was bruised from beating against the trunk lid, and the hazel eyes above the tape that covered her mouth were wide with fright.

Riley picked and tore at the duct tape covering the woman's mouth. His short nails just couldn't free her. He needed a knife.

The eyes above the duct tape widened still farther, and Riley turned just in time to see his father's pistol slam against the side of his head.

11

Criminal Imbeciles

Owen and Ruth had just finished eating when Buster began barking and Jeb Stuart Hobbs appeared at their door, out of breath and panting. "My mom's not home," he said through the screen door. "I waited, but she didn't come home for dinner."

"You poor thing," Ruth said. She opened the screen door and took Jeb Stuart's arm to lead him into the living room while Buster wagged his tail nonstop and danced on his hind legs around his old friend.

Jeb Stuart ignored Buster and looked around the living room like a boy who'd lost his bearings. He took a sheet of paper from his pocket and studied it as if it were a map filled with unfamiliar landmarks. "I found this note. In the mailbox."

Owen took the note. Letters had been cut from a variety of newspaper and magazine headlines, pasted on a sheet of paper, and photocopied. The cobbled-together message read

YOU'LL BE SORRY
IF YOU TELL ANYONE
YOUR MOM WILL DIE.

"When did this come?" Owen asked.

Jeb Stuart winced. "I don't know. It was in the mailbox. Mom always brings in the mail. When she didn't come home, I found it."

Owen had a sinking feeling. "So it could have been there all day."

The boy looked to be on the verge of tears. "I don't know. I just now found it. What'll we do?"

Owen refolded the note and held it by opposing corners. "We'll have to take this to the sheriff."

Ruth tried to lead Jeb Stuart to the couch but he resisted, stationing himself between Owen and the door. "It says there he'll kill my mom if I tell anyone."

"But you've already told the sheriff."

"Mr. Stokes might not know that."

"He'll know. His sister will tell him about our visit."

Jeb Stuart's hands fluttered away from his sides, then fell back against his jeans. "So he may have killed Mom already."

"We don't know that," Owen said. "I don't think Cable Stokes will hurt your mom."

"He says he will."

"He's trying to frighten you. To keep you quiet about Riley."

"But it's too late. I already told."

"Cable will know you told. And he'll know it's too late. He can't gain anything by hurting your mom. It will only make things worse for him."

Jeb Stuart's voice cracked. "It's too late. I know it's too late."

"We don't know that." Owen could see the boy wasn't likely to listen to any sort of reasoning. "We've got to take this note to the sheriff."

Ruth took Jeb Stuart's arm. "The sheriff will know what to do, hon."

Jeb Stuart pulled away. "Don't want to go to the sheriff. If Mr. Stokes finds out, he'll hurt Mom."

"Look, Jeb," Owen said. "I'll take the note to the sheriff. You won't have to be involved. You wait here. Stay with us tonight."

"Yes, stay," Ruth said. "I'll make up a bed."

Jeb Stuart started for the door. "No. I want to go home. Mom might call. He might call."

Ruth caught up with Jeb Stuart at the door and took his arm again. "I'll go home with you. We'll wait for Owen at your house. Have you had something to eat?"

Jeb Stuart shook his head. "He used to hit Riley. He'll hurt my mom. Because of me."

Owen took Jeb Stuart's other arm. "You haven't done anything wrong. Cable's got nothing to gain by hurting her."

Together, Ruth and Owen led Jeb Stuart back to the living room couch. "I'll bring you some milk and fix a sandwich," Ruth said. "Then we'll both drive to your house and wait for Owen. I'm sure your mom will be all right."

Ruth straightened, turned away from the boy, and shooed Owen away with the hand Jeb Stuart couldn't see.

Owen marveled at his mother. The hand making the shooing motion was shaking, and he could see the worry in her eyes. But the voice she used to soothe Jeb Stuart was calm and comforting. He tucked the note in his pocket and left to find the sheriff.

THAD READER SLIPPED the copy of the pasted-up threat into a clear plastic folder, laid the folder on his desk, and frowned. "That'll sure take the shine off your Saturday."

"What do you think?" Owen asked. "Will he hurt Mary Beth?"

Reader shrugged. "No way of knowing."

"We ought to be able to track him down, though. I mean, he's not exactly a criminal mastermind."

"Man's a criminal imbecile. Five kinds of crooked and ten kinds of dumb. In some ways that's worse. There's just no telling what he'll do."

"But the kidnapping doesn't make sense. If Cable harms Mary Beth, he'll never be able to show up to collect the insurance on Riley."

Reader shook his head. "The only place Stokes comes close to sensible is in the dictionary."

"Even there he's several pages behind."

"You got that right." Reader tapped the plastic-enclosed note.

"Don't forget, he took the Hobbs woman to try to silence her son. It probably never occurred to Cable that the kidnapping might not keep the boy quiet."

"Or that kidnapping raises the stakes a lot higher than insurance fraud."

"I tell you," Reader said, "the man's a criminal imbecile. Coal country's been breeding them like mosquitoes in a bog ever since mining jobs started to dry up. Lots of locals have gotten in over their heads by raising wacky weed, knocking over convenience stores, and running drugs."

"Well, this has always been moonshine country. Marijuana's just a form of horizontal diversification."

"Cable Stokes' boy Billy Joe is on probation for running weed."

"Boy's hauling dynamite while he's on probation?"

"Boy's no smarter than his old man. Maybe even dumber, if that's possible. Still claims he wasn't hauling dynamite over at Lyle Tanner's place. Even if he was, there's no law against it."

"Not even with his police record?"

"We catch him with drugs or guns, he's in trouble. We catch him with dynamite, though, he can claim to be a miner or a gardener busting rocks."

"Think he's still running dope?"

"Most likely. He's got lots of company. Weed grows good in our hollows. Lots of folks have started breaking the law with no head for criminal activity. Imbeciles just like Cable and his boy. There was a fire chief over in Mingo County who was supplementing his income by peddling pot and a little smack on the side. The FBI had him under surveillance from a boxcar in the railyard across from his house."

Reader smiled and scratched his forehead under the brim of his mountie's hat. "Man was oblivious. Thought nobody would notice the crowds lining up to score a little blow. One evening, business was so good the chief ran short of supplies. So he hung a sign on his door:

'OUT OF DRUGS

BACK IN THIRTY MINUTES.' "

Owen laughed. "You've got to be kidding."

"No. It's for real. The FBI snapped him up when he got back. Kept the sign as evidence. Made the papers all over the state."

"Even Cable's smarter than that."

"Not on the strength of his record to date." Reader held up the plastic folder. "He might as well have signed his name to this here note."

Owen nodded. "Imbecile, all right."

"*Criminal* imbecile. The fire chief's not all there is to my little cautionary tale, though. The news article on the chief caught the eye of a deputy sheriff from Wayne County who'd been dealing himself, working out of a parking lot across from an abandoned rail station.

"Thing about the chief's story that caught the deputy's eye was the feds' use of a boxcar for surveillance. So the deputy starts fretting about the cars in the railyard across from his drug stand. Instead of shutting down or taking his business elsewhere, he lets his fears fester.

"One afternoon, in mid-deal, he spots some movement in the railyard, takes a confiscated Uzi from the back of his van, and starts blowing hell out of the railroad cars. Took out a harmless hobo, crippled a livestock inspector, and turned six prize heifers into hamburger."

Owen's jaw dropped. "Jesus Christ."

"When he realized what he'd done, he swallowed the barrel of his own forty-five and joined the hobo and the heifers at the pearly gates."

"Cable's got to be smarter than that, doesn't he?" Even as he said the words, Owen felt himself doubting them. "His insurance fraud's already blown, and he's courting a kidnapping charge. There's no point in digging a deeper hole."

"He's just as likely to dig it deeper as to crawl out of it."

"But digging it deeper would mean . . ."

Reader cinched his chinstrap tight and rose from his desk. "Killing the Hobbs woman and finding a hidey hole in a hollow somewhere."

"What about his boy Riley?"

"For all we know, the boy's in on the scam. But if he's not, he's at risk too."

"Surely Cable wouldn't harm his own son?"

Reader took a set of car keys off a hook next to his office door. "You saw him light into Billy Joe. If Riley's a threat, I don't think Cable's likely to show any more concern for children than King Herod."

"Herod went after other people's children. Not his own."

"Well, take Abraham, then. He went after his own kid." Reader held his office door open for Owen. "You want to argue Bible stories or do something about that note of Cable's?"

Owen moved through the office door. "What can I do to help?"

The sheriff closed the door behind them. "Sounds like the Hobbs boy needs some bucking up. Go back to his home, help him cope. Could be Cable will contact him directly."

"Where'll you be if he does?"

"First thing, I'm going out to see Stokes' oldest boy, Billy Joe. That's where Cable's been holed up since the flood." Reader wrote a number on the back of his business card. "This will always reach me." He handed the card to Owen. "Next thing, I'm going to bring in the FBI. We've got a kidnapping here, and they've got lots more experience dealing with criminal imbeciles than I do."

"Guess we've got to hope Cable's more like the fire chief with his sign than the deputy sheriff with his Uzi."

"That hope's riding a slow horse. Don't forget, our imbecile's already taken at least one hostage."

BRADY JACKSON CHECKED his watch against the time on the grandfather clock standing in the corner of his law office. Ten minutes after two. "Not like Cable to be late when there's money to be discussed."

Lyle Tanner stretched his legs and shifted uncomfortably in an upholstered leather chair. He was wearing his security guard's uniform. "I'm due at the mall at three o'clock."

"What we've got to discuss shouldn't take too long," Jackson said. "Let's give Cable another five minutes."

"You said you've got an offer."

"Right. From Mountain View." Jackson squared the corners of a stack of papers and placed them back on his blue desk blotter. "If we wait for Cable I'll only have to go over it one time."

"See where Mountain View got fined a hundred and ten grand."

"By the feds, yes."

"Hardly seems like enough."

"It's the maximum allowed under the law."

Tanner shook his head. "Still doesn't seem like much. Not with all the damage they caused."

"We go to court, we should get a whole lot more than that out of them." Jackson lit a cigarette and blew a thin stream of smoke out of the side of his mouth. "I had a professor once, said lawyers only practice three kinds of law." He held up one stubby finger over a frayed shirtcuff. "First kind is 'pigs versus people.' You want to avoid that if you can."

A second finger joined the first. "Second kind is 'pigs versus pigs.' That's okay in a pinch. In fact, you can't avoid it if you want to make a living practicing law."

A thumb joined the two upraised fingers. "Third kind is 'people versus pigs.' That's the kind of case makes lawyering worthwhile. And that's the kind of case we got here. You, Cable, and your neighbors against Mountain View Development. People versus pigs."

The phone on Jackson's desk rang. He frowned, said, "Secretary's afternoon off," to Tanner, lifted the receiver, and announced, "Law Offices of Brady Jackson, Esquire."

Tanner could hear only a muted rumble on the other end of the line. Then Jackson said, "Cable? Where the hell are you?"

The muted rumble sorted itself into a three-word response that Tanner could understand. "Never mind that."

"How long will it take you to get here?" Jackson asked. "Lyle's got to get to his job shortly."

Lyle heard the words, "Can't make it," before Cable's response dissolved into indecipherable murmurs.

Brady Jackson shrugged and put his hand over the mouthpiece. "Says he can't come in. Says he wants to handle everything by phone."

139

Tanner checked his watch. "Long as it's quick."

Jackson pushed a button on the base of the phone and returned the receiver to its cradle. Cable's voice filled the tiny office. "What's so all-fired important?"

Jackson flicked the ash off his cigarette. "Mountain View has asked me to make you and Lyle an offer."

"Just us?"

"You two lost loved ones. They wanted to start with you."

Cable's voice came over the speaker phone. "How much?"

"One hundred thousand dollars for each death."

"A hundred grand?" A noise like a snort came out of the speaker. "Hell's bells. I got twenty-five grand just for my trailer. You telling me my boy Riley's not worth any more than four trailers?"

Jackson shrugged. "I didn't say it was a good offer."

"I'll say it's not a good offer." Cable's voice dominated the room. "You said we'd get at least a million."

"To get that much," Jackson said, "we'd have to prevail in court."

"Shouldn't have no trouble doing that. It was their dam water that drowned Maddie Tanner and my boy Riley."

"I agree," Jackson said. "But it will take time."

"And court isn't a sure thing," Tanner said. "We might not win. Or we might win less than a million."

"Lyle, you'll be a pussy all your life." Cable's voice dripped with disdain. "Let's take their hundred grand now and sue later."

"I'm afraid we can't do that," Jackson said. "In order to get the hundred grand you have to agree not to sue."

"Suppose we agree to give the hundred grand back if we win the suit?"

Jackson blew a stream of smoke at the speaker phone. "That's not the way it works, Cable."

"All right, how about this?" Cable said. "Lyle settles now and splits his hundred grand with me. I sue and split whatever I get with Lyle later. That gives us a little something now and something more later."

"That might work," Jackson said. "What do you think, Lyle?"

"If you say a hundred grand is a bad offer," Lyle said, "then it's a bad bet for either of us to take it. I never expected to get any money at all for Maddie's death. And I'm in no hurry. So if waiting gets a shot at a million, I'm inclined to wait."

"Pussy, pussy, pussy," Cable said. "Always thinking of yourself. Let me understand this. The hundred grand comes right now?"

"Right now," Jackson said.

"With no strings?"

"So long as you agree not to be part of a lawsuit." Jackson stared at the speaker phone. "You're not seriously considering it?"

"Don't tell me what I'm considering," Cable said. "Would I have to be there in person to get the money?"

"No. You could give me power of attorney."

"But then you'd take something off the top." The speaker phone went silent for a moment. "Maybe I better think on it a little and get back to you."

"That will be okay," Jackson said. "How can I reach you?"

"You can't. I'll contact you." Cable rushed his words. "I've got to run now. I'll be in touch."

The speaker phone buzzed with the sound of a broken connection.

Jackson stubbed out his cigarette. "Funny. Of the two of you, I thought you'd be the one who'd want to take the offer and Cable would be the one who'd want to sue."

Lyle got up to leave. "There's just no telling with that son of a bitch."

OWEN STOPPED AT home for a change of clothes before heading for the Hobbs house outside Contrary to spend the night with Jeb Stuart Hobbs. Canopies of trees covered the winding road between Barkley and Contrary, leaving the road and the creek below it shrouded in darkness and fog. Although Owen couldn't see the creek, he could hear the swish and gurgle of the water as he slowed to round the hairpin turns. There was a time, he remembered, when he'd been so anxious to see Mary Beth that he'd taken these same turns on two squealing tires. Tonight, though, he slowed his second-hand Saturn to an apprehensive crawl as his headlights picked their way through patches of tule fog illuminated by occasional slivers of moonlight.

An oncoming car swung wide on a curve and blinded Owen with its brights. He swerved off the road, braking to a stop just before the narrow berm tailed away to the creekbed. The unmuffled roar of the passing car faded in and out as it took the downhill curves.

Owen gripped the steering wheel hard, muttering "Asshole" after the roar had died down. He got out of his Saturn and inspected the thin strip of clay under his right wheels. It dropped off steeply about ten feet ahead of him. If he'd been going any faster, he'd be in the creek now.

He returned to his car and inched around the few remaining turns to the Hobbs' house. He was still tense when his headlights picked up the rural mailbox at the head of their driveway. A folded sheet of paper stuck out of the slot in the mailbox door.

Owen pulled into the driveway, parked, and walked around his car to the mailbox. Just before he reached it, he heard the roar of an unmuffled motor winding up the hill toward him. Bright headlights swept around the last curve and spotlighted him in their glare.

Owen froze.

The roar increased, the car slowed, and a gunshot ripped into the mailbox.

Owen dove for the cover of his car as two more shots tore into the mailbox. He crawled across the gravel drive and squatted behind his left front tire just as a fourth gunshot exploded it. He stayed there, crouched and trembling, as the car sped noisily down the hill.

12

A Poke in the Piggly Wiggly

THAD Reader shined his flashlight on the Hobbs mailbox. Bullets had pierced the *o* and the loops of the two *b*s in the name Hobbs. "Man who grouped these shots could easily have punched you a couple of new navels if he'd wanted to. My guess is, he was just trying to scare you."

Owen ran his fingers over the bullet holes. "Well, he did that."

"But you didn't get his license number?"

"I was too busy ducking. It was a Cadillac, though. Had to be Cable Stokes." Owen handed the sheriff the sheet of paper he'd retrieved from the mailbox. "Look at this note."

The note was a copy of the pasted-up threat Jeb Stuart had brought to Owen that morning. Scrawled across it in red magic marker was the warning I'M WATCHING YOU.

"Not much on originality." Reader glanced back at the porch steps, where a barefooted, pajama-clad Jeb Stuart sat shivering under a blanket held by Ruth Allison. The sheriff turned away and lowered his voice to ask, "How's the boy taking it?"

"He's scared and worried. He thinks it's his fault his mom's in trouble."

Reader folded his handkerchief over the note and pocketed it. "One good thing at least. If Cable's still sending threatening notes, his sister must not have told him we visited her."

"She will, though."

"Until she does, Cable can't be sure we know about Riley. I'll call Sheriff Cook in Middleburg, get him to take a few FBI types over to baby-sit Essie. If they get a wiretap warrant and scare her into cooperating, we may be able to track down Cable before he harms the Hobbs woman."

"So, in a way, it's good news that Cable left that note."

"But it's bad news that he recognized your car and followed you back here to underline his message."

"He doesn't know I was coming to see Jeb Stuart. For all Cable knows, I might have been trying to visit Mary Beth."

"What was it Cable called you when you upset his phony foundation claims? A limp-dicked brownnose? He's not likely to believe you followed a stiff pecker up that hill." The sheriff rapped twice on the mailbox. "Besides, he saw you going for the note in the mailbox. That's gotta tell him the pussy's out of the poke."

Owen and the sheriff trudged back up the driveway to the porch steps where Jeb Stuart and Ruth sat huddled under the plaid blanket. Reader tapped the pocket that held the warning note. "It's actually a good sign, son. If Cable's still trying to scare you, he probably hasn't hurt your mom."

"And he may not suspect we know about Riley," Owen said.

Ruth Allison drew the blanket tighter around herself and Jeb Stuart. "Stokes must suspect something. He wasn't shooting up that mailbox to protest poor postal service."

OWEN TOOK HIS mother to Mass at her home parish the next morning. In California, he usually spent Sunday morning on the tennis courts. Here in Barkley, though, his mother was a regular Mass-goer, and he accompanied her, finding the familiar ritual soothing.

This morning, his thoughts kept wandering from the ritual to images of Cable Stokes and Mary Beth Hobbs. The image of Cable Stokes that kept recurring was his hate-filled face as he raised a cinderblock overhead to throw it. The image of Mary Beth, on the other hand, showed her naked and vulnerable, standing at her bedroom window and staring through the Venetian blinds after their first evening of sex. The images alternated in his mind, triggered by the loosest associations. The priest's upraised arms during the Consecration reminded him of Stokes, while the clear contralto and long blonde hair of the lead singer summoned up Mary Beth.

Arriving back at Ruth's house after Mass, they found two men coming down the porch steps. One was tall and looked vaguely familiar to Owen. The other was short, pudgy, and wore a navy blue suit with a yellow necktie splashed with blue polka-dots.

"Dr. Allison. How nice. I was afraid we'd missed you," the pudgy man said in a high-pitched voice. He extended a hand with fingers as round as breakfast sausages. "I'm Hector Johnson. I believe you know my associate, Mr. Henry Clanton."

Shaking Johnson's hand was like clutching a cow's udders. When no milk came, Owen released the hand and looked uncertainly at the taller man. "I'm sorry, I'm afraid I can't place you."

"We met in the Tharps' backyard."

"Oh, yes." Owen smiled. "I didn't recognize you without your orange jumpsuit. You were running the cleanup dredge."

"For Johnson, Crane, and Associates," the pudgy man said. "That's my company. If you'll permit me, Dr. Allison, I'll get right to the point."

Johnson put so much backspin on the title "Doctor" that it managed to be both wheedling and dismissive at the same time. Owen usually asked people to call him by his first name rather than manufacture a title out of his Ph.D., but in this case he let the formal address stand and simply nodded.

"I believe you know," the man continued in his high-pitched voice, "that West Virginia's attorney general has been charged with the task of finding a firm to study the safety of the state's impoundment dams."

Owen nodded again.

"Well, my firm has been awarded the contract to undertake that study."

Owen was genuinely surprised. "I didn't see any official notice of the competition."

"There was no competition. To expedite matters, the state simply added funds to our existing cleanup contract."

"Congratulations," Owen said, keeping his voice even.

"Thank you. It's one of the benefits of having a current contract with the state. You understand how these things work, I'm sure. It's easier all round. State employees don't have to write proposal requests, contractors are spared the cost and tedium of proposal writing, and the state is saved the time and expense of evaluating proposals from a wide range of bidders."

"It certainly narrows the competitive field," Owen said. "But then, so do prearranged marriages, one-horse races, and uncontested elections. Trouble is, there's no guarantee they'll turn out well. Can I ask the size of the contract?"

"Two hundred thousand dollars."

Owen fought to keep his face free of the outrage he felt. The sum was more than twice the amount he had bid to do the same job. "You must be a heavy campaign contributor."

The pudgy man frowned. "Excuse me?"

"The attorney general offered me the same job," Owen said, "on the condition I kick back fifteen percent into his campaign fund."

"Hell, fifteen percent's cheap," Clanton said. "He must have wanted you pretty bad."

Johnson nodded. "Twenty percent's the going rate."

"And it usually goes straight into his pocket," Clanton said. "Not into any campaign fund."

"You just write a check?" Owen asked.

"Hell no," Clanton said. "It's cash on the barrelhead. His wife takes installment payments after dark in a supermarket parking lot."

"In a plain brown wrapper?"

"Shopping bag, usually," Clanton said.

Owen loosed a short laugh. "A poke in the Piggly Wiggly."

Clanton laughed. "It's a Big Bear, actually."

Johnson didn't join in the laughter. "Dr. Allison doesn't need to know the sordid details."

"Why do you put up with it?" Owen asked.

Johnson shrugged. "It's the cost of doing business."

"But if you blew the whistle, you could save twenty percent on every contract."

"We'd just lose it writing proposals," Clanton said.

"And the results wouldn't be nearly so certain," Johnson said. "How often have you seen a top-notch proposal lose to a mediocre effort with a lower bid? Or a competent expert beat out by somebody's inexperienced brother-in-law?"

Owen winced. Johnson's observations struck a nerve. He'd seen his first consulting business go belly-up when he'd lost a bid he later learned was rigged. "But this kickback system has to be worse. And illegal to boot."

"We prefer to think of it as enlightened cronyism," Johnson said. "Attorney General Boyer spreads the work around. And he sees to it that the jobs we do are done right. One screw-up and you're off his list."

"Seems like that's the least he should do for his share," Owen said.

"It's the attorney general's oversight that brings us to your porch steps this morning," Johnson said. "He'd still like to have you undertake the investigation. He feels you have the experience to do it right."

"The attorney general could have saved money by hiring me directly," Owen said. "There just would have been one less contribution to his campaign fund."

"Well, I'm offering to hire you for the same job," Johnson said.

"What about the kickback?"

"That need not concern you."

"We're taking care of it in easy installments," Clanton said.

"What's in it for you?" Owen asked.

"There'll be enough left over to make it worth my while," Johnson said. "And I'm hoping you'll train a few of my men to spot flaws in the state's impoundment dams."

"Wouldn't you rather have your own people do that?"

"I'm afraid no one on our staff has sufficient expertise."

"Then how'd you get the job?"

"As I explained, our cleanup contract provided a convenient legal channel for the state procurement office."

"So because you had an open-ended contract, you got the job without knowing how to do it."

Johnson seemed more amused than perturbed by Owen's remark. "We know how to do it. We're hiring you."

"What if I refuse?"

"We'll find somebody else. But we'd rather have you."

Owen didn't want to work for Johnson, but he couldn't afford to close the door on the possibility of a paying client. "I still have some working obligations with Anson Stokes."

"I don't see that as a conflict of interest." Johnson turned to his taller companion. "Do you, Henry?"

"Nope. If you're billing time to Anson, though, I'd advise you to get paid up front. Word is, if he don't get his mine reopened, he's likely to be stretched tighter than a fat lady's underpants."

"All the same," Owen said, "I'd like to talk to Anson before accepting your offer."

"I don't see that as a problem. We'll just wait for your answer." Johnson extended a pudgy hand. "I do hope we'll be able to work together, Owen. I trust I may call you Owen."

Owen shook the offered hand. "So long as you're hiring me for my expertise, maybe you better keep calling me Dr. Allison. Think of it as a kind of advertising."

SHERIFF THAD READER looked at Owen as if he'd just proposed they set out to scale Everest in their underwear. "You know how many Big Bear stores there are in this county? I'm not about to put them all under surveillance on the off chance we might witness a payoff to the attorney general's wife."

Owen lifted the nameplate reading RALEIGH COUNTY SHERIFF from Reader's desk and turned it so it faced the lawman. "Am I wrong? The sheriff's office still represents the law in this county, doesn't it?"

"Right now, the law in this county is concerned with a kidnapping, a mine explosion, three flood deaths, and Christ knows how many cases of insurance fraud. That doesn't even count the general run of DWIs and bar fights. On any given day, the sum total of political kickbacks in this county outnumbers my deputies by maybe ten to one. Even if I got lucky and caught one of the bagmen red-handed, they'd probably claim the money was a charitable donation or a legitimate campaign contribution."

"The public has a right to know about this kind of corruption."

"The public knows. They don't give a shit. They view it as a perk of office."

Owen sighed and shook his head. "I can't believe that."

"Look. I understand your outrage. You don't like the system. I don't like it either."

"It's more than that. My first company went under when I lost a rigged bid. Cost me my house in California and probably my marriage. Systems like that need fixing. Besides, I didn't much like Heck Johnson."

"I don't like him either. Nobody's forcing you to work for him, though. How'd you leave it with him?"

"I stalled. I told him Anson Stokes had first call on my services. I said I'd have to check with him."

The sheriff scratched his receding hairline. "Might not be a bad idea to talk to Anson anyhow. He might have some idea where Cable's gone to ground."

"You think so? Strikes me that'd be like asking Abel where to find Cain. The two aren't exactly close."

"Cain must have kept pretty close tabs on Abel just before he iced him. Maybe Anson knows about hideouts they shared before they had a falling out."

"They fell out pretty early. The only hideout they had in common before that was their mother's womb."

Reader rose from his chair. "Hell, it's worth a try. Let's drive out to Anson's place on the Little Muddy. It's a long shot, but it beats scanning Big Bear lots for suspicious shopping bags."

149

READER DROVE THE back roads of the county like a man who wasn't worried about speeding tickets.

"What about Cable's other relatives?" Owen asked. "Anybody who might provide him with a hideout? Or know where he'd go to find one?"

"We've got his sister Essie and his boy Billy Joe under surveillance." Reader took a switchback at full throttle. "Two other boys lit out as soon as they quit school."

"A real father figure." Owen braced himself in the passenger seat. "What about that neighbor, Lyle Tanner? How long have they known one another?"

"They've both lived in Drybone Hollow for quite a spell. I got the impression there's no love lost between them, though. To know Cable isn't exactly to love him. And the longer you know him, the more likely he is to piss you off." Reader honked his horn approaching a blind curve. "Still, Tanner's worth a shot."

"What about lady friends?"

"Since his wife left him, Cable's not held on to anybody very long. Got a reputation as a real chubby chaser."

"Excuse me?"

"Likes his women round, firm, and fully packed."

"How'd you come by that piece of news?"

Reader raised the brow over his glass eye. "I'm a trained investigator."

"Trained or not, I'd be curious to know who has that kind of information."

"Talked to Heidi Stamm. Runs the local bawdy house."

"I see. All in the line of duty."

Reader turned the corners of his mouth downward in mock seriousness. "Purely professional."

"Your profession or hers?"

ANSON STOKES' TWO-STORY brick house dominated a sparsely wooded stretch of bottomland formed by the confluence of the Little Muddy River and Tug Fork Creek. Sparkling white columns marched along the front of a long wooden porch and turned a corner to support a carport big enough to shelter a tank battalion. Beyond the carport, an attractive brunette in a warmup suit wafted a long-handled net over the surface of a large swimming pool.

"My God, it's a mansion," Owen said as Thad Reader steered his patrol car up the long winding driveway toward the carport.

"Old Anson's done all right for himself. Till now."

As the sheriff shut off his motor, Anson Stokes' head popped out from under the black Hummer parked between a powder blue Corvette and a tan Mercedes station wagon in the carport. He pulled himself out from under the Hummer, wiped his hands with a grease rag, and frowned at the sheriff's patrol car.

A half-smile replaced the frown when Owen emerged from the passenger seat of the sheriff's car. "Well, looky who's here. Welcome to my humble abode." Anson whirled the grease rag overhead and shouted to the brunette beside the pool, "Honey, come meet these here fellows."

The brunette laid the pool net down and came through the carport. The blue of her warmup suit was such a perfect match for the Corvette's color that Owen wondered which had been purchased first.

"This here's my wife, Mary Gil," Anson said. "Took me three tries, but I finally got it right."

Mary Gil smiled and shook the hands of Owen and the sheriff. "Third time's a charm."

The woman was short and slim, with high cheekbones and a narrow, open face that Owen associated with mountain-born women. He judged her to be at least twenty years younger than Anson.

Anson snapped the grease rag in the direction of his wife, who sidestepped it gracefully. "Honey, finding that oil leak's thirsty work. Why don't you fetch me a beer and get these good folks something too."

Owen asked for a Coke and Thad Reader said he'd settle for ice water. As the men watched Mary Gil walk off toward the house, Anson stuffed the grease rag into the hip pocket of his overalls and said, "Sure wish I'd met that little gal before I went and married my first wife. Course, Mary Gil was barely teething at the time." Then he arched his eyebrows and smiled. "Just gotta be glad the factory keeps on turning out new models."

When his wife had disappeared through the back door of the house, Stokes asked, "What can I do for you fellows?"

"We're looking for your brother Cable," the sheriff said.

Stokes squinted at the tree-lined ridge overlooking his valley. "Well, I hope to kiss a pig you've already covered the rest of the county, 'cause this is the last place I'd expect to find Cable."

"We thought you could have some idea where he might go to hide," Owen said.

"To hide? What's he done?"

"Insurance fraud, for one thing," the sheriff said. "He's been trying to collect death benefits on his boy Riley. But Riley's still alive."

Anson's face broke into a smile so wide two gold molars glittered in the sun. "You're telling me Riley didn't drown? Hot damn, that's great news."

Mary Gil returned with a tray full of drinks. "Guess what, hon?" Anson said, taking a beer from the tray. "These fellows are just now telling me Cable's boy Riley is still alive. He didn't drown after all."

"That's wonderful, Shug." Mary Gil handed Owen and the sheriff their drinks and gave Stokes an enthusiastic hug.

"By God, that's just great." Stokes clicked his beer bottle against the glasses held by Owen and Thad Reader. "I'll sure drink to that news. Let's go sit by the pool. I want to hear all about this. Where'd you find Riley?" He led them to a wrought-iron table with a huge parasol sprouting from its center. "What happened to the boy, anyhow?"

"Cable hid him at your sister's house in Middleburg and tried to collect on his insurance," the sheriff said.

Stokes took a long pull on his beer bottle. "Cable and Essie? Between them, they've barely got the brains to wipe their hineys clean. Wouldn't think they could *spell* fraud, let alone pull one off. You sure you got the right end of the stick here?"

"We're sure," the sheriff said. "When one of Riley's friends caught on, Cable kidnapped the boy's mother, Mary Beth Hobbs."

"Stony Hobbs' widow?"

"You know her?"

"Knew Stony right well. He was one of the last of the independents. Knew his wife to look at. Real easy on the eyes." Stokes shook his head. "Kidnapping don't sound like Cable neither. Man's barely got the gumption to collect his own welfare check."

"We're sure about the kidnapping. Cable left a note that could only have come from him." Owen recited the note from memory:

> "YOU'LL BE SORRY
> IF YOU TELL ANYONE
> YOUR MOM WILL DIE."

Anson's face clouded over. "You got a copy of that there note?"

Thad Reader went to his patrol car and returned with a copy of the kidnapping note. Anson had barely glimpsed the note when he shoved back from the table, upending his chair and spilling his beer. He stood and loosed a stream of invective that damned everything about Cable but their mutual ancestry.

When he finally sputtered to a stop, red-faced and gasping for breath, Anson pointed at Owen and the sheriff. "Wait right there. I'll kill that son-bitch."

Anson disappeared inside his house and returned with a single sheet of paper. "This come just after the judge shut me down."

He handed the sheet to Thad Reader. It was a photocopied composed of cut-out magazine and newspaper letters. The first line of the note, YOU'LL BE SORRY, matched exactly the first line of the note Cable Stokes left for Jeb Stuart Hobbs. The next two lines of Anson's note read:

> IF YOU REOPEN THE MINE
> IT WILL BLOW AGAIN.

13

One Leg at a Time

THAD Reader picked up Anson's note by opposing corners. "You say you got this just after your hearing?"

"Couple of days later."

"Why didn't you come to me? Or the court?"

Anson loosed a short, harsh laugh. "You kidding? The judge sees that note, he would have shut me down for good."

Reader laid the note on the iron table. "Instead you sat on it."

"I wanted to get the mine reopened. Nothing was going to blow before that happened. I thought I might be able to find the note writer."

"And now you have."

"So have you. Think there's enough here to put Cable away?"

"We've already got enough to put Cable away," Reader said. "The problem is finding him."

Owen nodded at the note. "That's just a threat. He didn't act on it."

"He might have acted on it already," Reader said. "Could be he set off the dynamite in the first place."

"Cable?" Owen asked. "Why would he do that?"

"To get at me," Arson said.

Owen shook his head. "I can't believe he'd flood out a hollow and kill three people just to get at you."

"Could be he was just trying to flood out my mine. Cable's got about as much sense of cause and effect as Mrs. O'Leary's cow."

Reader picked up Anson's note with a handkerchief and deposited it in the folder with Cable's note to Jeb Stuart. "I'll need to keep this."

Anson shrugged. "Long as it don't find its way into 'Lean to Green' Vereen's courtroom."

Reader got up to go. "If we find Cable quick enough, there'll be no sting to the threat."

Owen stood to join Reader. "I meant to tell you, Anson. Johnson, Crane got some grant money to look at all the shafts in the state that are near impoundment dams."

"Old Heck Johnson's got more connections than a six-way socket."

"Wants to hire me to help out. Maybe train a few of his people in the process."

"Couldn't have made a better choice."

"Thing is, I told him I still had some obligations to you."

"To me?" Anson walked with Owen and Thad Reader toward the patrol car. "Hell, Owen. I hired you to get at the why of the dam break. You spotted the blast hole first trip into my mine. Now you're working on the who of it with the sheriff here. I don't see you need to hold off working for Heck on my account."

Anson looked back over his shoulder and waved at Mary Gil, making sure she was out of earshot. "Truth to tell, if I don't get my mine open soon, I can't afford to pay you anyhow. Hell, go ahead and work for Heck. You need a place to train Heck's folks, use my shaft. Ain't nothing else going on there. Maybe you'll spot something you missed first time around."

ON THE WAY back, the car hugged the Little Muddy River, passing trailers on cinderblocks and clapboard houses sandwiched between the river and railroad tracks. "Anson sure raised the tone of this neighborhood," Owen said. "You think Cable would blow the mine just to get back at him?"

"I don't know. You saw Anson's spread. Cable must be jealous as Dolly Parton's sister."

"Tough to figure how they wound up so far apart," Owen said. "They sure started out even. In high school, you'd have been hard put to see any difference between them. Then they partnered up on their first business."

"And now Anson's living high on the hog, while Cable's a welfare case on the run from the law."

"Woody Allen says ninety percent of success is just showing up. Cable went missing the one day they took attendance."

Reader nodded. "And Anson showed up."

"Showed up, took the risks, and rode out the hard times."

"So Cable's bitter," Reader said. "That doesn't mean he'd blow Anson's mine."

"Is there any evidence at all linking him to the explosion? Besides the note, I mean?"

"I don't see the note as very compelling evidence. Judge Vereen had other notes threatening the same thing, all sent before the trial. They were computer generated and used high-falutin words like 'Impending Menace' and 'Sultans of Sludge.' Not a chance in hell they came from Cable."

"So you think the earlier note senders are better candidates for the mine-blowing experience?"

Reader didn't bother to wince at the pun. "Could be none of the note senders blew the mine. Maybe they both saw their notes as a low-risk way of shutting Anson down."

"Which leaves us back at the mouth of the shaft with no idea who blew it. Let's review what we do know about the blast itself."

Reader squinted as he rounded a curve and came face to face with the setting sun. "Dynamite composition. Turns out the same formula blew Anson's mine and Cable's truck."

"That's something, isn't it?"

Reader shrugged. "It is and it isn't. There's no DNA for dynamite. Most sticks would have left the same kind of residue."

"What about the chunks of plastic at both sites?"

"They match too. Same kind used in timing devices. Trouble is, the timing devices are pretty common."

"So it's possible Cable or Billy Joe blew Anson's mine and had an accident with the leftover dynamite."

Reader stopped at a railroad crossing and watched a loaded coal train rumble past. "Or maybe Cable and Billy Joe had nothing to do with anything. Maybe some third party had a grudge against both Anson and Cable."

"You mean whoever lit the fuse on Anson's mine might have blown Cable's truck as well. That the second explosion might not have been an accident."

Reader raised his voice to make himself heard over the train noise. "The Stokes brothers aren't going to win any popularity contests. In fact, they'd probably finish in a dead heat for last place. But I can't imagine any one person with a big enough grudge to light a separate fuse under each of them. It's just too messy. And they live in two different worlds."

"Maybe it's not a grudge. Who stands to inherit if they wind up dead?"

The caboose passed the intersection and Reader eased his patrol car across the tracks. "Mary Gil would probably come into Anson's money, but the blaster went after Anson's mine, not Anson. I guess Cable's boys would split any inheritance if he dies, but nothing split four ways still comes out nothing."

"Except Cable could win big with all those lawsuits. And I didn't detect a lot of mutual affection between Cable and his boy Billy Joe."

"So you think Billy Joe might have rigged the dynamite in Cable's truck? If that's the case, why was he still around when it blew?"

"Whatever plans he might have had would have been upset by our showing up at Lyle Tanner's and sending Cable and Billy Joe back to DPR with their load of cinderblocks."

"So with us following them, Billy Joe can't very well stop and say, 'Dad, I need to defuse the bomb under your seat.'" Reader shook his head. "No, I don't buy it. Billy Joe was the last one out of the cab when it came time to unload the cinderblocks and the closest to the truck when it blew. No way he could have intentionally set it off."

"Okay, if the truck explosion was an accident, what about Anson's mine? We've covered grudge and greed. What other motives are there?"

"Could be Moral Brody's rantings inspired a little ecoterrorism."

It was Owen's turn to shake his head. "I can't imagine certified tree huggers causing forty million dollars in environmental damage to protest underground mining."

"Maybe they planned the explosion without knowing the dam sitting on top of the shaft. Or maybe they had Cable's slippery grasp of cause and effect."

Owen sighed. "Nothing makes much sense. Does the timing of the blast tell us anything? What time did it happen?"

"The 911 call came in at 3:30 that morning."

"So the mine blew a little before that."

"Or a lot before that."

"And at 3:30 on that particular morning, both of the residents of Cable Stokes' household just happened to be out of harm's way."

"Riley was in Middleburg, and Cable was . . ." Reader pounded his palm against the top of the steering wheel as if sounding a silent horn. "Where the hell was Cable?"

"Maybe he was waiting for Riley at the bus stop."

"You say maybe. What are you thinking?"

"The 911 call came from the shopping center above the dam."

"And we don't know who made it."

"Maybe Cable made it. Suppose he did blow the mine. Suppose he set the charge to blow around 3:30 and called as soon as it happened."

"Doesn't make any sense," Reader said. "Why would he do that?"

"To limit the damage. If all he wanted to do was flood Anson's shaft, that would happen right away. The shaft itself limits the flow and the downstream damage. It's like a fire hose. Maybe Cable thought if they plugged the hole quickly enough there'd be no problems downstream."

"Trying to stop a flood's like trying to catch a hurricane in a bottle. Besides, the blast only flooded the abandoned shaft, not the working ones."

"Like Anson said, Cable's not too good on cause and effect."

The road left the riverbank and wound up the side of Moore's Mountain. Reader concentrated on two hairpin turns before responding. "If it was Cable out after revenge, why didn't he just dynamite a working shaft?"

"Maybe he thought all the shafts were connected. Maybe there was too much security in the working shafts. I'm just thinking with my mouth open. You listened to the 911 tape. Could it have been Cable?"

Reader chewed on his lower lip. "The voice was muffled. The accent was definitely coal country. It could have been Cable, I guess. But, hell, going by what I heard, it could just as easy been Johnny Cash."

"It'd be easy enough to get a voice print on Johnny Cash. Think we can get one on Cable?"

"If we can get Cable. I've got all my deputies and the FBI looking for his car."

"Anything I can do?"

Reader shrugged. "It's police business. Finding missing cars is one of the things we do best."

"In that case, I think I'll talk to a few of the people farther along the flood path, maybe get a better handle on the time it really hit. The closer the 911 call was to the blast, the more likely the caller was the blaster."

THE NEXT DAY, Owen tried to find someone who could put a time on the flood's onset while the sheriff continued to track Cable's car. Neither had any success. Cable's car had vanished from state roadways, and those people who had been awakened by the flood weren't sure how long the waters had been rushing before they heard them.

Tuesday afternoon was Jeb Stuart's third game of the season and the first home game. Owen arrived early to watch the teams warm up. He found the Contrary diamond had changed little in the thirty-odd years since he'd pitched for Barkley as the visiting team. The park was deep in a hollow, sandwiched between two softball diamonds and a dry creekbed. The surrounding ridges were so high and steep that the sun disappeared early, leaving the field shrouded in shadows and forcing umpires to call games on account of darkness as early as 5:30. Even now, during the pre-game warmups, shadows slanted across the bleachers and covered the field from home plate halfway up the first-base line.

The home team was turning the field over to the visitors for batting practice when Purvis Jenkins appeared at the shady end of the bleachers. He joined Owen in the seats behind the home team's dugout and asked, "Any word on Mary Beth?"

"None so far."

"How's my nephew taking it?"

"About like you'd expect. He worries a lot. Thinks it's his fault. He wanted to stay home from school yesterday in case his mom called. We talked it over, agreed it would be best if he followed his daily routine."

"Appreciate your looking after the boy."

"My mom's helping."

"Takes somebody with experience. I'd be useless as tits on a bull."

"We don't mind doing it."

Purvis shook his head. "Mary Beth could always take care of herself. A little too well sometimes. When we were kids, I was all the time being tanned in the coal cellar for something she did."

"She's the one in the coal cellar now. Or worse."

"Tried to blackmail Cable Stokes, you think?"

"Looks like."

Purvis sighed. "Three days now. Going on four. With no word."

"The sheriff's got all his men on it," Owen said, trying to put more hope than he felt into his voice. "The FBI's in it too. They find Cable, they'll find your sister."

"Likely holed up in a holler somewhere. Jesus, why'd she ever go after somebody like Cable Stokes?"

"Opportunity. She had something pretty big on him. And shady deals run in the family. How many years have you been bilking the government?"

"It's not the same thing. Shaking down someone like Cable is like shaking a stick at a rattlesnake. It's a lot easier to bilk the government. You just tap a spigot into that big green flow. If you're careful where you tap in, nobody even misses what you siphon off."

"I take it you got your new buses?"

"Easy. And a new water treatment plant's in the works."

Owen laughed. "Purvis, you're shameless."

"Contrary pays out good money in federal taxes. Only right we get some back."

"You get a lot more back than you pay out."

"No more'n our just due. West Virginia's gas taxes end up in Wyoming because they got more space to cover with roads and fewer people than we got. But we got more poor folks than most states. So it's only right the feds ship some of the taxes from rich folks in New York and California our way."

Owen smiled and echoed Purvis' twang. "Only right."

"I've never been able to figure out why we have to ship our money all the way to Washington in a leaky bucket, let them ladle it out any way they please, take their leavings, and follow their say-so in spending what little gets back to us."

Owen's smile wilted a little at the corners. He'd heard Purvis expound on leaky tax buckets several times.

"I just want to see we get our fair share back. Half the men over sixty-five in this state are toothless. That's a god-forlorn fact. Fluoridation and water treatment come too late for them. I'm seeing to it the next generation can chew into their eighties."

Owen reached for Purvis' knee as if he were squeezing an emergency brake. "Easy there, Purvis. No need to waste your campaign speeches on me. I don't vote in Contrary."

"You're turning on the tap at my sister's house. You ought to be concerned what's coming out."

AS THE HOME team took the field to start the game, Jeb Stuart crouched behind the plate, handling the pitcher's warmup tosses. He hadn't made eye contact with Owen since batting practice began. Maybe that's good, Owen thought. Maybe the boy can lose himself in the game and forget what's happening outside the foul lines.

Just after the umpire called "Play ball," the Cincinnati Reds' scout, Bill Anderson, climbed the bleacher steps and sat down next to Owen.

"Cops questioned me about Mary Beth Hobbs," Anderson said. "What the hell's going on?"

"They're trying to find anybody who's seen her since Saturday. She's missing."

"I gathered that. Tried calling her house. Some old lady answered."

"That was my mother."

"You moving in?"

"Just till Mary Beth returns."

"Helluva thing."

Purvis Jenkins introduced himself to Bill Anderson, and they shook hands across Owen's body. "Pleased to meet you," Anderson said. "I've been scouting your nephew for the Reds."

"What I hear, you've been scouting the whole family," Purvis said.

Anderson didn't respond. Instead, he opened his spiral-bound scorebook to a fresh page and turned his attention to the diamond.

The visiting team went down one-two-three in the top of the first. In the bottom of the inning, Jeb Stuart batted with one man on and struck out swinging at a pitch well wide of the plate.

Anderson made an entry in his scorebook. "Boy looks a little ragged."

"He hasn't been getting much sleep," Owen said. "He's worried about his mom."

"Gotta leave that behind when you step between the lines," Anderson said. "Gotta come to play. When the going gets tough, the tough get going."

Purvis and Owen exchanged glances. "Maybe I'll write that last bit down," Purvis said. "Use it in my campaign."

Contrary scored twice in the bottom of the second. Jeb Stuart batted again in the third and popped out weakly to shortstop. Anderson made another entry in his scorebook.

Purvis shook a cigarette into his hand from a pack of Camels. A woman seated behind him tapped him on the shoulder. "Second-hand smoke kills, you know."

Purvis put the cigarette between his lips. "Well then, it's lucky for me I intend to smoke this first-hand."

"Not here," the woman said. "This is a smoke-free park."

Purvis looked as if he were about to respond, thought better of it, excused himself, and disappeared behind the bleachers.

As soon as Purvis had left, Anderson turned to Owen. "I'm glad he's gone. I've got a favor to ask."

"What's that?"

"Well, it's kind of awkward. I left a shirt and a good pair of slacks in the bedroom closet at the Hobbs house."

Owen was more irritated than surprised by this confession. "And?"

Anderson made a sour face. "Well, I'd really like to get them back, but I don't want to go and ask for them while the boy's around."

"I can understand that."

"His mom and I tried to be careful that way. I'm hoping you can just put the clothes in a bag and leave them outside somewhere. On the porch, maybe. That way I could get them without bothering anybody."

Anybody but me, Owen thought. He stared at the field without responding.

"I mean, I wouldn't bother at all, but the shirt's a really good one." When Owen still didn't respond, Anderson added, "Ralph Lauren. The shirt's a Ralph Lauren."

"What size?"

"Sixteen-and-a-half, thirty-five. Why?"

"Want to make sure I get the right man's shirt."

Anderson seemed to miss the implication of Owen's remark. "You'll do it then?"

"I'll put your things in a bag and leave them in the driveway. You better pick them up tonight, though. If they're still around tomorrow morning, they're liable to have tread marks on them."

Anderson was silent for the rest of the inning. As the teams changed sides, Purvis returned, tipped his hat to the woman behind him, and said, "I sincerely hope you weren't breathing while I was smoking."

By the end of the fifth inning, the entire field was in shadows and the score was tied at two. Jeb Stuart had struck out a second time, and his passed ball with two runners on had set up both the visitor's runs.

Owen looked at the darkening ridge line. "It's a pitcher's game now. All they have to do is get the ball over the plate. The batters don't stand a chance in this dim light. Might as well be swinging blindfolded."

"Ought to have lights," Anderson said.

"Ought to have new textbooks, a watertight roof, and better teachers," Purvis said. "Takes tax money, not some damnfool complaint."

The first batter up for the visiting team in the top of the sixth swung and missed at a third strike, but the ball skipped by Jeb Stuart and the hitter took first before Jeb could retrieve it. The next batter bunted. Jeb Stuart pounced on the ball and tried to get the force at second, but his throw sailed over the shortstop's glove, putting runners on first and third.

Anderson slapped his scorebook shut. "That's it. I've seen enough."

"The shortstop was late covering the base," Owen said.

"A lower throw would have gotten the out anyhow." Anderson stood and started down the bleacher steps.

Owen followed Anderson down the steps. "Cut the boy some slack."

Anderson kept walking toward the parking lot. "The game doesn't cut anybody slack. The best players fail two times out of three. You've gotta come prepared to play."

"We're talking about a sixteen-year-old boy here. His father's dead and his mother's missing. He's got more on his mind than a ball game."

Anderson picked up his pace, as if he were trying to outdistance Owen's argument. "Everybody's got problems. Gotta take them in stride. Leave them outside the foul lines."

"For Christ's sake, do you have a cliché for everything? I know the boy. He puts his pants on one leg at a time, comes with his game face on, and always gives a hundred and ten percent." Owen lengthened his stride to keep up. "I can match you bromide for bromide. We're talking about a real human being here."

Anderson didn't look at Owen. "Boy's not ready."

"Not ready? He's just having a bad day. He's the same boy you've been drooling over for weeks. Or was it his mother generating all that saliva?"

Anderson stopped and slammed his scorebook down on top of his two-tone Chevy. "You questioning my professionalism?"

"Your professionalism, your judgment, your decency, and your common sense." Owen could feel his anger mounting and knew he wasn't helping Jeb Stuart's cause, but he was too far gone to stop. "Hell, I'd question your manhood if I thought you had any."

A tight, ugly smile cut across Anderson's face. "Just ask Mary Beth about my manhood. She seems to be what's really bothering you."

"What's bothering me about Mary Beth is that she's missing. This isn't about her. It's about her son's future."

Anderson opened the car door and flung the scorebook onto the passenger seat. "Her son's future doesn't concern me. Or my ball club." He squeezed behind the steering wheel and gunned the motor. "That's all over." The Chevy sprayed gravel backing out of the parking lot.

"It isn't over till it's over, asshole," Owen shouted after the disappearing taillights. He felt exhausted, as if he'd just run hard to lose a rigged race.

By the time Owen returned to the bleachers, Contrary was just coming to bat in the bottom of the sixth. "What did I miss?" he asked Purvis.

"Runner on third scored on an infield out. What happened with the scout?"

"We swapped clichés. I think I got the worst of the deal."

"You never had a chance. That man's a walking cliché."

CONTRARY'S BATTERS FLAILED at pitches they could barely see in the bottom of the sixth and the umpires called the game because of darkness before the seventh inning started, leaving the home team on the short end of a three-to-two score. Owen and Purvis waited in the bleachers until most of the players had cleared out and then joined Jeb Stuart in the dugout. He sat alone at the far end of the worn wooden bench, stuffing his chest protector into a dusty duffel bag.

"Anything new on Mom?" Jeb Stuart asked as the two men approached.

Owen shook his head.

"Tough game," Purvis said. "You'll get 'em next time."

"Should have had them this time. Might have if I'd played that bunt safe and gone to first with it."

"Your shortstop was a little slow covering second," Owen said.

"My throw sailed. It wasn't his fault." The boy shoved his mask into the duffel bag and yanked the drawstring tight. "Did Mr. Anderson leave?"

"He saw most of the game," Purvis said.

"I don't blame him for leaving. I stank."

"You've got a lot on your mind," Owen said.

"Mr. Anderson says I can't let that bother me."

Owen glanced at Purvis. "Well, it certainly didn't seem to bother him."

"Nothing outside the lines bothers our boy Bill," Purvis said.

Jeb Stuart swiped at a streak of grime on his forehead with the back of his wrist. "I really blew it, didn't I?"

"You had a bad day." Owen looked across the darkening field at the headlights blinking on in the parking lot. "More like a bad night, actually. You'll have better days. Lots of them. You're too good a player not to."

"But Mr. Anderson won't be back, will he?"

"The Reds aren't the only team. There are twenty-nine others. You're just a junior. Plenty of time left to strut your stuff."

Jeb Stuart stood and shouldered his duffel bag. "But the Reds are my team."

"Mine too. It's their loss." Owen put his arm around the boy. "Come on, I'll give you a ride home."

WHILE JEB STUART showered and Ruth fixed dinner, Owen went to the closet of the master bedroom and located Bill Anderson's slacks and shirt. He unzipped the fly of the slacks and used a pair of scissors to cut the pants in half along the crotch seam, separating the two legs. Then he put the shirt and bisected pants in a bag with a note explaining that this particular pair of pants could *only* be put on one leg at a time. For a more traditional pair, he referred Anderson to the adage, "When the going gets tough, the tough go shopping."

As he'd promised Anderson, Owen left the bag in the Hobbs' driveway, hoping that the scout's angry departure from the game wouldn't keep him from reclaiming his abandoned clothing.

After dinner, Jeb Stuart cleared the table while Owen loaded the dishwasher and Buster sat panting at his feet, waiting patiently for dropped crumbs. Suddenly the dog left his post and ran yapping to the front of the house.

"Somebody's in the driveway," Ruth called from the living room.

"Maybe it's Mom." Jeb Stuart ran to look.

Owen went on loading the dishwasher. Buster returned first, followed by Jeb Stuart.

"It looked like Mr. Anderson," Jeb Stuart said. "But he didn't stay."

Owen allowed himself a smile to ward off an outright laugh. "No. He wouldn't."

"I knew I blew it today."

Owen knelt to feed Buster some table scraps. "In the long run, I think Anderson blew it."

"But what'll I do in the short run?"

"Tell you what. Tomorrow we'll start looking for a college that needs a catcher."

"Colleges cost money."

"If the Reds thought you might be worth a contract, there ought to be a lot of colleges that'll think you're worth a scholarship. The majors are drafting more prospects from college than from high school now anyhow."

The phone rang. Jeb Stuart ran to answer it.

"Let it ring four times," Owen called after him. "That way the FBI will have everything set up."

Jeb Stuart lifted the phone halfway through the fourth ring. His face told Owen and Ruth that the caller wasn't his mother. He handed the phone to Owen. "It's the sheriff. For you."

On the phone, Reader rushed his words as if he were trying to shove them over the wires personally. "We've found Cable's car. Pick you up in ten minutes."

14

God's Enema

THE car's in a creekbed just beyond the bone pile," Reader said, gunning his patrol car around the wooded curves. "Some kids called it in."

The roadside trees disappeared and the police car's headlights swept over the top of the bone pile, where smoldering shale waste dumped by local miners fell away to the creek below. The slate-covered slope reflected slivers of moonlight and patches of dull orange flame where deep-burning fires slowly consumed the mine waste.

The bone pile had been burning there for most of Owen's lifetime. Local preachers used the smoldering shale to remind their congregations of the fires of hell. From time to time local drunks would illustrate the analogy by curling up near the bone pile for a warm nap and suffocating in the sulphur fumes.

"It's a blight," Owen said. "These slate dumps have been outlawed for twenty-five years."

"It's just taking the EPA's bureaucrats a little time to clean up after the lawmakers," Reader said. "At least nobody's starting any new dumps."

Beyond the bone pile, the road sloped downhill. Just as it leveled out to parallel the creekbed, flares guided traffic around two parked patrol cars. Ahead of the parked cars, a dirt path dipped even closer to the creek. Reader edged onto this path, which hugged a limestone shelf and soon dropped out of sight of the main roadway.

The creekbed beside the path was filled with debris the flowing water had failed to flush. A gnarled cedar root held a ladder-back chair captive, while an upended sofa with exposed springs formed a small island in the center of the stream. Beyond the sofa, an old-fashioned refrigerator half sunk in silt left its cylindrical crown of coils above the muck like a beaconless lighthouse.

The sheriff parked his car just ahead of a dip where the creek waters claimed a portion of the path. "We better walk it from here."

Outside the car, frogs croaked and the smell of burning sulphur assaulted their nostrils. Reader shined his flashlight on a rump-sprung car seat, sending frogs slithering for cover inside its stuffing. "Once the mines started using the creek for a dumping ground, the locals followed suit."

Splintered slats from discarded furniture poked through the dark waters like severed limbs.

"It's like following the alimentary canal of some chair-chewing giant," Owen said.

"Alimentary, my dear Watson. You've got the anatomy right. If God wanted to give the world an enema, this is where he'd stick it."

They rounded a bend and came upon yellow crime-scene tape stretched across and alongside the creekbed. Spotlights on either bank focused on Cable Stokes' Cadillac, sitting up to its floorboards in creek water.

"Followed the path as far as he could and then drove it in, looks like," Reader said.

Two deputies and a man in a dark blue suit and hip-high waders surrounded the car, their flashlight beams criss-crossing in a spastic semaphore.

Owen remembered the taller of the two deputies, Jeffreys, from the mineshaft. Jeffreys waded over to the sheriff and directed his flashlight beam back at the Cadillac's rear wheels. "Inside's picked pretty clean. But you better take a look in the trunk."

Owen's heart sank. His apprehension must have shown on his face, because the deputy said, "Nothing there now. But somebody was in there recent."

Owen and the sheriff rolled up their pantlegs and followed the deputy into the shin-high water. He popped open the trunk and shined his light on a dark stain at one end of the metal ridge that crossed the underside of the trunk lid. A few blonde hairs clung to the stain. Black scuff marks covered the other end of the metal ridge.

"Somebody kicked up a storm at that end," Jeffreys said.

"Likely skinned their head on the other," Reader said.

The thought of Mary Beth kicking and squirming in the confined space caused Owen to look away. He forced his eyes to return to the trunk, which was empty except for the spare tire and six half-gallon milk cartons filled with a clear liquid.

"Water," the deputy said. "Think maybe he had a radiator problem?"

"More likely, he's holed up somewhere with no running water," the sheriff said.

The deputy reached in with a gloved hand and lifted the flap that covered the spare tire well. "Tool kit's gone, but look at this." He lifted the spare itself to reveal two sticks of dynamite.

"Almost too pat," the sheriff said. "Have Robbins dust them for prints."

The deputy started to drop the flap covering the spare when Owen pointed to a scrap of paper dislodged by the movement. "What's that?"

The deputy picked up the scrap. "Grocery receipt from Big Bear. Dated three days ago."

"The same day he fired on you," Reader said to Owen.

The deputy read the list. "Canned chili, beef jerky, trail mix. Man planned on roughing it."

"Around here?" Owen asked.

"Nothing around here I know of," the sheriff said. "No homes, that's for sure."

"What about hunting cabins?"

The deputy shrugged.

"First light, get some men and fan out from here," the sheriff said. "See what you can find. He must have left some kind of trail."

"Think he dumped the car and backpacked somewhere?" Owen asked.

"More likely, he drove to some hidey hole and offloaded his supplies before he dumped his car," the sheriff said. "But the hole could be around here."

"Or he could have gotten another car."

"Check and see if any have turned up missing," the sheriff said to the deputy. "Cable's not likely to be a member of the Hertz Number One Club."

"Another car means someone may be in this with him," Owen said.

The sheriff nodded. "To drive here to pick him up, you mean. One of his boys, maybe."

Owen made a sound like a slow leak. "We couldn't find Cable when he was driving this wired-up clunker. How are we going to find him when we don't know how he's traveling?"

"He's probably not traveling at all," the sheriff said. "From the look of that shopping list, it's more likely he's gone to ground."

"If he's gone to ground, why'd he leave all this water in his trunk?"

"Could be he really did have a radiator problem," the deputy said.

"Something smells, and it's not just this place," Owen said. "It doesn't make any sense."

"We'll wring some sense out of it," the sheriff said. "We'll start by checking out the Big Bear where he bought his supplies."

The cold water on Owen's ankles sent shivers through his body. "On the way here, I thought we were finally closing in on him. Now it seems like we're even further away."

"It's this place," Reader said. "It would make Dracula's blood run cold. You'll feel better after a good night's sleep."

The creekbed stank of desiccation, decay, and disappointment. Owen knew he'd carry the stench with him a lot longer than overnight.

THE NEXT MORNING, Owen drove to Charleston to see his brother George, who occupied the office of state highway commissioner once held by their father. He found his brother staring out of his office window at the golden dome of the state capitol.

"Pretty impressive view," Owen said. "Your office has improved at least. How's the rest of it going?"

George turned his back on the view and shrugged. "Eleven months sober. Nine months separated. Both live-ball records."

"Good to hear you're still on the wagon. How's the separation going?"

"We'd get a divorce, but neither of us wants to make the other that happy."

"In my experience, divorce and happiness aren't even in the same neighborhood."

"Well, Barb's not in the same neighborhood as your ex-wife, either."

"Divorce is an expensive neighborhood no matter who lives there."

George moved a stack of papers and sat on the edge of his desk. "What brings you to town? It's not Mom, is it?"

"No. Mom's okay. They've cut back on her chemo. They'll quit altogether in a couple of weeks."

"You know, I really appreciate your taking time off to live with her."

Owen waved him off. "It's all right. It's been good for both of us."

"Maybe I'll drop down this weekend."

"That'd be great. Bring Billy. Mom loves to see her only grandchild. And we've got a boy with us who could stand to see a real live college student. His high school doesn't produce many."

"Thundering Herd's got a game Saturday. I'll see if I can pry him loose Sunday. But you didn't make the trip just to invite me home."

Owen twirled the graphite pencil sharpener on the drafting table that had once been his father's. "I'm trying to help the Raleigh County sheriff put an exact time on the explosion that flooded Drybone Hollow and took out the Crawley Creek Bridge."

"How can I help?"

"I thought you might have a fix on the time the bridge broke. I could work backward from that."

George wrinkled his brow. The corners of his mouth turned upward in a smile that wasn't reflected in his eyes. He opened a file cabinet and pulled out a hefty folder bound up with two thick rubber bands. "Turns out I know more than I want to about the Crawley Creek Bridge."

"Why's that?"

"The Dempsters. They're the parents of the new bride that drowned. They're suing the state. Claim the bridge was defective."

"No bridge is built to take a side blow from a flood-scudding mobile home. It would have hit like a wrecking ball."

"Tell me about it. Want to be an expert witness if the case goes to trial?"

"Sure."

"Course, you might be accused of bias. Your brother's the highway commissioner and your dad built the bridge."

"It was one of Dad's bridges? I'll give you the family discount."

"The Dempster's lawyers will love that." George slipped the two rubber bands off the file folder. "This country's come to a crappy pass. In Dad's day, parents who lost a child would blame bad luck and look to their pastor for support. Nowadays they look to blame somebody with deep pockets and get support from a lawyer."

"Litigation's today's liturgy. Still, you have to feel for the parents. Their daughter was an only child."

"How do you know that?"

"Met them at the memorial service."

George leafed through the papers in the file. "I'll have my secretary get you a copy of the bridge plans and the relevant paperwork." He pulled out a stapled sheaf of forms that Owen recognized as an accident report from the state police. "Turns out there was a witness. A nurse at St. Vincent's, Kathy Brown, was coming home from her seven-to-three shift and was close enough to the honeymoon car to see its taillights disappear downstream."

George flipped to a second page of the sheaf of forms. "She called the state police right away on her cell phone. "Call logged in at 3:32."

"County got a 911 call at 3:30 reporting the dam break."

"That checks then."

"Except the 911 caller was too far upstream from the dam to have seen the flood from his phone booth."

"How'd that happen?"

"We think he knew it was coming."

OWEN STOOD AT the entrance of Anson Stokes' abandoned mineshaft with Hank Clanton of Johnson, Crane, and Associates, waiting for the new trainees to arrive. He'd asked Clanton to come a little early, partly to be filled in on the trainees' background, but mostly because he hoped to learn more about the kickback arrangements that greased Johnson, Crane's contracts.

"We skimmed the applications for the best we could find," Clanton said, handing Owen a clipboard holding three employment forms. "Got us a mining engineer, an ex-miner, and a civil engineer."

Owen flipped through the forms. The top form, lettered in a neat script, was from a recent WVU graduate named Emile Kruk. "This Kruk sounds like a good prospect," Owen said. "You were lucky to find a mining engineer."

"Half the county's out of work. Surprised we couldn't find more."

"Johnson, Crane doesn't appear to be hurting, though. Guess it pays to have connections."

"*Costs* to have connections, more like. Sometimes it costs more than it pays."

"I can't believe you make payoffs in parking lots. Sounds risky and antiquated."

"Tradition. The attorney general's superstitious. He's handled payoffs that way ever since he was a ward heeler."

"Wasn't there a governor that came to grief making payoffs that way?"

Clanton flicked a cigarette ash through the chain-link fence Anson had recently built around the mine entrance. "Governor Banning. You don't look old enough to remember him. He and his highway commissioner and a few cronies were indicted for bid rigging and kickbacks back when the Interstate came in."

"I remember the highway commissioner. My dad had the job for a while."

"That's right. I disremembered that. Well, the jury found everybody guilty. Everybody but the governor, that is."

Clanton took a drag on his cigarette and smiled through the smoke. "Turns out the governor had paid off a juror. Had his wife give the juror's wife twenty-five grand in a paper sack. Made the payoff in a parking lot."

"Same parking lot the attorney general's wife uses?"

"Nah. The AG's wife needs an upscale lot. One with high-tone fashion stores. Besides, it'd be bad luck to use the same lot as Governor Banning's wife."

"Payoff didn't take?"

"Payoff took too well. Trouble was, the juror went right out and bought himself a lime-green Cadillac. Paid cash on the barrelhead. Over ten grand. Raised a few eyebrows. Up until then, the man had cashed more relief checks than paychecks."

"People had questions?"

Clanton stubbed out his cigarette. "People had a lot more questions than the juror had answers. They got the governor for jury tampering and sent him to jail with his cronies."

"You'd think the AG might have learned from that."

"Oh, he did. The lesson he learned was to keep payoffs small. Small and regular. His wife might buy a dress at Lazarus, but any big purchases get put on the installment plan. They take their payments the same way."

Owen filed away the name of the Lazarus Department Store. Before he could question Clanton further, a balding, burly man with a potbelly hanging over the belt of his blue jeans appeared at the top of the hill and started down the slope toward the two men. "You the folks from Johnson, Crane?" the man asked as he approached.

Hank Clanton nodded and fished another cigarette out of his pocket.

"I'm Virgil Gibbs. Got me a letter said to show up here at one o'clock."

Owen introduced himself and Clanton. "You've been a miner," Owen said as they shook hands.

"Man and boy, I've spent the better part of forty years underground. Missed a lot more sunsets than I've seen. Lately, though, there just ain't been enough work to go around."

"We didn't hear you drive up," Clanton said.

Gibbs scuffed at the dirt and looked back up the hill. "Walked up from Blue Creek."

"Blue Creek," Owen said. "That's what? Eight miles or so?"

"Thereabouts. It were good exercise."

A dusty Camaro coasted down the grade and parked next to Clanton's company van. A tall, thin man wearing a brown windbreaker emerged from the car. He sighed audibly and asked "Johnson, Crane?" through pinched lips that gave him a look of perpetual dissatisfaction.

"This is the place," Clanton said.

"I'm Reynolds," the man said. "Elmer Reynolds."

Clanton looked at the man's loafers. "Ever been in a mine?"

"I was told that wasn't necessary."

A bright red pickup cleared the rise as if it were auditioning for a movie chase scene, thumped onto the downhill slope, ground into a lower gear, and swerved to a stop beside Reynolds' Camaro. The driver wore heavy work boots, tight-fitting jeans, and a miner's helmet that matched the red of the pickup. When the helmet was removed, auburn hair cascaded to the driver's shoulders.

"Kruk?" Hank Clanton asked. "Emile Kruk?"

The driver smiled. "It's Emily, actually."

"Your form says Emile."

"If you look closely, it says Emily. I shorten the tail on the y on applications in case somebody's superstitious about women in mineshafts. It's not a problem, is it?"

When Clanton didn't respond, Owen said, "No problem at all. We're glad to have you."

Owen led the introductions and handed helmets and battery packs to Virgil Gibbs and Elmer Reynolds. Gibbs, the ex-miner, helped Reynolds connect his battery pack to his cap light.

When the group was outfitted, Owen explained that they were assembling a team to examine all the mineshafts in the state that were under impoundment dams to determine whether there was a risk of flooding. They were going to explore the Stokes' shaft so that they would know what to look for and make certain, to Johnson, Crane's satisfaction, that they could handle underground work.

"Been handling underground work for forty years," Virgil Gibbs said. "Sometimes I wisht I never had to."

Owen unrolled a map of the Stokes' Canaan II shaft on the hood of his Saturn. "The place to start the investigation is outside the mine with the plans, if they're still around."

The group gathered around the map as Owen pointed to the end of the abandoned shaft, where the explosion had occurred. "This is the point that was closest to the dam site. You'll need to compute the distance from the shaft to the impounded water. Anything under a hundred feet would be a flood risk."

Virgil Gibbs looked worried. "How do we figure the distance?"

"If the maps are good enough, just draw a line and measure it."

"You could survey it if need be," Elmer Reynolds said. "Get the coordinates, then there's a formula to calculate the distance."

Virgil had the look of the last man left in the baggage claim area after the bags have stopped coming.

"It's a real simple thing," Reynolds said.

"We could program a pocket computer to do it for you," Owen said. "All you have to do is punch in a few numbers."

"Nobody said nothing about using no computers," Virgil said.

Emily put her hand on Virgil's shoulder. "Don't worry, it's a cinch. We'll help you."

The young woman's hand seemed to have a healing effect on Gibbs. "You won't be alone out there," Owen said. He decided to move the group inside the shaft, where Virgil would feel more at home. As he led the way into the mine, dank air wrapped around the five bobbing cap lights. They kept walking until they had moved about a hundred feet beyond the first stubbed-off break that marked an aborted attempt to cut out a side shaft. Then Owen stopped and faced the other four.

"All right," He said. "For those of you who have never been in a mine, let's turn the lights out."

One by one, the cap lights switched off. Elmer Reynolds' light was the last one to go out.

Darkness weighed in on them. It always unsettled Owen. You waited for your eyes to adjust, but there was no light to adjust to. Just a deep, shadowless dark that amputated your hand in front of your face.

"All right now." Owen's voice echoed in the darkness. "Without using your cap lights, see if you can find your way back to the last break in the wall."

He heard scuffling noises, and a giggle that had to be Emily. When the noises stopped, he said, "Now turn on your lights."

The cap lights flashed on to show Emily and Virgil standing at the corner break. Hank Clanton was about halfway there, feeling his way along the wall. Elmer Reynolds didn't appear to have moved.

"It's a real simple thing," Virgil said. "Just find the wall and walk it."

"It takes some practice," Owen said. "But it's good to know you can navigate in darkness if you need to."

He began leading them deeper into the shaft, lecturing as they went along. "One of the signs that a nearby dam might be ready to break through is seepage." He ducked his head to shine his cap light on a puddle in the center of the mine floor.

"That puddle is left over from last month's flood. If the dam hadn't already broken through, that black water would be a warning sign that it might be about to."

A track at the edge of the puddle caught Owen's eye. He knelt to examine it.

"What are some of the other warning signs?" Reynolds asked.

"Basically some of the same signs that would warn of a collapse even if you weren't under an impoundment dam," Owen answered, still kneeling. "Emily, you're a mining engineer. What are some of those signs?"

A single tread mark led out of the puddle. He didn't remember seeing it on his last trip into the shaft. He wracked his memory, barely listening to Emily's answer.

"Popping roof bolts," Emily was saying. "Dust trickling from ceiling cracks. Falling rocks."

Owen stood. "That's good, Emily." He couldn't imagine he would have missed such an obvious track, but the shaft had supposedly been locked shut after the sheriff's crew left. "Anything else?"

"Used to be, when they used timber supports, you could hear the mountain working." Virgil said. "It'd talk to you in low, steady moans and creaks. When it started crackling like popcorn, though, you knew it was time to skedaddle."

"You mean these things could still cave in?" Reynolds asked.

"Most of the shafts you'll be looking at have been abandoned for some time without collapsing," Owen said. "If you're careful, there shouldn't be any problems."

"Mountain can always sit on you, though," Virgil said.

Virgil seemed to enjoy needling Reynolds, exacting some small measure of revenge for his own lack of computation skills. Between the two of them, Gibbs and Reynolds might make one competent investigator, Owen thought. As he led them deeper into the shaft, his cap light picked up a second tread mark. He was sure now he couldn't have missed it before. It had to be recent.

They passed another break in the wall. A ladderlike crib supporting the side shaft had splintered and the ceiling sagged around a popped roof bolt like a hammock holding two Sumo wrestlers. A crudely lettered

DANGER

KEEP OUT

sign had been hung over the shaft entrance.

Owen aimed his cap light at the spavined ceiling. "Now there's a real sign of trouble."

As his light swung back toward the main tunnel, he noticed another tread mark beyond the DANGER sign. "Wait here," he told the group.

"I wouldn't go in there," Emily said.

Owen crouched under the DANGER sign and stepped carefully

around the splintered roof support. The humpbacked ceiling squeezed down on him, and he squatted as low as he could without crawling.

He saw it about twenty yards ahead of him. A wheelbarrow had been shoved as far as it could go under the sagging ceiling. A pair of feet shod in heavy work boots dangled over the edge of the wheelbarrow.

Owen hunched over and crabwalked forward. His cap light swept beyond the clogged boot soles to shine on the mangled and barely recognizable face of Cable Stokes.

15

Where the Pick Hits the Seam

After leading Thad Reader and his deputies to Cable Stokes' body, Owen stood outside the main shaft with Reader while his deputies swarmed over the scene, taking photographs and bagging those bits of evidence large enough to catch their attention.

"Better tell your men to be careful in that side shaft," Owen said. "It's ripe for a cave-in."

"Maybe we ought to back out and let it happen," Reader said. "Save the state the cost of burying the son of a bitch."

"Better find out who killed him first."

Reader took out his pocket notebook. "I'll just write that down so I don't forget it." He tugged on the chain-link fence around the shaft entrance. "Pretty solid fence. This gate locked when you got here?"

Owen nodded. "And there was a guard at the entrance off the main road."

"You think the guard would have noticed a body in a wheelbarrow passing his station?"

"I doubt he was there when the body went past. The main gate is locked most of the time now. The guard's only on duty when the mine is open, like today. But the surveillance cameras operate around the clock."

"We'll need to check your tapes for sure. Whoever did this, though, had to get past two locked gates. Be easiest for a person with the keys."

"Anson, you mean?" Why would he hide a body in his own mineshaft?"

At that moment, Anson's black van cleared the hump and started downhill toward the two men. "That's a question we can ask the man himself," Reader said.

A deputy flagged down Anson's van.

Anson rolled down the driver's window. "Out of my way, sonny."

"You'll have to back up, sir," the deputy said. "You're entering a crime scene."

"It's my goddamn mine. It's my goddamn brother. Stand aside or your boss'll have another murder to solve."

"Let the man come through," Reader called.

Anson smirked at the deputy, parked his van, and joined Owen and the sheriff at the gated fence, a miner's helmet under his arm. "What the hell happened here?"

"That's what we're trying to find out," Reader said.

Anson went through the gate toward the mine entrance. Reader caught up with him, slowing him down. "Just wait here," the sheriff said. "They'll be bringing him out soon."

"How'd he die?"

Owen glanced at Reader, then answered, "Looks like somebody hit him pretty hard with something big and solid."

"In the mine?"

"Not likely," Reader said. "Looks like it happened outside. Then somebody trundled him into the mine in a wheelbarrow."

"In a wheelbarrow?"

"Any idea who'd want to kill him?" Reader asked.

Anson grimaced. "About half the people in this hollow, around a quarter of the people in the county, and maybe a tenth of the people in the state. Hell, I'd have killed him if I could have found him. But I never found him."

A deputy emerged from the mine, pushing the empty wheelbarrow and blinking in the sunlight. Two deputies carrying a stretcher followed. They set the stretcher and its bundled burden down outside of the chain-link fence.

"Can I look?" Anson asked.

Reader nodded.

The deputy at the head of the stretcher unzipped the top of the body bag. Reader joined Anson beside the stretcher. Owen hung back. He'd seen enough inside the mine.

Anson wilted as if someone had let the air out of him. "Jesus. They just didn't stop hitting him." He turned away. "Jesus."

Reader nodded at the deputy, who zipped up the bag. Then the sheriff closed the gate to the chain-link fence. "Who had keys to this gate lock?"

"Me. The shift foremen." Anson pointed over his shoulder with his thumb. "There's one in the tool shed."

"And the gate across the road in?"

"At the guardhouse? Same people. Plus my security chief."

"And the guard records whoever goes in and out?"

"When it's necessary. Haven't had much traffic lately. Being shut down'll do that to you. Keep the gate locked most of the time. Just use the guard when we're expecting visitors. Like today. But those security cameras Owen installed should tape everything."

The two deputies loaded the stretcher into a waiting ambulance.

"Jesus," Anson said. "They just kept beating on him."

The tall deputy, Jeffreys, approached, holding a large spanner wrench in rubber-gloved hands. "Found this in the weeds behind that shed."

Owen stared at the wrench, which had two long black hairs caught in its jaws. He'd watched Anson using a similar wrench on his continuous mining machine.

Anson was also staring at the wrench.

"Recognize it?" Reader asked.

"It's my wrench," Anson said. "There's 'C-III' scratched on the handle. Should be a couple more like it in the tool shed."

"Who has keys to the tool shed?" Reader asked.

"Me. My foremen. Damn near everybody who ever worked for me used the shed keys at one time or another."

"Bag the wrench and tag it," Reader told the deputy. "Have Robbins dust it for prints and check the DNA on those hairs."

"Likely you'll find my prints on it," Anson said.

"You use it?" Reader asked.

"I saw him tightening the treads on his miner with one like it," Owen said.

Reader smoothed his uniform front, leaving one hand resting on his holster. "Maybe you better come down to the station with me, Anson."

Anson's expression faded from disbelief to annoyance. "You fixing to arrest me?"

"Hell, Anson. It's your mine. You've got all the keys. I've heard you threaten Cable in public at least twice myself. Now you're telling me your fingerprints are on that weapon."

"It wasn't a weapon when I used it."

Reader took a step toward Anson, getting close enough to reach out and cuff him if he had to. "So you say."

Anson didn't back away. "You've got to be kidding. Cable was my brother."

Reader took Anson's arm and turned him until he faced the sheriff's patrol car. "You'd be well advised to think up a better line of defense. That one hasn't worked since Cain cold-cocked Abel."

THE DARK SKIES and rain pelting down on Owen's windshield the next afternoon mirrored his mood as he parked his car a block away from Thad Reader's office. He wasn't anxious to confront the sheriff over Anson's arrest, and was dripping wet by the time the deputy on the front desk pushed the button that gave him access to Reader's office.

Reader looked up from behind his desk. "I'd ask you to sit, but there's no flood insurance on the office furniture."

"I hear Anson made bail."

"He send you around? You still on his payroll?"

"Just came by to see if there's anything new on Mary Beth or Riley."

Reader removed his glass eye and laid it in the center of an empty ceramic ashtray. "Wet weather makes my socket ache. One of these days, I'm going to get me an eye that fits."

"You need that one for your image."

Reader rubbed the scar over the missing eye from the grenade burst that had killed men on either side of him. "And to remind me I'm lucky to be here."

"What about Mary Beth and Riley?"

Reader stared at his glass eye as if it were a crystal ball. "It hurts me to think on it. I just can't see any good outcome."

"Why not?"

Reader closed both eyelids and rubbed them with his thumb and forefinger. "Cable's death has been all over the TV and newspapers. That's like a free ticket home for Mary Beth and Riley. But they haven't shown up."

"Maybe somebody's still guarding them."

"Game's over. No point in keeping them now. Should just let them go. If they're still alive."

"I still can't believe Cable would harm his own son."

Reader picked up his glass eye and rolled it between his thumb and index finger. "Then why haven't they shown up?"

"Maybe Cable locked them away somewhere. He'd bought supplies for a hideout."

"That's one good sign. Nobody's going to go hungry. He bought enough supplies to keep a small regiment alive through a tough winter. Stripped the shelves clean of beef jerky. Clerk at the Big Bear remembered him. So'd Lyle Tanner."

"His neighbor?"

"Lyle works security at the mall where Cable bought his supplies. He remembers seeing Cable and talking to him, but the trail goes cold there." Reader returned his glass eye to its socket and stared up at Owen. "You actually came here to hector me about Anson, didn't you?"

"You don't really think he killed Cable, do you?"

"We're talking about a West Virginia coal mine here, not some locked English drawing room. In this county, if a man threatens to kill someone and his prints wind up on the murder weapon, it's a good bet he did it."

Owen shook his head. "But Anson's the one who suggested we use his shaft for training. Why would he hide a body there knowing we'd find it? And why wouldn't he hide the murder weapon a little better?"

"Anson may have been a lot richer than Cable, but he never was a whole lot smarter. Around here, murderers don't usually top the Mensa charts."

"It doesn't take a Mensa member to ditch a wrench where it won't be found."

"Anson had a guard on the main gate. Since the time Cable shot at you, Anson's the only one logged in or out. He's the only one on the tapes, too." Reader handed Owen the log book from the guard house. "Except for your training crew."

Owen traced his finger along the log. "Couple of days with no activity at all."

"Guard says the gate was locked tight those days. Tapes show Anson coming in once without bothering to sign in."

Owen's finger stopped on his own name. "There's something wrong here. We had three trainees, plus Hank Clanton. This log only records two."

"Who's missing?"

"Virgil Gibbs. An old-timer miner. He walked up."

"Maybe the guard didn't count walk-ups."

"Or maybe there's another way in. I think we ought to talk to Virgil."

"What do you mean 'we'? You so hard up for consulting contracts you're thinking about taking up law enforcement?"

"It's about time somebody in this county did." Owen smiled to show he was kidding. "Don't you think?"

———

RAIN PINGED OFF the fenderless pickup in Virgil Gibbs' yard and dotted the muddy puddles in front of his clapboard house. Planks laid down in a zigzag pattern provided a puddle-free path from the road to the narrow front porch.

Virgil answered the door wearing an undershirt, faded jeans, and thick cotton socks. As he held the door open for Owen and Thad Reader, a voice from the rear of the house asked, "Who is it, hon?"

Virgil scratched his stomach. "The sheriff and the man from the mine job."

"Praise Jesus."

A rug hand-hooked in a checkerboard pattern covered most of the living-room floor. Camera portraits of John L. Lewis and Jack Kennedy flanked a painting of the Sacred Heart of Jesus on one wall. An adjacent wall held high school graduation photos of four boys and two girls.

"Hope you didn't come to cut off the job," Virgil said.

"The job's still yours," Owen said. "You'll be getting an inspection schedule soon. We came because you walked to yesterday's training session."

"I walked to save gasoline. That's my pickup out front. I could of drove if I'd wanted to. I can get to wherever the job needs me on my own hook. I told the Johnson, Crane people that."

"When you walked to the mine, did you pass the guard station?" Owen asked.

"The path cuts in beyond it."

"We'd like you to show us that path," Reader said.

Virgil looked through his front window at the pelting rain. "Now?"

The sheriff nodded. "Now."

"We on clock time?"

"We can be," Owen said. "I'll get a signed time sheet to Johnson, Crane."

"That'd be a good thing, all right," Virgil said. "I'll just get my shirt and shoes."

As the patrol car wound uphill to the mine site, Virgil asked, "You fellows think whoever killed Cable Stokes walked in?"

At the wheel, Reader just shrugged.

"We don't know," Owen said. "We want to see how hard it would be."

Reader slowed, rounded a hairpin turn, and pulled up in front of the guard station on the side road leading to the Canaan mines. The gated fence across the road was padlocked shut.

"They weren't expecting anyone," Reader said. "Why don't you take us to the path, Virgil."

"Just keep a-going along this here road."

Reader drove slowly, his wipers barely able to keep his windshield clear.

"Turn off here," Virgil said, pointing to a half-hidden fire trail.

Reader splashed onto the muddy trail, which grew narrower and narrower as the surrounding trees closed in to choke it off. After about a half mile of switchbacks, the trail became too narrow for the patrol car and the sheriff braked to a stop. "Have to walk it from here."

"It's not far," Virgil said. "Can't we wait for the rain to stop?"

"That could take all day," Reader said. "Tree cover's pretty good here. Let's go now."

The thick overhead branches provided some shelter from the rain as Virgil led the way through the sucking mud. "Trail's wide enough for a wheelbarrow," Owen said.

Reader pulled aside an eye-high limb, loosing a shower of stored raindrops. "Rain will have washed away any traces of one, though."

"Here we are," Virgil said, stepping out of the woods and into the clearing behind the mine's tool shed.

Owen and Thad Reader followed Virgil into the clearing. As they emerged from the woods, the rain suddenly stopped.

"Should have waited," Virgil said.

Reader dumped the water from the crease of his mountie's hat. "Then it wouldn't have stopped."

"How many people know about this path?" Owen asked.

"Just about anybody who ever worked here, I imagine," Virgil said. "It's a shortcut to the highway."

"So just about anybody could have brought Cable's body in along the trail," Owen said.

"Could have parachuted it in too," Reader said. "That's no proof anybody did. My money's on the man with the keys. Anson had the motive and the access, and his prints are on the likely murder weapon."

"His prints are on his own damn wrench," Owen said.

"Which was locked inside his own damn shed," Reader answered.

"Oh, hell," Virgil said. "That shed lock's about as useful as a screen door on a submarine." He walked over to the toolshed, felt around the top of the door sill, and pulled down a key which he used to open the hasp lock on the shed door.

"Location of that key common knowledge?" Reader asked.

Virgil returned the key to its hiding place. "Weren't no secret. Anybody who knew about the path would likely have known about the key too."

The three men walked down the hill to the abandoned shaft where Cable Stokes' body had been found. Yellow crime-scene tape decorated the chain-link fence around the shaft's entrance.

Reader pointed to the locked gate on the fence and asked Virgil, "Don't suppose you can find us a key to that lock as well?"

Virgil shook his head. "That's a new one on me. That fence wasn't around when I worked here."

"Anson told us there was a key in the toolshed," Owen said.

Reader thumped the fence with his open palm. "Makes that shaft about as hard to get into as the Book-of-the-Month Club."

Owen looked out over the valley below. Black scum tracing the flood's high-water mark still bracketed the creekbed, but the rain-swollen creek waters ran clear, flushing whatever mine waste remained into the Little Muddy and the Ohio rivers. A rainbow arched over Drybone Hollow, one end floating near the empty foundations that had held Cable Stokes' trailer and his hopes for a pot full of fraudulent settlements.

"Holy Christ," Owen grabbed Reader's arm. "Do you still have those phony claims Cable filled out?"

"FEMA has them. Why?"

"He dummied up the foundations and made up some names, but he used real social security numbers. Different ones for each claim."

"Yeah. He got his friends and relatives to contribute."

"He had to use different home addresses as well."

Reader nodded, then smiled, seeing where Owen was headed. "But he couldn't make those up."

"Otherwise FEMA wouldn't be able to deliver the checks."

They were already heading back up the hill, leaving Virgil in their wake. "So FEMA has four or five different addresses on Cable's fraudulent claims," Reader said. "Addresses where he could expect to pick up checks."

"And he filled out those forms before he snatched Mary Beth Hobbs, so one of those addresses might lead us to her."

Owen and the sheriff rushed past the tool shed and plunged back into the wooded shortcut. "Hey, wait up," Virgil shouted, but the two men didn't slow down until they reached the sheriff's car. While they waited for Virgil to catch up, Reader called the FEMA office on his cell phone.

With Virgil in the back seat, Reader bounced and splashed his way back out the fire trail and was turning onto the paved road when FEMA called back with the addresses. Owen tried to keep his ear to the cell phone and write the addresses in his pocket notebook while Reader whipped around the mountain curves.

The first address was the Middleburg, Ohio home of Cable's sister, while Reader recognized the second as the home of Cable's son Billy Joe. "FBI's already staked out those places," Reader said.

Owen was beginning to think the FEMA forms might not lead them anywhere when the next address came through, on Ennis Street in Morgantown. "Don't recognize that one," Reader said. "It's at least three hours from here, though. We'll let the FBI handle it."

The last address was RD 5, Spruce Run. "That's down-county," Reader said. "It's one of our ten-two-and-four hollows. Easy to hide somebody there."

Owen scrawled the address in his notebook. "What's a ten-two-and-four hollow?"

"Hollow's so deep and the ridges are so steep that the sun doesn't rise until ten, sets at two, and gives you four hours of daylight. The whole scene is godforsaken."

Owen pocketed his notebook. "Godforsaken fits Cable. Let's check it out."

As they were dropping Virgil Gibbs at his house, Reader called the Morgantown address in to the FBI. Then he ordered his duty deputies to meet him at the head of Spruce Run Road, turned on his flashing light bar, and sped down county with his siren blaring.

The sun had vanished behind the steep ridge line and fireflies blinked in the narrow hollow by the time the sheriff and Owen reached the head of Spruce Run Road. Two patrol cars were waiting for them, and two more arrived while Thad Reader was tracing maneuvers in the roadside clay with a tree branch and a flashlight beam.

When the deputies had finished asking questions, Reader opened the trunk of his patrol car, pulled out a Kevlar vest, and put it on. As his deputies followed suit, he handed Owen a vest.

"Is that necessary?" Owen asked.

"I don't know. I do know I'd a lot rather have it and not need it than need it and not have it."

Reader doused his headlights and his deputies did the same. Then he led the way down the narrow dark road, driving in silence so that the only sound Owen heard was the crunch of wet gravel under their tires.

After about a mile, Reader pulled off the road, stopped, and stared into the blackness. "Back there," he said, pointing out of his side window, "You can just make out a light."

Owen could barely see the outline of a small house set well back from the road in a stand of trees that backed up against a steep, wooded hillside. From the roadway, the lone window light looked no brighter than a firefly's flicker.

Two of Reader's deputies left the road and drove as close as they could to the stand of trees that sheltered the house, then parked facing their target. Mutt and Jeff, the other two deputies, parked behind Reader, then separated so that they could flank both sides of the property on foot, and disappeared into the darkness.

Reader took a bullhorn from his back seat. "Wait here," he said to Owen.

"Why can't I come? It's probably just a scared teenager watching over Mary Beth."

"Maybe. Maybe nobody's home. Or maybe it's just a friend of Cable's providing a mail drop. But could be it's Cable's killer. Or some hyped-up kidnapper overanxious because Cable isn't coming back." Reader pulled his revolver from its holster and checked its cylinders. "Either way, this is where the pick hits the seam and I don't need any amateurs wandering near the flying sparks."

"This amateur's the one that got you here."

"I won't argue that. I won't argue this, either. You probably haven't fired a weapon since the Boy Scouts, if then. That makes you more a target than a hunter." Reader closed the car door and mouthed, "Keep your head down," through the window.

Owen slid down so his chin was even with the dashboard. "Watch out for your own damn head."

Reader walked slowly toward the house, holding his bullhorn against his hip. When he was abreast of the two patrol cars facing the house, he stopped and signaled the cars' drivers. Two pairs of head-lights flashed on, illuminating their target, which Owen could now see was a tiny log cabin.

As the headlights pierced the darkness, Reader raised his bullhorn. "This is Sheriff Reader. My deputies have your cabin surrounded. Please come out with your hands empty and in plain view."

The two deputies flanking Reader pointed shotguns at the cabin and edged away from their vehicles. Reader lowered his bullhorn and waited. There was no response from the cabin.

Reader raised his bullhorn and repeated his message. Still no response. The sheriff dropped his bullhorn, crouched, and ran zigzag-ging toward the cabin.

Owen heard glass breaking.

Reader took cover behind a tree and waited while his two deputies joined him in the first line of trees.

Someone shouted from inside the cabin. Owen couldn't make out the words.

The cabin door swung open and the tall deputy, Jeffreys, appeared in the lighted doorway. The sheriff and the two flanking deputies lowered their guns and hurried into the cabin.

Owen left the patrol car and ran toward the open doorway. As he reached the first line of trees, two deputies came out through the door, supporting a barely conscious teenage boy between them. The boy's head drooped and both feet dragged the ground.

"Is he all right?" Owen asked as the two deputies shouldered their burden past him.

"Needs a hospital," the nearer of the two deputies answered.

Reader intercepted Owen at the doorway. "You don't want to go in there."

Owen shoved by him. The cabin stank of urine and decay. A bare light bulb dangled from a cobweb-covered cord in the center of the room. Bleached skulls of small animals grinned from the horizontal studs lining the side walls. Rusting tools lay scattered on a wood workbench that ran the length of the rear wall, supported by two thick posts. Severed lengths of clothesline rope coiled like sleeping snakes around the base of one post.

It was the other post that gripped Owen's attention. A grimy army blanket covered a slumped human form bound to the base of the post. A pair of bare legs the color of the straw covering the concrete floor stuck out from one end of the blanket.

Owen looked from the slumped form to Thad Reader, who shrugged and looked away.

Owen lifted the upper edge of the blanket. Mary Beth Hobbs' mouth was covered with strapping tape and her sightless eyes looked as if they'd seen death coming on a long, slow march.

"Cable must have tied them up and gone to get supplies," Reader said. "He never made it back. She never made it either."

Owen sank to the floor. "I should have figured it out sooner."

"You figured it out in time to save the boy."

"The address. It was right there in front of me."

"It was in front of all of us."

The dust and straw covering the concrete floor had been cleared in an arc around Mary Beth's legs, as if she'd tried to make half of a snow angel. Owen felt drained. He took off his windbreaker and covered the bare legs. "What a sad way to die."

Reader held out his hand to help Owen to his feet. "There aren't many happy ways."

16

Sultans of Sludge

"AND how's Jeb Stuart taking it?" Judith asked, on the phone from California.

"I waited until he was asleep before I called. I could still hear sobbing in his bedroom at 11:30. He blames himself."

"He blames himself. You blame yourself. The two of you are well matched. From everything you've told me, the woman was trying to blackmail a sociopathic lout. How can either of you be to blame for that?"

Owen carried the phone to the front porch so he wouldn't wake his mother or Jeb Stuart. The night was overcast and starless. A lone firefly reminded him of the hollow at Spruce Run. "I should have figured it out sooner."

Judith sighed. "You figured it out in time to save the boy, what's his name?"

"Riley."

"You figured it out in time to save Riley."

"But not Mary Beth."

"Owen, for heaven's sake." Judith paused, and Owen could imagine the look of exasperation on her face. He recognized the tone of voice. "With you, every silver lining has a cloud. It's not your fault. The woman was kidnapped, right? That means the FBI was on the case. Your buddy, Sheriff Reader, had his men looking for her. They're law-enforcement professionals. You're not. You're a consultant in failure and risk analysis. And you're risking the failure of more than your business if you don't get back here soon."

Judith paused again, waiting for a response. When Owen failed to reply, she said, "That's why you called, isn't it? You're not coming back."

Owen tightened his grip on the telephone. "Not soon."

"You want a son. The boy needs a father. You feel responsible. Is that it?"

"That's part of it."

"What about his family? He's got an uncle right there in Contrary."

"I like Purvis, but he's got the paternal instincts of a riverboat gambler. He'd give the boy a deck of cards and turn him loose on the world."

"There are worse legacies."

"I promised the boy's father I'd see that he got an education."

"There are high schools here in California."

"This isn't a good time to uproot him. Besides, he's not the only reason I need to stay. There's Mom."

"Is her cancer worse?"

"No. But she's forgetful. She repeats herself."

"I'm forgetful. I repeat myself."

"It's not the same thing."

Judith's voice softened. "No, you're right. It's not. Have you had her diagnosed?"

"She doesn't believe it's serious enough."

"What do you believe?"

"She ought to see a specialist."

"Then take her. Did I tell you I repeat myself?"

Owen couldn't muster a smile. "Have you seen someone about it?"

"I was hoping to see my ex-husband."

"Judith, I'm needed here."

"And you don't feel needed here?"

"It's not the same thing."

"Now you're repeating yourself."

For Owen, the solution was simple. But he'd tried to get Judith to leave her California law practice once before, when they were still married. He'd lost the rigged bid that had cost him his consulting practice and had taken a job in Washington, D.C. He'd pleaded with her to come with him then, but she'd stayed put. The distance had poisoned their marriage.

Without much hope, he said, "Look, I know there are high schools in California. But there are law firms here in West Virginia."

Judith interrupted him. "We've had this conversation before. Do you really want me to repeat myself?"

"I was hoping we wouldn't repeat ourselves."

"It's too late. We already are."

OWEN SAT ON the porch steps for a long time, staring at the silent phone, wondering if there was something he could have said differently, some argument that might have worked. A lone bullfrog croaked somewhere in the dark. "Can't find a mate?" Owen asked. "Or just having trouble sleeping? Either way, I can sympathize."

He started to rise from the porch steps. His knees ached and he had to use the banister to pull himself upright. "At least nobody's likely to hunt me down for my legs," he said to the frog in the darkness.

He went into the house and was startled to see Ruth standing in the darkened stairwell, wearing her quilted robe. "Heard you talking to someone," she said.

"Just a bullfrog." He held up the cordless phone. "And Judith before that."

"What did Judith have to say?"

"Same old thing. Wants me to come back to California."

"Don't you think you should?"

"I've got responsibilities here, Mom."

"I've only got one week of chemo left. And the boy doesn't have to be your responsibility."

"I think he does."

"Then take him with you to California."

Owen moved to the living room sofa and sat down without turning on the lights. "It's not a good time to uproot him."

"Raising a child's a two-person job."

"You raised two alone. George was younger than Jeb Stuart is now when Dad died." Owen smiled in the dark. "You did all right."

"I didn't have a choice. Or a full-time job."

"I don't feel like I have a choice. I promised his father. And his mother would still be alive . . ."

"You've got to stop troubling yourself over that." Ruth moved behind the couch and put her hand on Owen's shoulder. "You did all you could."

Owen sighed. "We've done all right with Jeb Stuart the past few weeks."

"He's a good boy."

"We should stay right here, I think. Not move him. Let him live here in his own home." Owen pulled a sofa pillow onto his lap. "At least until school's out. Then we could all move back to Barkley."

"I've only got one week of chemo left."

"You said that."

"Did I? What I mean is, there's only one week when I'd need to make the trip back to St. Vincent's. And this house is handy to Jeb Stuart's school. It might be best for him to stay here. If it doesn't remind him too much of his mother."

"We'll see how it goes." Owen reached up and clasped Ruth's hand. "If it takes two, I count two people right here. One with good experience raising kids."

"Oh, Owen. You need Judith."

"Judith's not here. And she doesn't want to come. And it's not clear she wants a child anyhow."

"It's not clear she wants someone else's full-grown child, you mean."

"It's not clear she wants any child."

Ruth's voice was soft behind him. "Oh."

"So what do you think?"

Ruth squeezed his hand. "Well, I've managed to raise two pig-headed boys. Maybe I could get it right this time around."

Owen smiled in the darkness. "Third time's the charm."

AFTER RUTH HAD retired to the downstairs bedroom, Owen sat for a while on the sofa, staring into the darkness. Then he went out onto the porch and inhaled the clear night air. It smelled of creek water and freshly cut grass. Staying in West Virginia felt right.

The bullfrog croaked again, then was silent.

"Done for the night, old buddy?" Owen said. "Time for me to join you."

He went back inside the house and took off his shoes so he could get up the stairs without waking Ruth or Jeb Stuart. He'd made it halfway up when the banister creaked loudly.

Owen released the banister as if its sound had delivered an electric shock. He stood quietly for a moment before tiptoeing up the rest of the stairs. Jeb Stuart's bedroom door swung open and the boy appeared, wearing a maroon Cincinnati Reds T-shirt and gray pajama bottoms.

"I'm sorry," Owen whispered. "I was trying to be quiet."

"That's all right. I was only half asleep. For a minute, when I heard the noise, I thought it was Mom. Whenever she tried to be extra-quiet, she'd forget about the banister squeak." The boy blinked twice and rubbed his eyes. "As soon as I opened the door, I remembered."

"Next time I come upstairs, I'll rattle around a lot. That way you won't make that same mistake again."

"Rattling around's what Dad used to do." Jeb Stuart's lips trembled and his shoulders shook. "I don't want to be alone."

Owen gathered the boy in his arms, hugging him fiercely. "You won't be. I promise you. You won't be."

_201_

THE FUNERAL SERVICE for Mary Beth Hobbs was held in the Reverend Moral Brody's Church of Jesus Christ of the Redeemed Earth. The cinderblock building that was Brody's church had once been the lumber warehouse for a nearby sawmill. Felt banners depicting green mountains, silver rivers, and white streams hung like medieval standards from rough-hewn wood crossbeams. Small rectangular panes in the high warehouse windows had been filled with colored glass of every hue. A gold plaque under each window identified the Blenko Glass Company as the donor.

Owen and Ruth Allison flanked Jeb Stuart in the front pew on the right-hand side of the altar. Purvis Jenkins sat between Owen and the closed casket in the center aisle. On the other side of the aisle, the front pew held four pallbearers wearing navy blue jackets with the yellow insignia of the Contrary Comet Bus Company.

By the time the service started, all the pews were packed with people and lines of mourners stood in the two side aisles under the multihued glass panels. Six black-robed choir members filed down the center aisle past the casket, took their places at the side of the altar, and led the congregation in the hymn, "Here I am, Lord." When the hymn ended, the Reverend Moral Brody ascended the steps to a pulpit made of the same rough-hewn lumber as the overhead beams.

The Reverend's bald head glistened in the glare of an overhead spotlight as he ran one hand around the tattooed band circling his forehead, which for the purpose of the day's sermon was a halo, "just like the one newly earned by the deceased." The Reverend reminded the mourners that Mary Beth Hobbs was a baptised child of God who had spent most of her life in Contrary, graduating from the local high school as the class salutatorian and marrying another native, Stonewall Jackson Hobbs, shortly after graduation.

Owen watched Jeb Stuart out of the corner of his eye. The boy sat with his head bowed, barely breathing, hands clasped on his lap. He blinked once at the mention of his father's name, but otherwise showed no outward reaction as the preacher listed the highlights of his mother's life, from her marriage to the birth of her only child, and from her night-school degree in accounting to her career with the Contrary Comet and the death of her husband.

After lamenting Stony Hobbs' death, the Reverend Moral Brody gripped the sides of the pulpit so hard that his knuckles whitened. "The life of this good woman," Brody said, "this proud mother, this devoted churchgoer, ended suddenly, brought to a close by an act of incomprehensible evil."

The choir master led the congregation in a round of "Amens." Jeb Stuart's shoulders buckled slightly, and Owen and Ruth each took one of the boy's arms.

"The evil of a senseless kidnapping," Brody continued. "Too often, it seems, good cannot survive in this county. It is overmatched by evil. The evil that surrounds us. The evil that blackens the veins of our homeland. The evil of Big Coal."

Brody stretched out his arms toward Mary Beth's coffin. "Big Coal made this woman who lies before us a widow before her time."

"Amen," intoned the black-robed choir leader.

"Big Coal has poisoned our waterways. Big Coal has left half the county unemployed."

Owen couldn't believe his ears. Brody was turning the funeral service into an environmental rant.

"Big Coal has turned good men so desperate they succumb to impenetrable evil." Brody raised his fist toward the wooden rafters. "I tell you, brothers and sisters, it's time to say 'NO TO COAL!' "

"NO TO COAL!" the choir echoed.

"It's time to tell these outsiders, these coal barons, these sultans of sludge, these kings of contamination, that they no longer have a place in our county. That we will not stand for the evil they spawn."

Owen was so outraged by Brody's posturing that he almost missed it. Amid all the "Amens" and shouts of "NO TO COAL" that followed, he still wasn't quite sure he'd heard it. But he felt someone staring at the back of his neck and turned around to look.

At the rear of the church, Thad Reader stood holding his mountie's hat, his jaw clamped shut, his one good eye locked on Owen. The sheriff had heard it too. "Sultans of sludge," the phrase from one of the early letters to Judge Vereen threatening to blow up Anson Stokes' mine. The phrase that had convinced Reader the letter couldn't have come from Cable Stokes.

Owen couldn't keep his mind on the remainder of the funeral service. Even as a pallbearer, leaving the church with the weight of Mary Beth's coffin on his arm, he wondered whether the single phrase "sultans of sludge" was enough to prove Moral Brody had written the threatening letters that had caused Anson Stokes' mine to be shut down.

Listening to the Reverend's graveside eulogy, which contrasted the beauty of the surrounding hillside with the festering black seams beneath their surface, Owen took his speculation one step further. If Moral Brody's zeal for the environment led him to threaten Anson's active mine, could he also have set the timer that blew up Anson's abandoned shaft?

When the coffin had been lowered into the grave and the crowd prepared to leave, Owen left Jeb Stuart with Ruth, caught up with Thad Reader, and asked, "Did anyone besides you and the judge see the 'sultans of sludge' letter?"

"If they did, I didn't show it to them."

"Time to pay the Reverend a visit?"

"It would seem so."

OWEN DROPPED JEB Stuart and Ruth at the Hobbs home and joined the sheriff outside Moral Brody's house, which was located next to the warehouse the preacher had converted into a church.

"Harley's in the driveway," Reader said. "The Reverend must be home."

The Reverend Moral Brody answered their knock himself, wearing a white T-shirt under a black dickey topped by an unbuttoned clerical collar. Black suspenders hung in loops around his hips.

The clergyman seemed momentarily surprised to see Owen and Thad Reader, and checked over their shoulders as if he were expecting other visitors to follow them up the driveway. When no one else appeared, the Reverend hitched up his suspenders and invited the two men into his study, a small dark room with a half-filled bookcase, a leather sofa and an easy chair, and a rolltop desk. Pictures of the Reverend Moral Brody with the governor, the attorney general, Dusty

Rhodes, and several local civic leaders surrounded a crucifix on the wall above the desk, which held a boxy, gray Macintosh computer and printer.

With Owen seated in the easy chair and the sheriff on one end of the couch, Brody leaned against the edge of the rolltop desk and asked, "How can I help you gentlemen?"

"We've come to discuss today's sermon," Thad Reader said.

"Was there some special aspect of my message that kindled your spirit?"

"I found your message a little off the point," Owen said. "But full of thought-provoking images."

Brody waved his hand over the printer on the rolltop desk. "I can get you a copy if you'd like."

"That won't be necessary," Reader said. "I already have a copy of the part I'm interested in. I'd seen it before."

The Reverend smiled and raised his eyebrows. "Surely the sheriff's office hasn't sunk to prosecuting people for plagiarism?"

"No, but we do prosecute people who threaten to blow holes in mines."

Brody's smile disappeared and his eyebrows dropped to squint level. "I don't understand."

"We think you sent Judge Vereen a letter threatening to blow up Anson Stokes' mine if it wasn't shut down," Reader said.

"And why do you think that?"

"The phrase 'sultans of sludge,'" Owen said. "It appeared in the threatening letter. You used it in your sermon today."

"Three little words." Brody made a series of slow, tight circles with his right hand as if he were erasing a blackboard. "Inconsequential. I linked the words 'coal barons' and 'land butchers' too. They're common usage."

"'Coal barons' is certainly common usage. I got five hundred hits looking it up on the Internet." Owen improvised, making up research results on the fly. "I didn't get a single hit on 'sultans of sludge.'"

"That's absurd. It doesn't prove a thing. I've used the phrase before. One of my parishioners could have picked it up. Anyone could come up with those words." Brody swept his right arm overhead like a magician about to pull a rabbit out of an empty hat. "It's simple alliteration. 'Pirates of peat,' 'sovereigns of slag,' 'masters of muck,' 'dukes of . . .'" He dropped his arm to his side. "Well, you get the idea."

"Dukes of deceit," Owen said. "You're right, it's not too hard." He rose and moved to the computer on the rolltop desk. "There's an easy way to settle this. The note was composed on a computer. Why don't we take your Macintosh and let an expert go over it."

"Wouldn't you need a warrant for that?"

"I imagine Judge Vereen will give us one," Reader said. "Might not need one, though. After all, you invited us in. Do you really want to stand in the way of justice here?"

Owen started to disconnect the computer leads. "Even if you erased the file, there'll still be a record of it on the hard drive." He knew that wasn't necessarily the case, but from the age of the Macintosh, he didn't expect Brody to be an expert in disc storage. "Shouldn't take long to locate the record. After all, we know what it looks like."

Brody sighed. "That won't be necessary. I wrote the note."

Owen stepped back from the computer and the sheriff rose from the couch.

"Don't look so surprised," the Reverend said. "That's what brought you here, isn't it? Did you expect me to lie? To bear false witness?"

The sheriff measured Moral Brody with his good eye. "In my business, I expect everyone to lie."

"I can tell you, I take the Eighth Commandment seriously," Brody said.

"That the one that forbids lying?" Reader said. "How about one forbidding false threats? Guess that didn't make the top ten."

"I see no need to apologize," Brody said. "Those miners defile the God-given earth. I knew a few letters to Judge Vereen would give him the leverage he needed to shut down Stokes' mine."

"So you had no intention of blowing up Stokes' working shaft?" the sheriff said.

"None whatsoever. My letters achieved their purpose. There was no need . . ."

"What about blowing Stokes' abandoned shaft?" the sheriff broke in.

Brody flinched. For the first time that evening, he seemed out of his element. "I don't understand."

Reader took a step toward Brody. "Somebody blew up Stokes' abandoned shaft and caused the black flood that killed Maddie Tanner and that honeymoon couple from Tennessee."

The suggestion that he might be responsible for more than a little letter writing seemed to outrage Brody. "Surely you don't believe I'm responsible for that abomination?"

The sheriff took another step forward. "You wanted his mine shut down. You wanted it badly enough to threaten to blow it up." Another step and it looked as if the sheriff might reach out and grab Brody's suspenders. "Where were you the night of the flood?"

"I wasn't here. I was at a healing mission in Morgantown."

"All night?"

"The program lasted until ten o'clock or so. I was on the program."

"And after that?"

"After that?"

"Can anyone vouch for your time after that?"

Brody backed away from the sheriff until the rolltop desk blocked his retreat. "I'd rather not say."

The sheriff pursued Brody, pinning him against the desk. "So you're taking the fifth?"

"I take the Fifth Commandment seriously, yes."

"That the one about killing?"

"That's right."

"All right, Reverend. So far we've got you seriously observing the Fifth and Eighth Commandments. How are you doing on the other eight?" The sheriff looked back at Owen. "You went to a religious school. What commandment covers screwing around?"

"Sixth and Ninth," Owen answered.

"Two of them?"

"Need to cover committing and coveting both. Get you coming and not coming."

The sheriff pushed forward, causing Brody to put his hands behind him on the desk and lean backward. "You screwing around, Reverend? That why you don't want to account for your time after the mission?"

Owen had watched several of Reader's interrogations. The sheriff seemed to be taking a deliberately crude approach in the hope of unnerving the clergyman.

Brody straightened, forcing the sheriff to back off. If the Reverend was unnerved, he didn't show it. "I was registered at the Morgantown Arms. You can easily check on that."

"That wasn't what I asked," the sheriff said.

Brody's face had become a rigid mask. "That's what I'm answering."

Owen stepped forward. "That was a Saturday night, Reverend. Who tended your flock Sunday morning?"

"Why, I did. I left an early wake-up call and made it back in time for the service."

"You traveled almost two hundred miles Sunday morning on your motorcycle?" the sheriff asked.

"That's right."

"And no one traveled with you?'

"No one."

"Why not just make the trip Saturday night?"

"I wanted to get some sleep before I took to the road."

Reader pushed forward again. "And you slept alone?"

Instead of bending backward, Brody sat upright on the edge of the desk. "I don't see how that can possibly concern you."

"It concerns me that you can't account for your time when the shaft exploded."

"The hotel people may be able to tell you what time I checked out, but I don't really see that it matters. Whoever set the fuse in the shaft wasn't in the mine when it exploded. In fact, I'd guess that whoever set the timer to blow the mine would have an airtight alibi for the time it went off."

The sheriff backed away and smiled. "You know, you're absolutely right, Reverend. It's a wonder we law-enforcement professionals never thought of that. It must have taken some divine guidance."

If the Reverend Moral Brody thought he was being mocked, he didn't show it. Instead, he answered, "I always try to remain open to Divine Guidance."

"Well, next time you talk to God, or vice versa, you might ask him or her who blew up Anson Stokes' mine. In the meantime, I'll ask Judge Vereen what he wants to do about your anonymous threat."

"The judge is a good friend. We share a common vision."

"If he's such a good friend, why didn't you sign your letter? Just one of those commandments you didn't take too seriously?"

Moral Brody stood up straight. "I see no point in continuing this interview."

"Neither do I. Don't bother to show us out." The sheriff took two steps toward the door. "One more thing, Reverend. Next time you write a letter like that, I'd advise you to sign it. It helps us poor law-enforcement types to know whether we're dealing with a serious threat or some shrub-cuddling clergyman who leads his flock wherever his pecker points."

Outside, Reader shuddered in the cool night air. "God save us from those righteous folks who know what's best for the rest of us."

"You don't really think he blew up Anson's mine?" Owen asked.

"As some sort of misguided environmental protest? I'll grant you that motive doesn't make much sense. But then, how many sensible motives can you think of for blowing up an abandoned mineshaft?" Reader cinched the strap of his mountie's hat and zipped up his windbreaker. "Brody's wrong about the bomber having an airtight alibi, though. When the shaft blew, whoever set the fuse was right there on the phone with the 911 dispatcher."

17

Where's Waldo?

Afew days after Mary Beth's funeral, Ruth and Owen talked Jeb Stuart into attending a showing of *Matewan* that a local theater was running as part of West Virginia History Month. After the movie, they exited onto the main corridor of a shopping mall.

"Quite a show," Ruth said. "They filmed it just up the road in Thurmond."

"Why not in Matewan?" Owen asked.

"Matewan has been flooded out three times since the mine wars. It doesn't look the way it did then."

"Mines don't look the way they did then," Owen said. "Machines give you straight, flat walls, and you don't need all those timber supports."

"It's still a tough life," Ruth said.

"My dad worked a mine like that one in the movie," Jeb Stuart said. "Smaller, but Mom never sold the property it was on. I guess it belongs to me now."

"Your dad wanted you to get out of the mines," Owen said.

"I've been thinking about that," Jeb Stuart said. "You're working in mines now, aren't you?"

"Just for a little while," Owen said. "We're doing a study for the state."

"With some mining engineers?" Jeb Stuart said.

"One or two."

"What's it take to be a mining engineer?"

"A college degree and a tolerance for dark holes."

"WVU offers a degree," Ruth said.

"I used to help my dad bring the coal out. It was kind of fun."

"Mining killed your dad," Owen said.

"Maybe if I got to be a mining engineer I could keep it from killing more people."

"That's a wonderful idea," Ruth said. "Owen, why don't you bring one of your engineers home to dinner some night?"

"I could do that," Owen said. He thought of Emily Kruk. "It might be fun."

A man approached wearing the navy blue uniform of a security guard. He carried a brown nightstick, which he touched to the brim of his cap as he passed.

"He looks familiar," Owen said.

"That's Mr. Tanner," Jeb Stuart said. "He was a neighbor of Mr. Stokes. His wife was killed in the flood."

"I didn't recognize him in uniform," Owen said.

It was late enough so that all the stores were closed except a Big Bear at the far end of the mall. They passed a row of lit window displays marking a Corbin's outlet store, Banning's Hatbox, and a women's fashion boutique Owen had never seen before.

Ruth stopped to look at the boutique's window display, which grouped three mannequins wearing cocktail dresses in front of an enlarged poster featuring the Eiffel Tower.

"That was quite a movie," Ruth said again. "You know they filmed it just up the road in Thurmond. Matewan had been flooded and rebuilt so many times since the mine wars, it doesn't look like it did then."

212

Owen gave her a sideways glance and tried to keep his response light, to hide his worry. "I think I heard that somewhere."

"Oh, really?" Ruth said. "Where?"

"You just told me. On our way out of the theater."

"I did?" Ruth adjusted her knitted cap. "Oh, well. I was just trying to see if you were really paying attention."

"I was paying attention," Owen said. "I'm always paying attention."

It didn't dawn on him until they'd reached his car. From the Big Bear store to the fashion boutique, the mall fit the description of the payoff location Hank Clanton had described, the parking lot where the attorney general's wife collected his kickbacks.

THAD READER'S GLASS eye seemed to bore through Owen. "That description must fit at least five shopping malls in this part of the state. The only reason it doesn't fit more is the state's too poor to support more malls."

"I'm not asking for a lot of help here," Owen said. "Just support me and move in if I find something."

"It's a waste of your time. Kickbacks are a way of life here. Nothing you can do will change that."

"I can make life miserable for one kickback artist."

Reader drummed his fingers on his desk. "And all this righteous zeal comes because you lost one rigged bid in California?"

"It was a little more than that. The CALTRANS evaluators had picked me for the job before the politicians stepped in and threw it to my competition. I was counting on the work. When it didn't come in, my business went belly-up right away and my marriage only lasted a little longer."

"For the want of a nail, the shoe was lost, and so on through the horse, the rider, the battle, and the war." Reader shook his head. "You're connecting a lot of dots there. I've never been big on linking lost horseshoe nails to lost wars. Ever stop to think that your marriage might have folded even if you'd gotten the job?"

"If I'd gotten the CALTRANS job, I wouldn't have had to move to D.C. If I'd stayed in California instead of moving, my marriage wouldn't have gone down the tubes."

"If my dick were an inch longer and my wallet a pound heavier, I would have married Jacqueline Bisset." The sheriff opened his hands, palms outward, in surrender and asked, "What do you want from me?"

"I'm going to put a surveillance camera up in the mall parking lot. If I can document the payoff schedule, I want you to move in."

"So you don't need me until you've got hard evidence."

"Right. Except you could do me a small favor right now."

"What's that?"

"Find out what kind of cars the attorney general and his wife drive and get me their license numbers."

"I guess I can donate that amount of effort to your wild goose chase."

"Take it from the time you're spending trying to convict Anson Stokes. That's *your* wild goose chase."

"Anson's still the lead candidate in Cable's murder." The sheriff held up three fingers and ticked off the points one at a time. "First, he threatened Cable in public. More than once. Second, he had a motive, and third, his car's the only one on record going into the mine site where you found the body."

"We both know there's another way into the mine site."

"Doesn't mean anybody took it. Why push a wheelbarrow overland if you can just drive right up to the mine entrance? Be like hiking up and down a roller-coaster track shoving the cars instead of riding in them."

"Pushing a wheelbarrow would avoid the cameras."

The sheriff held up a fourth finger. "Besides, whoever slugged Cable really had it in for him. The medical examiner says the killer was still clobbering the skull after Cable had been dead a spell. Takes a powerful lot of hate to do that. I'd say Anson qualifies there, too."

"If Anson's wrench was used for the postmortem clobbering, it could have been an afterthought, just to plant evidence."

"I'll ask the examiner to sort out the timing. No matter when it was used, though, it's still Anson's wrench with Anson's fingerprints."

"So you figure Cable blew the mine to spite Anson and Anson killed Cable to get even."

"Makes a neat package."

"Cow flop in a neat package is still cow flop. What did Cable stand to gain from the flood?"

"He'd see his brother brought down to his level. Right after the flood, he was front and center with phony claims for lost property and Riley's death."

"Other people besides Cable figured to gain from the flood."

The sheriff leaned back in his chair and clasped both hands behind his head. "Like who?"

"Johnson, Crane's been overcharging the state for their cleanup contracts. Dusty Rhodes parlayed his dam leak into a twenty-million-dollar federal grant."

Reader shook his head. "Much as you might like to pin a rap on both those folks, I can't see either of them blowing the mineshaft. Johnson, Crane didn't have a lock on the cleanup business, and Dusty's looking at a few lawsuits to balance his federal grant."

Owen sighed. "I guess it is pretty far-fetched. One other thing, though. Even if we don't know who blew Anson's abandoned shaft, we've tracked down both of the threats to blow up his working mine, one to Cable and one to the Reverend Moral Brody. Cable's not a threat to anything but groundwater, and the Reverend's not likely to blow anything but his own horn."

"Your point being?"

"Seems like Anson ought to be able to start mining again."

"What do you want *me* to do about it?"

"Tell it to the judge."

Reader smiled. "I already did. He's lifting the injunction against Anson's mining operation first thing tomorrow."

OWEN CAUGHT UP with Anson in the trailer that served as an office for the Canaan mines.

"They're giving me my mine back? Hot damn." Anson squinted at the dial of a squat safe, twirled the dial twice, swore, twirled the dial again, levered the door open and pulled out a green tackle box that he set on a scarred metal table next to a half-empty bottle of Jack Daniels. The cap from the bottle was nowhere to be seen.

Anson reached into the tackle box and pulled out two packets of bedraggled bills that looked as if they'd survived a mine blast. "Now I can get a little cash flow going to pay off some of my bills."

He pulled a thick rubber band off one of the packets, licked his thumb, and began counting the bills into stacks. "How much I owe you, anyhow?"

"Don't worry about it," Owen said. "I can wait until the mine's up and running again."

"This here's my rainy-day stash." Anson picked up four hundred dollars in fifties, folded them over, and held them out to Owen. "At least let me give you a little something on account."

When Owen didn't reach for the bills, Anson leaned over the desk and stuffed them into Owen's shirt pocket, giving him a hefty whiff of whiskey breath.

"On account," Anson said. "On account of I owe you, old buddy. It's your doing the judge is reversing hisself. Don't think I don't know it. You figured it out who was writing them threatening notes, showed they come from dickless wonders who'd never heft a blasting cap."

"I wouldn't exactly call Cable and Moral Brody dickless wonders. And Cable had certainly hefted a few blasting caps in his day."

"His day's done done." Anson pulled two glasses out of his top desk drawer. "Now if we could just find out who done him in, my worries would be over." He splashed Jack Daniels into each of the glasses and shoved one across the table to Owen. "Hell, I'd sure drink to that."

"Too early for me," Owen said. He'd never seen Anson drunk. It was hard for him to believe a sober Anson could have killed Cable. But he'd seen liquor shove at least one killer over the edge.

"Too early for me too. But we got good news to celebrate." Anson swilled down the contents of his glass.

Owen turned away from the glassy-eyed Anson and scanned the framed photographs on the wall of the trailer. He remembered noticing one of the pictures on his last visit. It was a newspaper photo of Cable and other union men pounding on the hood of Anson's car. In the picture next to it, six men were at the entrance of a mineshaft, staring out at the camera.

Owen stood and examined the picture. Cable and Anson knelt together in front of the group.

"Happier days," Owen said.

"First mine. We was together then. Till coal prices tanked and damn near busted us."

"But you stuck it out."

"I did. Cable didn't."

"Is that Lyle Tanner in the back row?"

"Yeah. Lyle worked in our first mine. He got out of the hole early though."

"Saw him a couple of nights ago, working security at the Contrary mall."

"Lucky bastard. Wasn't for that late-night job at the mall, he'd be under the mud with his wife."

"Talking about the shopping mall, I want to borrow one of those surveillance cameras we set up at your mine entrance."

"Go ahead. Don't see we need them now. We know them threats was as empty as my glass here." Anson poured more bourbon into his glass and held it up as a toast to Owen. "Take the cameras. Welcome to 'em."

"I'll take them off your bill."

"Leave them on. Like I said, I owe you."

OWEN TOOK ONE of the rented video surveillance units from Anson's guardhouse to the shopping mall. The unit was housed in a single-axle trailer about the size of the ice-cream freezers that vendors peddled through Owen's neighborhood when he was a boy. Instead of ice cream, the aluminum trailer held a tangle of electronic equipment and a video recorder and monitor. The split-screen monitor displayed a picture from two video cameras mounted on a collapsible pole bolted to one end of the trailer.

Owen chained the other end of the trailer to a water meter on the side of a Rexall Drug Store facing the mall entrance and raised the collapsible pole to its full height, about fifteen feet above the ground. He was adjusting the picture on the monitor when a voice behind him said, "Don't think I'd stay tuned to that channel very long."

Owen turned to see Lyle Tanner, wearing his security guard's uniform and peering at the monitor, which showed the cars waiting to turn at the stoplight controlling traffic entering the mall.

"I'll grant you there's not much plot," Owen said, "but we've got the potential for quite a few car chases."

Tanner rested his hand on a wooden baton strapped to his belt. "Still don't think it'd hold my interest. What's the point?"

Owen was glad the cameras were still fitted with the zoom lenses they'd used for mine surveillance rather than the wide-angle lenses that would cover the parking lot. He waved his hand toward the intersection the cameras were recording. "We're monitoring traffic at that stoplight. City wants to see if it's worth putting in a video system to ticket red-light runners."

"They can do that?"

"Oh, yes. They photograph the driver and the license plate whenever a car runs the signal. Then the driver gets a ticket in the mail."

"That Purvis Jenkins, he'll do anything to get money for the city."

Owen just nodded and turned his attention back to the monitor.

Tanner cleared his throat. "You're the fellow that was down in Drybone Hollow with the sheriff, talked to me and Cable Stokes."

"That's right." Owen held out his hand. "Name's Owen Allison."

"Lyle Tanner. This shopping mall's my beat. I like to know what's going on."

"Well, I'll be leaving these cameras up for a couple of weeks."

"Batteries last that long?"

"Batteries last about 48 hours. I'll come back before they run out, put in new ones, and pick up the data."

"Doing this for Purvis Jenkins, huh?"

Owen nodded again. He'd have to tell Purvis what he was really up to in case the story got back to Contrary's City Hall.

"You're the fellow found Cable Stokes' body."

"That's right."

"Hear he was beat up pretty bad."

"Worst I'd ever seen." Owen turned from the monitor to face Lyle Tanner. "You know him long?"

"Neighbors fifteen year. Played poker with him once a month most of that time."

"Worked in Anson Stokes' mine with him, too."

Tanner frowned. "Who told you that?"

"Saw your picture on the wall of Stokes' office."

"Oh, that. Back when I worked it, the mine belonged to Cable and Anson both. I didn't work it long, though. Couldn't take the dark and the damp. Told them if they wanted to keep me they'd have to put in skylights and central air conditioning."

"Cable kept on working it though."

"Till coal prices went south and Anson bought him out for a song."

"Hear Cable was pretty bitter about that."

"Bitter?" Tanner spat on the asphalt. "Bitter's not the word for it. Bitter's just a bad taste in your mouth. Cable let it rot his soul."

"Think Cable took it hard enough to blow up Anson's shaft?"

"Cable? He was high on sly and mean as a cornered snake. He'd go behind your back for your money, your wife, and anything that wasn't nailed down, but I can't believe he'd blow Anson's mine. That what the sheriff thinks?"

Owen felt he was beginning to give out more information than he was taking in. "I'm not sure what the sheriff thinks."

"If Cable blew that shaft, I wouldn't blame Anson for killing him. Hell, Mister, I lost my wife Maddie in that flood. If I thought Cable had blown that shaft, I'd have killed him myself."

Owen laughed once. "Seems like half the people I talk to tell me they could have killed Cable."

"I said *if* he blew the shaft. That's a mighty big if."

"You don't think he could have done it?"

"Hardly seems so." Tanner shook his head slowly, then frowned. "Come to think on it, though, I remember Cable saying his boy Billy Joe had filched some of Anson's dynamite. For stump removal, he said."

"Any stumps on Cable's property?"

"Not on Cable's. Never seen Billy Joe's." He shook his head again. "Don't make sense for either Cable or Billy Joe to blow Anson's shaft. Makes more sense for Anson to do it himself."

"How's that?"

"Anson was all the time disappointed he never hit a paying seam in that first shaft. Always wanted to drill a little deeper."

Owen remembered Cable advancing the same theory on the witness stand. "If Anson just wanted more coal, he wouldn't have set a charge on a timer and left the mine."

"Maybe there wasn't no timer on the charge. Maybe the flood come well after the shaft was blown. Could be the blast just weakened the wall, and the water pressure blew through later. That's possible, ain't it?"

"Possible, but not very likely." The picture on the TV monitor began rolling. Owen tried adjusting the tracking knob, then slapped the monitor in frustration. The picture righted itself.

"Just like my set at home," Tanner said.

"It's all in knowing where to hit it."

"Like a lot of things, I reckon."

Owen looked from the monitor to Tanner. "Word is, Cable was shopping here the day he died."

"Bought supplies at the Big Bear. I helped him load them."

"Supplies never made it to his hideout."

Tanner shrugged. "I guess Cable didn't neither. Damn shame about the Hobbs woman. Wish I'd known what Cable was up to when he was here in the lot."

You're not the only one, Owen thought. "What shift did you work then?"

"Three to eleven, same as now. When Maddie was alive, I worked the late shift, eleven to seven, to give us more daylight time together. No point in losing sleep on the late shift now she's gone." Tanner checked his watch. "Talking about shifts, I got to get on with mine."

He took his wooden baton from its holster and waved it near a button-shaped chip behind the drug store's water meter. The baton emitted a short, high-pitched beep.

"That's how they keep track of me." Tanner touched the tip of his cap with his baton, put it back in its holster, and went off down the line of store fronts.

When Tanner was out of sight, Owen installed wide-angle lenses on the two cameras and replaced them in their weather-proof housings, which had been disguised to look like overhead lights. Then he raised the collapsible pole and adjusted the cameras and monitor to give a 140-degree view of the parking lot. Finally, he set the recorder, locked the trailer, and hung a HIGH VOLTAGE sign on it to discourage prying eyes.

It was a long shot to expect to record payoffs that might or might not be taking place in the parking lot. But a long shot was better than no shot at all.

IN THE BREAKFAST room of Jeb Stuart's house, Owen fast-forwarded through the first twenty-four hours of the forty-eight-hour recording looking for a yellow Cadillac in the mall parking lot. The sheriff had given him the car's description and license number, as well as the home address of the attorney general, and Owen had taken a photo of the target auto and taped it to the top of the monitor.

At least the car's distinctive enough to stand out, Owen thought. Even so, it had taken him nearly three hours to review a full day's recording. He was lucky that nothing much happened in the parking lot between the time the last movie ended and the time Dunkin' Donuts opened for breakfast.

Owen was kneading his tired eyes when Jeb Stuart wandered into the breakfast room wearing his Cincinnati Reds T-shirt, gray sweatpants, and white athletic socks. He was munching Cheerios straight out of the box and asked, "Whatcha doing?" between mouthfuls.

Owen tapped the photo taped to the monitor. "Trying to spot this car."

"What for? They running drugs?"

"No."

"They kill somebody? You got a line on Mr. Stokes' killer?"

"Not that either."

"What then?"

"They're part of a payoff scheme that's swapping state contracts for kickbacks."

Jeb Stuart's cheeks puffed out with Cheerios as he raised his eyebrows and shoulders in a "who cares?" shrug.

The boy's reaction didn't surprise Owen. The payoff scheme didn't pass Thad Reader's "who cares?" test either, and the public at large seemed to take kickbacks for granted.

He tried to explain the problem in a way that would catch Jeb Stuart's imagination. "Somebody who has no right to sell a public job is taking money from somebody else who has no right to do the job. It's as if your coach sold the starting pitcher's job to the highest bidder and left Riley Stokes sitting on the bench."

"The team would suck. Unless every coach did the same thing."

"Then the league would suck."

"So you're helping Sheriff Reader fight the bad guys?"

"Sort of. I had to sit on the bench once when a state official sold a job I really needed."

"So it's payback you're after."

So much for his imagination-catching baseball analogy. "As much as anything, I guess."

"I'm into that." Jeb Stuart set down the Cheerios box. "How do you control that picture?"

Owen showed the boy how to fast-forward the image and slow it down for a frame-by-frame search.

"Cool," Jeb Stuart said. "Can I help?"

"How's your homework?"

The boy shrugged. "Done enough. This looks like more fun."

Owen rose from his kitchen chair. "Be my guest."

Owen fixed himself a pot of tea and settled down in the living room with the latest Jeremiah Healy mystery. He figured he'd be able to get a few chapters in before Jeb Stuart tired of screening the surveillance video.

An hour later, he realized he'd become so engrossed in the book he hadn't heard a peep out of the boy. He peeked into the breakfast room. Jeb Stuart was hunched over the controls of the monitor, peering at the screen as if it were a video game.

"It's kind of like a video version of *Where's Waldo?*" Jeb Stuart said when he sensed Owen's presence. "There aren't too many yellow cars."

"Want me to take over?"

"Heck no. I'm just getting the hang of it."

Owen went back to the Healy mystery. He was into his second pot of tea and more than halfway through the book when Jeb Stuart came into the living room.

"I finished the whole tape and didn't see the car. You sure it's there?"

"No. I guess that makes it less like a real video game."

The boy laughed. "Not necessarily. Half the games I try I don't get far enough to know whether the prize is really there. You going to get more tapes?"

"We're recording even as we speak."

"You let me know when there are more to watch, okay? I want to help out."

Owen sipped his tea. "Oh, I'll let you know. Don't worry about that."

The boy stood uncertainly at the foot of the stairs. "You're still working with the sheriff, right?"

"Right."

"So what's he doing about Cable Stokes' killer?"

"He thinks Stokes' brother Anson did it."

"What do you think?"

"I'm not so sure."

"Whoever killed Mr. Stokes caused my mom to die."

"I know that, Jeb Stuart."

"And almost killed Riley Stokes."

"How is Riley?"

"He's better. He's back pitching. Thing is, if Anson Stokes didn't kill his brother, whoever caused my mom's death is still out there."

Owen felt the weight of the boy's frustration. "You're right."

"So maybe we could work on that a little." The boy paused, looking embarrassed. "After you get your payback, I mean."

"Jeb Stuart, finding Cable Stokes' killer is lots more important than my payback. But the sheriff thinks he's got the killer and he could well be right." Owen set his book aside. "There's an old joke about a man who loses his wallet on one street but looks for it on the next street over because the light's better there." He wasn't sure the analogy held, but he went on with it because it was easier than admitting he didn't have many ideas about where to look for Cable's killer if the sheriff was wrong. "Right now, I feel like the light's better on this payback problem. But I haven't forgotten your mom. And neither has the sheriff."

"That's good, 'cause neither have I." The boy bit his lip. "Well, good night." He started up the stairs, then stopped. "I'm glad you're here."

Owen smiled. The tea and the sentiment warmed him. "Good night, Jeb Stuart. I'm glad I'm here, too."

TWO NIGHTS LATER, Owen set up a schedule that had he and Jeb Stuart reviewing videotapes on alternating one-hour shifts. Owen had just finished his second shift and was channel-surfing through the local TV offerings when the boy burst into the living room. "I got it. Come see."

Owen watched over Jeb Stuart's shoulder as the boy reversed the frames on the monitor and pointed to a yellow Cadillac convertible backing in jerks and starts through a half-full parking lot. The display in the corner of the screen showed the time of the recording to be just after noon on Thursday, the previous day. When the frame reversal had taken the Cadillac back to the entrance of the parking lot, Jeb Stuart let the image run forward in real time. The car entered the lot and parked, but no one got out.

Two minutes later, a tall, well-dressed woman with streaks of gray in her brunette hair approached the yellow car carrying a red, white, and blue shopping bag. She leaned over and spoke briefly to the driver, then lifted the bag into the back seat of the car and walked away.

"See there," Jeb Stuart said. "She made the drop."

"Leaving Mrs. Boyer holding the bag."

"Who's Mrs. Boyer?"

"The attorney general's wife."

A short time after the tall woman left, an attractive blonde in a tailored beige pantsuit emerged from the Cadillac, looked up and down the rows of parked cars, and headed toward the row of shops.

"She's a nice-looking woman," Jeb Stuart said. "What'll happen to her?"

"Nothing yet. I have to show the tape to the sheriff."

"Will he arrest her?"

Owen could imagine Thad Reader's reaction, right down to the glass-eyed stare and skeptical voice. "Not on the strength of what we've just seen," Owen said. "We don't know what was in the bag. What we've got here is the first link in a chain of evidence. The sheriff will need to keep an eye on the lot himself, so he can intercept a future payment."

"So we're not done?"

Owen could hear the disappointment in Jeb Stuart's voice. He patted the boy's shoulder. "No, but that's a great start you've given us." His long shot was leading at the first turn.

OWEN WAS RIGHT about Thad Reader's reaction to the tape. "For all we know," the sheriff said, "there's dirty laundry in that shopping bag, or borrowed Tupperware, or somebody's anniversary gift." But Reader was impressed enough with the possibility that they were watching a regularly scheduled payoff to agree to have a deputy cruise by the parking lot every day around noon.

For the next six days, Owen and Jeb Stuart fast-forwarded through the parking-lot tapes without catching a glimpse of the yellow Cadillac. Exactly one week after they had recorded the shopping bag hand-off, Owen was home reviewing the layouts of a few of the mines on his inspection list when the phone rang. Thad Reader's voice said, "Owen, you better get over here to the shopping center."

Owen checked his watch. It was nearly noon. "What happened? Did you intercept a payoff?"

"Not quite."

"Don't tell me you confiscated a shopping bag full of dirty laundry."

The sheriff's voice was flat, giving nothing away. "Not that either. Just get over here."

Owen left the mine layouts unrolled on the kitchen table and rode the accelerator on his Saturn trying to get to the mall as fast as he could. When he turned into the parking lot, he spotted the sheriff's patrol car parked beside the Rexall Drug Store where the surveillance cameras had been set up.

But there were no surveillance cameras in sight. The collapsible pole supporting the cameras had been severed, leaving only a short stump with dangling cables poking above the top of the trailer. The HIGH VOLTAGE sign that was supposed to deter vandals had been flipped over and the message LET IT BE scrawled on the reverse side.

"Looks like somebody hacked right through the pole," the sheriff said.

Owen swore, then asked, "What about the cameras?"

"Nowhere to be seen."

"When did it happen?"

"Must have been last night. Store manager says it was that way when he opened up."

"But he didn't bother to tell anybody?"

"Not in his job description, evidently."

Owen lifted the scrawled sign. "Let *what* be?"

"Whatever you thought you were videotaping, most likely. Who knew what you were up to here?"

"You. Jeb Stuart, but I can't imagine he'd tell anyone. And Lyle Tanner, but he thought I was recording intersection traffic."

"Well, somebody must have figured it out."

"What about your deputies? What did you tell them?"

"Just to cruise by around noon and keep an eye out for a yellow Caddy. They thought they were working a drug bust."

Owen replaced the HIGH VOLTAGE sign. "It doesn't make any sense."

The sheriff stared over Owen's shoulder. "I have a feeling it's about to make even less sense."

Owen turned and looked in the direction the sheriff was staring. A yellow Cadillac convertible was sitting at the traffic signal, waiting to make a left turn into the mall parking lot.

18

Moon Shot

THE yellow Cadillac passed Owen's parked car and headed down the shopping center's entry road. The car's convertible top was open to the noonday sun and its driver was the blonde from the surveillance video, the attorney general's wife, wearing the same sunglasses she'd worn a week earlier.

The sheriff watched the Cadillac go by and raised his eyebrows in a "What the hell?" look.

"There's always somebody who doesn't get the word," Owen said.

The blonde parked the Cadillac in the same section of the lot where the last payoff had taken place. Reader nodded toward the severed stump on the aluminum trailer. "Too bad your cameras went missing."

"I've got one in my trunk for mine inspections." Owen retrieved the video camera, flipped it on, and looked through the viewfinder at the sheriff. "Maybe you ought to get close enough to find out what's in the bag."

"My uniform will scare them off."

"Take my car." Owen tossed him the keys. "They won't notice you without your light bar."

The sheriff ducked into Owen's Saturn, removed his mountie's hat, and drove off down the entry road the Cadillac had followed.

Owen took the camera and stood behind the shoulder-high shrubbery next to the aluminum trailer with the severed stump. He trained the camera on the yellow Cadillac. So far, the blonde hadn't left her car.

Owen looked up from the viewfinder. The sheriff had driven the Saturn to the row of cars where the Cadillac was parked and sat with his engine idling.

Owen's eyes returned to the viewfinder. Still no movement from the blonde in the Cadillac. Then he saw the brunette, walking through the rows of parked cars, carrying a green shopping bag with gold edging.

The sheriff must have seen the brunette as well, because the Saturn began rolling forward, approaching the Cadillac at a slightly slower speed than the woman with the shopping bag.

Just as the brunette reached the yellow convertible and hefted the bag over its side into the passenger seat, the sheriff pulled the Saturn up to block the Cadillac and hopped out of the car, holding his badge aloft.

The brunette froze for a few seconds, then leapt at the sheriff, clawing and scratching and pinning him against the Saturn. Reader managed to grab both the pinioning claws and seemed to have the woman under control when she kneed him in the groin. His knees buckled and he stumbled forward, wrestling the brunette onto the hood of the Cadillac.

The blonde flung open the convertible door and began running, hopping first on one foot and then the other to shuck her high-heeled sandals.

Owen kept the camera trained on the sheriff and the brunette as she tried to squirm out from under his weight. Reader managed to keep her pressed against the Cadillac and they slid along its side until the woman tumbled backward over the door and into the passenger seat, pulling the sheriff down on top of her.

The blonde cleared the rows of cars and sprinted toward the main exit, her arms windmilling like broken kite struts in a gusty breeze.

Half hidden behind the shrubbery and the trailer next to the exit, Owen recorded the blonde's approach. When she was almost on him, he stepped out from behind the trailer into her path, keeping his viewfinder on her and bracing himself for a collision.

On seeing Owen and his camera, the blonde stopped so suddenly that her sunglasses tilted forward to the tip of her nose. She peered over the edge of the glasses, patted her hair into place, and said into the lens, "And who the fuck are you, Candid Camera?"

THE TV NEWS that evening bleeped out the word *fuck,* although they showed Reader's struggle with the brunette wife of contractor Heck Johnson in slow motion from the time she kneed him in the groin to the time he wrestled her over the edge of the convertible and they disappeared into the passenger seat with her legs wrapped around him. Asked to comment on his wife's shoeless flight from her yellow convertible, the attorney general sidestepped questions about the ten thousand dollars found in the green shopping bag and raised issues of police brutality and warrantless searches. The governor could not be reached for comment.

By the time the morning papers arrived, the governor had gone on record with several comments, chief among them a demand for the attorney general's resignation. The story was front-page news in both the *Charleston Gazette* and the *Barkley Democrat.* Both newspapers printed an enlarged frame from the videotape showing Heck Johnson's wife toppling backward into the convertible, her legs wrapped around Thad Reader's waist. Reader's eyes were squinting and his mouth stretched open in a grimace that might have been misinterpreted as orgasmic release by anyone who had not seen the videotaped knee to his groin.

Owen was reading the *Democrat* and finishing his breakfast tea when Reader called. According to the sheriff, the governor's public demand for the attorney general's head had been prompted by a private viewing of the earlier videotape establishing a payoff pattern and a copy of Owen's proposal offering to undertake the mine inspections at a price substantially lower than that bid by Johnson, Crane.

"So you nailed them," Reader said. "How's it feel?"

"Pretty good. I'd feel a lot better, though, if I didn't have to replace surveillance equipment that runs at least twenty grand on the open market." Owen glanced at the picture of Reader wrestling with Johnson's wife. "I'm looking at the front page of the *Democrat*. Seems like I should be asking *you* how you feel."

"That damn picture makes me look like a pervert caught in midstroke. Whoever runs against me next election is going to have a field day with that photo."

"Should get you in solid with the Bubba vote, though."

"That might have been enough a while back, before they outlawed inbreeding and gave women the vote. These days, I figure it'll cost me a thousand votes across the board."

"At least nobody's going to say you're soft on crime."

Reader laughed. "I'll give you that. Think 'hard on crime' might make a catchy slogan?"

"I think there's a good reason nobody's used it before. On a related subject, I'm guessing the attorney general didn't confess to cutting down my cameras?'

"Seems pretty clear he had no idea they were there. Maybe it was just random vandalism. Lot of that going around."

"Why would vandals leave a note?"

"Damned if I know. Could be there's more happening on the lot than we know about. Maybe you should take a closer look at your tapes."

"I took a close look at the tape just before the system went down. Whoever did it sneaked up behind the trailer and cut the lead from the cameras to the recorder. Happened at 3:41 in the morning."

"Don't suppose the perp wound up on the tape?"

"No. He must have figured out which way the cameras were pointing. It's not obvious from the ground."

"Man didn't want to be photographed." Reader let his voice drop an octave. "Hmmm. Sounds like we're up against another criminal mastermind."

"One thing I don't get, though, is why the mall watchman didn't see anything. Cutting through that pole was no quick job."

"The woman who runs mall security used to work for me. Maybe we ought to pay her a little visit."

THE HEAD OF security at the Contrary mall was April Downey, a tall, wiry woman with wrinkles around her eyes and mouth that gave her a pinch-faced look of perpetual skepticism. She showed Owen and Thad Reader the dime-sized chip behind the drugstore's water meter that activated the wands carried by her security guards. To demonstrate, she leaned over the meter and waved a wand close enough to the chip to cause the wand to emit a short, sharp beep. "The wands our people carry record the time of day they pass these checkpoints," she explained. "When their shift ends, they dump the data into our computer and we print out a record of their activity."

Owen watched April struggle to right herself after leaning over the water meter in a tight space made even tighter by untrimmed shrubbery and his surveillance trailer. "You've almost got to be a contortionist to get at that chip. How come it's so hard to reach?"

April brushed away a shrub branch that had caught in the pocket of her blue pantsuit. "When the chips are out in plain view, they invite vandalism. Besides, we want our security people to extend themselves a little. We don't want them sleepwalking through their shifts."

Owen lifted the severed cable on the surveillance trailer. "This lead was cut at 3:41 in the morning. Where would your security person have been then?"

"During the week, the graveyard shift's security man is Rollie Gordon. Rollie hits this chip on the half hour and a chip behind the Big Bear at the other end of the mall on the hour."

"So he would have been gone from this checkpoint about ten minutes when the cable was cut.

April nodded. "If he hit the chip on time."

"How much latitude do you give them?"

"Long as they're within fifteen minutes of the schedule, we figure they're doing their job. We just need to know they hit all their marks in order and don't rush through them to create goof-off time."

"So far as you know, then," the sheriff said, "this Rollie Gordon was on time when the cameras vanished."

April shrugged. "I can check the printout. Rollie's usually spot on, though. You could set your watch by him."

"Maybe somebody did," Owen said.

April squinted, adding a few more lines to her face. "Excuse me?"

"Could be somebody clocked his tour. Seems strange the cameras went down just after he left the area."

"It would be a big help if you checked the printout," Reader said. "Find out what time he passed here night before last."

"If it's not too much trouble, could you get us the records for the last two weeks as well?" Owen said.

"If it will help, sure." April walked off toward her office in the center of the mall.

The sheriff watched April thread her way through the parking lot. "She was a hell of a deputy. Really thorough. I hated to see her leave for this mall job." He turned his good eye on Owen. "How come you want two weeks' worth of April's records? Won't the guards show up on the tapes you recorded?"

"Just trying to be thorough myself. Whoever cut the cameras down didn't show up on the tapes. I don't have any idea what's going on, but we made somebody antsy enough to cut the recorder feed and leave us a note."

Owen squeezed in behind the shrubbery and examined the chip. It was in the center of a metal plate bolted to the drugstore wall behind the water meter. A narrow ledge ran the length of the wall below the plate. The top of the water meter was scuffed and gray paint had been scraped off the ledge just under the plate.

"See something?" the sheriff asked.

"Nothing that makes any sense."

April returned with a sheaf of computer printouts. "I've got two week's worth of records here, one page for each shift. I scanned them while I was making the copies. Didn't look like there was anything unusual. Everybody hit their marks pretty close to schedule. The night your cameras vanished, Rollie Gordon logged in here right at 3:30."

Owen took the records. "Thanks for checking."

"What'll you do now?" April asked.

"Watch a lot of videotape. There must be something on the recordings that upset somebody."

"WHAT ARE WE looking for this time?" Jeb Stuart asked.

Owen took the photo of the yellow Cadillac down from the TV monitor. "We don't know. Anything that might explain why someone would cut down the camera pole. Did you tell anyone what we were doing?"

"Just Riley."

"Do you think he told anyone?"

"I don't know. I could ask."

"Ask tomorrow. For now, why don't you watch the tapes I reviewed and I'll watch the ones you looked at. Maybe we'll see something."

Jeb Stuart frowned. "Why don't we just watch the same tapes again?"

"Fresh eyes. You might see something I missed, and vice versa."

Jeb Stuart still seemed reluctant. "I don't know . . ."

"Look, if you don't want to help, it's all right. I can watch the whole batch myself."

"No. That's okay. I want to help."

Halfway through his second hour of tape watching, Owen saw why Jeb Stuart had been reluctant to swap viewing responsibilities. The tape in the monitor, which had been recorded the day after the boy started to help reviewing tapes, showed Jeb Stuart driving his car into a parking space directly in front of the surveillance cameras.

As Jeb Stuart opened the driver's door and got out, Riley Stokes emerged from the passenger seat. Both boys were wearing their baseball uniforms and, from the time on the tape and the dust on their outfits, Owen guessed that they must have just come from afternoon practice.

Jeb Stuart pointed up at the cameras and waved, while Riley Stokes extended his middle finger skyward in the universal salute. Jeb slapped at Riley's upraised finger, and the two boys walked toward the surveillance trailer, disappearing from the bottom of the screen as they passed under the cameras' field of vision.

A few minutes later, the boys reappeared, walking back toward the parked car. Jeb Stuart waved again and slipped into the driver's seat. As the car backed out of the parking space, Riley thrust his bare, hairy buttocks out of the passenger window, mooning the cameras.

The car swerved and braked to a stop. Riley's rear end disappeared from view, and Lyle Tanner appeared in the picture, running toward the car and brandishing his baton. The car burned rubber out of the lot, leaving Tanner standing in a cloud of white exhaust fumes.

The security guard shook his baton overhead and shouted after the disappearing car. As the engulfing exhaust vanished, he turned and looked up at the cameras before starting toward them and disappearing from view. The tape logged the time as 4:30 in the afternoon, time for Tanner to record his presence by waving his wand at the disc behind the water meter.

"I'm sorry. I didn't know Riley was going to moon the cameras," Jeb Stuart said over Owen's shoulder. Owen had been so engrossed in the taped drama that he hadn't heard the boy approach.

Owen reversed the tapes and froze the image at the instant Riley thrust his rear out of the passenger window. "It's not your fault. It's hereditary. I recognize that butt. It's the same one Riley's father used to shove up against the window of the school bus to moon passersby."

Ruth appeared in the doorway wearing a quilted robe. "Jeb Stuart, it's past your bedtime."

Jeb Stuart straightened as if he'd just been goosed and moved to stand between Ruth and the TV image of Riley's rear end. "I was on my way. I just wanted to talk to Owen a little."

"Well, hurry it up. And don't forget, Owen invited one of his mining engineers to dinner tomorrow night. It'll be a good chance for you to find out what you have to do to be one."

"I won't forget."

"Well, good night then." Ruth pulled her robe sash a little tighter and nodded toward the TV monitor. "If that's the Internet porn everybody is so concerned over, I don't see that there's much to get excited about."

RUTH HAD FIXED pot roast, and Buster sat expectantly beside Owen's chair, hoping for a few choice morsels.

"Ignore that dog's soulful look," Ruth said. "You know we don't feed him table scraps when there's company for dinner."

Jeb Stuart sat across from Emily, whose auburn hair reflected flashes from the logs blazing in the fireplace as she listed some of the schools that offered degrees in mining engineering. "Near home, there's WVU and Kentucky. But there's quite a few out West. Arizona, Utah, most of the mining states have programs."

"Where'd you go?" Jeb Stuart asked.

"WVU."

"Lots of girls in your class?"

Emily smiled. "I was the only one. Three guys got degrees with me. We all got jobs right away. I went to work in Colorado."

"But you came back home," Ruth said.

"My mama needed me."

"Is your mother ill?" Ruth asked.

"She's better now, thank you."

"What kind of courses did you have to take?" Jeb Stuart asked.

"Basic engineering courses. Physics, chemistry, geology, mine systems, four semesters of calculus."

"Four semesters of calculus." Jeb Stuart frowned. "I had a tough time with sophomore algebra."

"Calculus isn't as tough as it sounds," Owen said. "I can help you prepare for it." He'd looked at Jeb Stuart's high school courses, which were light on math. It was a common failing in rural areas of the state, where few teachers had adequate backgrounds in math and science. He remembered his own algebra teacher, an elderly nun who waited until the last day of class to unveil the Pythagorean theorem, and then treated it as the revealed word of God, to be entrusted only to those four of her thirty students who were likely to go to college.

"When do you get to go down in the mines?" Jeb Stuart asked.

"Sophomore year. Half the kids that started with us as freshmen changed majors before the underground mine class ended."

"I wouldn't change," Jeb Stuart said. "My dad had a mine. I used to work with him."

Owen knew that Jeb Stuart's father had wanted him to escape from the mines. At least engineering would mean an escape from the tight picking and loading and the dust at the mine face that had led to his father's black lung disease.

As if she sensed Owen's ambivalence, Ruth changed the subject. "I see the attorney general resigned today."

"It was our tapes that did it," Jeb Stuart said.

"You were the ones that videotaped that woman running out of the mall?" Emily asked.

"That's right," Owen said.

"But aren't we working for Johnson, Crane?"

"Right again."

Emily dabbed at her lips with a napkin. "So isn't that like biting the hand that feeds us?"

"The hand was dirty," Ruth said, in a tone that closed off the topic of conversation.

After dinner, Jeb Stuart and Emily chatted in the living room while Owen cleared the table and Ruth loaded the dishwasher. Buster stationed himself below the sink, and Owen slipped him a few slivers of roast beef from each of the cleared plates before rinsing them.

Owen was wiping down the dinner table with a damp cloth when Emily entered the dining room and asked, "Can I talk with you?"

Owen folded the damp towel. "Sure."

Emily glanced back at Jeb Stuart in the living room, looked pointedly at Ruth in the kitchen, and said in a voice a little louder than a whisper, "Alone?"

"Buster could use a walk." Owen retrieved Buster's leash from the drawer above his supper dish. "Be right back," he said to Ruth, who was staring impassively at the dishwasher as he led Emily and Buster out the back door and into the cool night air.

While Buster sniffed at the rhododendron bushes lining the driveway of the Hobbs house, Emily asked, "Since Johnson, Crane bribed the attorney general to get our contract, will the state rescind it now that he's resigned?"

"They can always rescind the contract any time for almost any reason. There'll certainly be some political pressure to take it away from Johnson, Crane. Even if they jerk the contract, though, they'll have to rebid it. The job really needs to be done."

"When will we know what's going to happen?"

"It will probably be at least a couple of weeks before anything official happens. Bureaucrats never move any faster than they have to."

Emily looked down at Buster, who was sniffing a dark spot in the center of the driveway. "I didn't want Jeb Stuart to hear, but it hasn't been easy for me to get work back here in West Virginia."

"Why don't you want him to hear that? That's exactly what he needs to know."

"It's nothing that will affect him. It's because I'm a woman. It was a lot easier out West. But it's still a man's world here. I can't tell you how many jobs I interviewed for before you hired me."

"I'm surprised to hear that. You're easily the best worker we've got on the inspection team."

"What I wanted to know, was, could we move the inspection schedule up a little? Check a few more mines before they pull the plug on the contract?"

"I don't see why not."

Emily was still addressing the back of Buster's head. "I kind of need the money." she looked up at Owen. "I've got a little girl. That's really why I came back. My mama watches her while I work."

"How old's your little girl?"

"Eighteen months."

Owen checked Emily's left hand. There was no wedding ring. He hadn't thought so, but he wasn't sure.

She saw where he was looking. "I wasn't apologizing, just explaining. My mama doesn't work, so I'm the only wage earner in the household."

Owen felt his face flush. He was glad the moon was just a sliver and that there were no streetlights to illuminate his embarrassment. "I'll work in as many inspections as possible the next couple of weeks. They may cancel the contract, but we'll get you as many hours as we can before they do."

Emily knelt and scratched Buster behind the ears. " 'Preciate it."

BACK IN THE house, Emily joined Jeb Stuart in the living room, while Owen returned Buster's leash to its kitchen drawer. Ruth stood next to the stove, pouring tea. Scowling, she thrust a mug at Owen so hard that the hot liquid sloshed over the brim. "That girl is closer to Jeb Stuart's age than to yours."

Owen tried to handle the mug without touching the hot overflow. "I know how old she is. What are you saying?"

"Pick on someone your own age."

"Mom, she's just part of my inspection team. That's why she's here. You thought it was a good idea to invite her. Remember? So Jeb Stuart could see a mining engineer close up."

"I have two eyes. You just spent a lot of time alone with her."

"You have two eyes and one overactive imagination. We walked Buster. We talked about work. There's nothing going on between us. That's preposterous."

Ruth poured another mug of tea and passed it to Owen more carefully. "The young lady drinks tea too. You have that in common."

"That, the same employer, and identical zip codes. I can see why you'd think we're intimate."

Owen returned to the living room and handed Emily the tea. She looked up from her conversation to thank him. He'd never noticed her eyes before. They were the soft violet of hyacinths and seemed perpetually amused.

He sat across the room and watched Emily talk with Jeb Stuart about one of her WVU professors. When she laughed, she lost herself in it and her whole upper body shook, bouncing her red hair away from her shoulders. Jeb Stuart was hanging on every word. Was the boy smitten with her? Jesus, what was he thinking? He was as bad as his mother.

When the evening ended, Owen walked Emily to her pickup. The smell of the river and fresh-mown grass hung in the air. He did the math. Emily was almost twenty years younger than he was, and at least ten years older than Jeb Stuart. Was twenty years too much of a difference? He'd stopped buying *Playboy* when he realized most of the Playmates of the Month were young enough to be his daughter.

Hell, his mother was probably right. Emily would have grown up listening to rock groups he had never heard of. Owen was out of his teens before they took hold and couldn't tell Nine Inch Nails from Electric Orgasm. And if Emily was like Jeb Stuart, she wouldn't know Steven Sondheim from Lorenz Hart.

Emily turned on the ignition of the pickup and Owen was surprised to recognize the song on the tape deck. "Walk the Way the Wind Blows," he said. "Kathy Mattea. Pure country. She's a West Virginian, you know."

He must have sounded a little too pedantic, because Emily looked down from the driver's seat and mimicked his cadence. "And Ella Fitzgerald is an African American, you know." Then she laughed, tossing her auburn hair. "The cut I really like is 'Come from the Heart,' where the father is giving advice."

Owen quoted one of the lines. "Dance like nobody's watching."

Emily nodded. "That's the one. 'And love like you've never been hurt.' I saw that on a T-shirt somewhere."

"It's better when she sings it."

Emily lowered the volume on the tape deck, turning Kathy Mattea into a background murmur. "Well, thank you again. It was a nice evening. Between Susan, that's my little girl, and my mom, I don't get out much."

"We'll have to do it again."

She smiled. Her smile was like her laugh. It was all there. "I'd like that."

Ruth was waiting at the front door when Owen returned to the house. "That girl is closer to Jeb Stuart's age than to yours."

Owen edged by her into the living room. "Mom, you're repeating yourself again."

"Damn straight."

AFTER RUTH AND Jeb Stuart had gone to bed, Owen sat down at the TV monitor to review more parking-lot tapes. Something they recorded had made someone angry enough to cut down the cameras and leave a note saying LET IT BE. But what had they recorded? And who had cut the camera leads?

He began by watching tapes from the graveyard shift. It was easy to fast-forward through those tapes. Most of the time, nothing moved in the parking lot. Then, once an hour, Rollie Gordon would show up, disappear under the cameras to wave his recording wand at the chip behind the water meter, and then reappear a short time later.

April Downey was right. You could set your watch by the rounds of the roly-poly black security guard. As each night wore on, his uniform buttons tended to pop open around his midsection, so that you could even guess how late it was in his shift by the amount of white undershirt puffing out above his belt.

The midday tapes were more difficult to decipher. It had been a lot easier when all he was trying to do was spot a yellow Cadillac. Now he had no idea what he was looking for.

He started fast-forwarding through the midday tapes. Then, afraid he might be missing something, he slowed his review down to real time. Cars came and went. Shoppers left their cars empty-handed and returned laden with packages. At the rate he was going, it would take him two weeks to watch a week's worth of tapes. What was he missing?

After two hours of fast-forwarding, slowing, and rewinding the midday tapes, one thing that was missing dawned on Owen. On the late-night tapes, Rollie Gordon was a regular presence, appearing every hour on the half hour, letting Owen know how much he'd watched and how much he had left to view.

On the midday tapes, though, Lyle Tanner's appearances were much more sporadic. Sometimes he was fifteen minutes early. Other times he was fifteen minutes late. One time he didn't show up on the tape at all when he was supposed to log in.

Where you could set your watch by Rollie Gordon's appearance, Lyle Tanner was so undependable you could barely set your calendar by him. But that undependability hadn't shown up in April Downey's printouts. Or had they both missed it?

Owen checked the printouts April Downey had given him. According to the computer records, Lyle Tanner had logged in at 4:30 p.m. on the second afternoon the surveillance cameras were running. But he didn't appear on the videotape at all between 3:50 and 5:10.

Owen rewound the tape and reviewed it carefully. It was the peak shopping period and the lot was nearly full of people coming and going. He wanted to be sure he wasn't missing anything.

At 3:50, Tanner showed up on the tape, passing under the cameras headed toward the checkpoint behind the drugstore's water meter. According to the day's printout, he'd just logged in at 3:45 at the other end of the mall, fifteen minutes early for his 4:00 pm check-in behind the Big Bear. He reappeared briefly a minute later, disappeared into the mall, and didn't show up again on the tape until 5:10, just five minutes before the printout showed him logging in behind the Big Bear at the other end of the mall.

There was no sign of Tanner at 4:30, when the printout said he had logged in behind the drugstore's water meter. Of course, he could have come up to the checkpoint from behind the cameras without being seen. Whoever had cut the camera leads had done just that to avoid appearing on the tape. But why would Tanner hide out behind the mall's shops?

When he finally appeared on the tape again at 5:10, Tanner came from inside the mall, passed under the cameras, and reappeared almost immediately, headed across the mall parking lot. In the view from the rear, Owen saw that the security guard was wearing a bulging backpack. He hadn't noticed the backpack when Tanner had disappeared under the cameras a minute earlier.

Owen rewound the tape and looked for the backpack. It was there on the tape. He hadn't noticed it from the front view, because the pack's straps matched Tanner's uniform and the backpack wasn't bulging.

241

Something else was wrong with the picture. Owen froze the image and studied it. It was the baton. Tanner's baton was missing. As he walked under the cameras toward the checkpoint, Tanner's backpack and baton holster were empty. When he returned, the backpack was bulging and his baton was back in its holster.

Suddenly Owen understood why Tanner's log-in times were so erratic. And he was pretty sure he knew who had cut down the surveillance cameras.

19

The Law of Maximum Cussedness

Owen unfolded the morning newspaper and lifted his mug of tea, scanning the headlines as he sipped. "Son of a bitch!" He thumped his mug down on the table, splattering hot liquid on the newsprint. "God damn, slippery-assed son of a bitch."

He realized his voice must have carried well beyond the breakfast room when Ruth appeared in the doorway wearing her gardening gloves and Jeb Stuart pounded downstairs in his stocking feet.

"Owen, what on earth?" Ruth asked, pulling off her gloves.

Owen slid the morning paper across the breakfast table toward his mother. The headline below the fold read GOVERNOR APPOINTS DUSTY RHODES ATTORNEY GENERAL.

"They've replaced one son of a bitch with a bigger son of a bitch."

Ruth glanced at Jeb Stuart, who stood framed in the kitchen doorway. "Owen, your language."

"What about my language?" He followed his mother's glance to Jeb Stuart. "Was there some word you didn't understand?"

Jeb Stuart smiled. "Not so far."

"Owen has issues with Dusty Rhodes," Ruth explained to Jeb Stuart.

"Issues." Owen slapped his hand down on the folded paper. "High school debaters have issues. Saying I have issues with Dusty Rhodes is like saying Sitting Bull had issues with General Custer."

"Isn't Dusty Rhodes a baseball player?" Jeb Stuart asked.

"This Dusty Rhodes is a flim-flamming politician," Owen said. "He's crooked as a snake swallowing a corkscrew. He's a murdering, conniving scumbag who's scamming the taxpayers out of millions to clean up the mess made by his mining dam."

Ruth nodded. "As I said, issues."

Jeb Stuart backed out of the doorway. "I've got to get ready for school. Let me know if you need help bringing this new guy down."

"It's likely to take a lot more than a shopping mall videotape to do Dusty Rhodes in," Owen said.

When Jeb Stuart had gone back upstairs, Ruth said, "Imagine, that boy really looks up to you. He believes you can bring down any politician you happen to have issues with."

"You don't know how sorry I am he's mistaken."

As SOON AS Jeb Stuart had left for school, Owen called Thad Reader. He'd been looking forward to telling the sheriff what he'd learned about Lyle Tanner, but the newspaper headline had squashed his enthusiasm.

"Suppose you've seen the morning paper," Owen said.

"Almost makes you wish we hadn't collared Hayes Boyer and his wife," Reader said. "It's the law of maximum cussedness."

"Is that some hill-country version of Murphy's Law?"

"It's Murphy's squared. Not only does your own bread fall butter side down, your worst enemy inherits a bakery."

"That posits a world where your worst enemy prospers."

"Him and all the other bad guys. If 'posits' means what I think it does."

"There's one bad guy who may not prosper much longer. I think I know who cut down the cameras at the mall."

"If you tell me it's Dusty Rhodes, we're going to have a tough time finding anybody in the attorney general's office to prosecute him."

Owen didn't laugh. "No. It's Lyle Tanner, the security guy. He's been rigging his sign-ins to give him time to goof off." Owen explained how Tanner would sign in early behind the Big Bear store, go directly to the drugstore and disappear from sight until he returned as late as possible to make his next Big Bear stop. "I think he rigs some kind of mechanical device to bring his baton in contact with the drug store chip while he's away goofing off."

"And that buys him what? A half hour or so of freedom?"

"More like an hour and a half. From quarter till one hour to quarter after the next."

"But your cameras don't show him rigging this mechanical thingamajig or goofing off." Reader's voice was noncommittal.

"No. They were pointing at the parking lot, not at the chip behind the water meter."

"Tell me again why you feel this is of interest to law enforcement?"

"I think Tanner cut down my cameras. He found out I was taping the parking lot and must have thought I was trying to catch him goofing off."

"How'd he find out you were taping the lot? You told me he thought you were watching the intersection for red-light runners."

"He saw Riley Stokes mooning the cameras from the parking lot."

"Mooning the cameras?" Reader stretched out the *moon* syllable until he sounded like a contented cow. It was the first time he sounded at all interested in Owen's Tanner report.

"Jeb Stuart showed Riley where the cameras were hanging and where they were pointing."

"And Riley showed Tanner the cameras and his bare bottom as well." Reader paused. "Look, Owen, this is all very interesting, but as sheriff I really don't care if Tanner has rigged a robot to take over all his rounds. That's between him and April Downey."

"As sheriff, you should care if he's vandalized a twenty-thousand-dollar piece of equipment. Look, I know this sounds crazy, but I've got a really bad feeling about this guy Tanner."

"That seems clear. Any idea why?"

"He's overreacting. Cutting down my cameras is way over the top. There's no need for it. I told him they'd only be up for a couple of weeks."

"Maybe he didn't believe you."

"He could have waited to see. What's he doing with his hour off that's so important he'd cut down my cameras to keep from being exposed?"

"Maybe he's got himself a holler honey somewhere."

"He's a widower. He doesn't need to sneak around."

"Maybe the holler honey's got a holler hubby."

"Another thing. He lied to us."

"Us?"

"You and me. Way back when we asked him and Cable Stokes whether they'd ever worked in Anson's mine. He said no."

"Cable lied too. Maybe it was contagious. Look Owen, even if you add lying and screwing around to Tanner's rap sheet, it's still a matter for April Downey, not for me."

"There's still the vandalizing."

"But you don't have him on tape doing the vandalizing. You don't even have him on tape blowing off his check-ins. It's all happening off camera."

"Now that I know what he's doing, I can rig a camera to record it."

"Even if you do, it's still a matter for April Downey."

"If I get him on tape, will you have a look and maybe question him about the missing cameras?"

Reader sighed audibly. "Owen, I'm trying to run a murder investigation and figure out who caused the flood that made Lyle Tanner a widower."

"I thought you had Cable pegged for the flood and Anson pegged for Cable's killing."

"I'm beginning to have my doubts. Or your doubts, actually. The coroner says you were right about the late hit coming from Anson's wrench."

"So whoever killed Cable could have picked up Anson's wrench when he planted the body in the mine and whacked the corpse one more time to incriminate Anson."

"Could have. Or Anson could have whacked his brother one last time as an afterthought."

It was Owen's turn to sigh audibly. "How likely is that? If you're really having second thoughts, why not drop the charges against Anson?"

"Anson's still the man with the motive, the mine, and the opportunity. Dropping charges now would violate the wingwalker's first rule: Don't turn loose the strut you're holding until you've caught hold of another strut."

"That sounds like good advice for switching jobs and maybe even ending relationships, but it seems like a poor way to run a system of justice."

Reader's voice turned frosty. "You let me worry about justice. Go on back to clocking your security guard."

"At least I've got my eye on the right man." Owen thumped the receiver down so hard it bounced in its cradle. It was barely past breakfast time, and he'd already managed to promote an asshole to attorney general and have an argument with Thad Reader. The day could only go uphill from here.

As THE DAY wore on, it didn't get much better, but at least it didn't get any worse. Owen spent the morning on the phone rescheduling mine inspections, moving dates up to get as much work done as possible in case they were shut down. Around two in the afternoon, he drove his Saturn to the Contrary mall and took one of the time-lapse recorders from the vandalized trailer. He rigged the recorder to operate with his own video camera using power supplied by the car's battery through an adaptor plugged into the cigarette lighter outlet. Then he left the Saturn parked with the recorder under a duffel bag on the back seat and the camera on the back ledge pointing at the drugstore checkpoint. He covered everything but the camera lens with his Cincinnati Reds jacket and jogged four miles to the house he and his mother were sharing with Jeb Stuart. He'd have the boy drive him back later that evening to pick up the car and check out the videotape to see if he'd caught Tanner scamming the system.

Owen was in the kitchen tearing lettuce into a salad bowl while Ruth dusted a chicken breast with flour when Jeb Stuart came into the kitchen through the back door. He'd just come from baseball practice, and his mud-splattered jersey hung loosely outside his uniform pants.

"Can I talk to you two a minute?" Jeb Stuart asked.

Ruth wiped her white hands on her apron. "Sure hon, what is it?"

"I was wondering, can Riley Stokes stay with us?"

"You mean, like a sleepover?" Ruth asked.

"No, not exactly. I mean could he, like, live here?"

Ruth cast a wary glance at Owen, who stopped shredding lettuce and asked, "Where is Riley now?"

"He's right outside, in my car."

"No. I mean, where's he living now?"

"With his brother, Billy Joe. But it's not a good situation."

"Why not?" Owen asked.

"Billy Joe's dealing dope. And he wants Riley to help. Either that or put up rent money."

"Oh my goodness," Ruth said. "What about the boy's mother?"

"She's living with some man in Tennessee. She wants to wait and see how all these lawsuits settle out before she decides whether to take him in."

"Is Riley likely to have money coming from lawsuits?" Owen asked.

"Billy Joe thinks Riley and all his brothers will come into some money. Their dad was a part of a whole slew of class-action lawsuits."

"That's just horrible," Ruth said. "Expecting a sixteen-year-old to pay his own way."

"Riley's seventeen, actually," Jeb Stuart said. "He got held back a year."

"You've got Riley waiting outside," Owen said. "What have you told him?"

"I told him it would be all right." Jeb Stuart paused, then added, "Probably."

"Probably?" Owen felt an edge coming to his voice. "You told him it would be all right to stay here without asking us?"

Jeb Stuart took a step backward toward the kitchen door. "Well, I mean, it's my house, you know."

Sensing Owen was about to blow up, Ruth said, "We know that,

Jeb Stuart. We thought it would be easier for you to go on living here for the rest of the school year. And your uncle put us in charge of you."

"It's your house," Owen said. "But you're our responsibility."

"Why don't you go wait with Riley and let us talk this over," Ruth said.

"All right." Jeb Stuart shrugged and left through the kitchen door.

"I don't like it," Owen said.

"Why not, Owen? It seems as if the boy has nowhere to go."

"He's a bad influence on Jeb Stuart. That was his hairy butt hanging out of the car window on the video the other night."

"You did some pretty foolish things yourself when you were his age."

"I just have a bad feeling about letting Riley stay here."

"You've been out of sorts all day, starting with that Dusty Rhodes business." Ruth nodded toward the calendar over the pantry door. "We'll be moving back home when the high school year ends. What if we let the boy stay until then? It's only a few months, and it would give us a chance to size up the situation."

Owen felt as if his mind had been vacuumed clean. He didn't want to assume any responsibility for anyone named Stokes, but Ruth's logic seemed so reasonable. And Jeb Stuart clearly wanted it. He shrugged. "All right. But only until the school year ends."

Owen went out through the kitchen door. Riley was pitching to Jeb Stuart from a practice mound Owen and Jeb Stuart had built using the side of the garage as a backstop behind home plate. Buster ran yipping back and forth between the two boys, following the flight of the baseball.

Seeing Owen, Jeb Stuart held the ball and rose from his catcher's crouch. "Well?"

"Riley can stay until the school year ends. Then we'll have to work something out."

"Oh, boy," Jeb Stuart said. "Thanks, Owen."

Riley tilted his head and hung his pitching arm until he looked lopsided. "Yeah, thanks," he said, following Jeb Stuart's lead.

"What about after school's out?" Jeb Stuart asked.

249

"We'll worry about that when the time comes. Let's see how the next couple of months work out first." He turned to Riley. "What about your uncle Anson?"

"What about him?"

"Could you stay with him?" Owen asked.

"Him and Dad didn't get along."

"Doesn't mean you and Anson wouldn't get along. He might like the idea. I could ask him."

"For now, though, you're staying here." Jeb Stuart underhanded the ball to Owen. "I told Riley you could help him with a cutter."

Owen caught the ball and shook his left arm. It felt tight, as if a piano wire had been strung between his shoulder and wrist. "Now?"

Jeb Stuart smiled. "Why not now?"

Owen gripped the ball with his fingers across the seams, walked to the makeshift mound, and showed Riley the grip. "See, you hold it like a four-seam fastball. When you throw it, though, you put a lot of pressure on your middle finger, as if you were using it to cut through the ball. You being right-handed, the extra pressure will give the ball a little movement away from a right-handed batter."

Riley checked Owen's grip with the look of an atheist examining a rosary and stepped back off the mound. "Show me."

Owen toed the rubber with his street shoes and stared down at Jeb Stuart behind the plate. In the back of his mind, he heard the nasal twang of Wait Hoyt, the Reds' radio announcer when he was a boy. "Now pitching for the Cincinnati Reds . . ."

Owen wound up and drove hard off the mound, putting everything he had into the pitch. The ball sailed high over Jeb Stuart's head and splatted off the garage siding just under the eaves.

"Oh, yeah. I see," Riley said.

Buster leapt happily on the loose ball, grabbed it in his mouth, and started back toward Owen.

"Hey, drop it. That's a good baseball." Riley threw his glove at the bounding dog.

Buster dodged the glove, brought the ball to the edge of the mound, and used his nose to nudge it uphill toward Owen.

Jeb Stuart retrieved Riley's glove. "Watch that stuff. The dog didn't hurt you."

"That's right," Owen said. "You're lucky you didn't have any more control over your glove than I had over the ball. If we ever see you mistreating that dog, you'll be looking for another place to stay."

Riley thrust out his chin and chest in a stance that reminded Owen of the young Anson Stokes. "That's a good ball. He slobbered all over it."

"Buster's used to chasing old tennis balls where slobbering isn't a concern." Owen picked up the baseball, wiped it clean with his shirt-tail, and rubbed it up with both hands. "Let's try it again."

Jeb Stuart crouched behind the plate. This time Owen held back a little, making sure of his control, and he hit Jeb Stuart's glove with a satisfying pop.

"It just moved a little bit," Riley said.

"That's all it has to move to fool a batter." Owen caught Jeb Stuart's underhanded toss and handed the ball to Riley. "You try it."

Riley stepped up on the mound and showed his grip to Owen. "Like that?"

Owen nodded. "Like that." He stepped back. "Steve Carlton said that the best way to make it cut at the last minute is to 'throw the shit out of it.' "

Riley's face wrinkled with concentration. "Who's Steve Carlton?"

"Geeze, jerkoff, don't you know anything?" Jeb Stuart said.

Riley flung the ball as hard as he could at Jeb Stuart.

"Nice pitch," Owen said. "Good and hard with a little movement right at the end."

Jeb Stuart threw the ball back to Riley. "Steve Carlton's just the best left-handed pitcher in the last twenty-five years."

"Hell, I'm only seventeen. How do you expect me to know that?"

Owen could see that being a surrogate father was getting to be more complicated than he had anticipated. He walked up onto the mound and checked Riley's grip. "Fingers across the seams. You follow any big-league teams?"

"No. Never had time." Riley wound up and threw the ball at the catcher's target. Just before it reached Jeb Stuart, the ball darted to the left and bounced off the thumb of his glove.

Buster bounded after the loose ball, but Jeb Stuart got to it first.

"Another nice pitch," Owen said. "Ever see a big-league game?"

"A few. On TV."

"Maybe we can get the two of you to a Reds' game. Keep practicing that cutter. Dinner will be ready in about twenty minutes." Owen slapped his leg twice. "Come on, Buster, let the boys practice. We'll find you some used tennis balls to chase."

AFTER DINNER, OWEN asked Jeb Stuart to drive him back to the shopping center so that he could pick up the car he'd left with the camera in back recording Lyle Tanner's checkpoint activity.

"What time do you want to go?"

"Tanner's shift ends at 11:00, but that's a little late for you, and my car's battery may not last that long. If Tanner's going to goof off, he's more likely to do it in mid-shift. Why don't we wait until he's finished his 9:30 check-in."

"Can Riley come?"

Owen had waited until Riley was out emptying the garbage to ask Jeb Stuart for a ride. "Let's just keep it between us. The fewer people who know what we're doing, the less likely anyone will tip off Tanner."

"I don't think Riley will tell anyone."

"I'd rather not take the chance."

In the car on the way to the shopping center, Jeb Stuart said, "You don't like Riley much, do you?"

"I was hoping it didn't show."

"Can I ask why?"

"I knew his father."

"Is that fair?"

"It's how I feel. I don't know that 'fair' enters into it."

"You've always been fair with me."

"I knew your father."

"I know Riley's a little rough around the edges."

"From what I've seen, he's rough clear through."

"Thing is, he's had a pretty tough time lately."

Owen smiled. "I'd say that's an understatement."

"What I'd like is, if you could be as fair with him as you have been with me."

Owen's face flushed. He was embarrassed that the boy would have to make such a request, but proud of him for asking. He looked away, out the passenger window. "I'll try, Jeb Stuart."

"It's only a couple of months till school's out."

Owen reached out and patted the hand the boy had rested on top of the steering wheel. "I said, I'd try, Jeb Stuart. And I'll try to find a home for Riley when the two months are up."

Owen's car was the only one left in the last row of the parking lot when Jeb Stuart pulled up beside it. They'd tried to arrive at a time when Lyle Tanner was scheduled to be at the other end of the mall, but Tanner was so unpredictable that Owen piled out of Jeb Stuart's car and into his own as quickly as possible. He'd brought jumper cables in case the recorder had run down his car's battery, but the Saturn started on the first turn of the ignition key, and Owen burned rubber getting out of the parking lot.

Back home, Owen fast-forwarded the tape through the times Lyle Tanner was scheduled to check in beside the drugstore. Tanner made each of his stops exactly on the half hour, waving his baton at the chip and returning to his shopping center rounds right away. If the security guard had discovered a way to scam the system and create free time for himself, it certainly wasn't obvious from that day's tape.

THE NEXT MORNING, Owen left early for McDowell County to make the first of the mine inspections he'd rescheduled at Emily's request. He drove alone, hoping they'd finish early enough so that he could leave his car and camera in the Contrary mall for most of Lyle Tanner's shift. He hadn't met with Emily since the night they'd shared dinner and a walk with Buster, and he found he was looking forward to seeing her again. He'd loaded his glove compartment with Kathy Mattea tapes and was singing along with "Lonesome Standard Time" as he swung the Saturn around the hairpin turns leading to the Stone-broke Mine.

He stopped at the Chink Creek Dam above the mine to check his GPS readings and make sure the location of the dam had been recorded accurately on the map the state's Department of Environmental Protection had provided.

By the time he pulled up in front of the chain-link fence surrounding the abandoned mine entrance, he saw that Emily had already arrived and left the fence gate open for him. He parked beside her pickup, went through the fence gate, and shouted, "Hello in there" at the mine entrance.

Nobody answered.

He thought it a little strange that Emily would move very far into the mine without him, but she'd probably driven down with Virgil Gibbs, and the two of them must have decided to get started without waiting. They knew he'd be stopping at the dam site, and Emily and Virgil were certainly capable of starting the inspection on their own.

Owen checked his battery pack, connected it to his mining helmet, and shouldered the black leather case holding his video equipment. He stopped at the mine entrance, shined his cap light on the brown limestone walls, and called in, "Emily, Virgil, I'm here."

Still no answer.

Had he missed something? Had Emily and Virgil taken a hike around the mountain face while waiting for him? Had they left a note? There was no note visible on the pickup. They must have just gone so deep into the mine they couldn't hear him shout.

He started into the dark cavern, shining his cap light on the walls and ceiling, looking for signs of seepage, and between the parallel rails on the tunnel floor, looking for signs of Emily and Virgil.

Stale, dead air weighed on Owen. He thought he heard a skittering noise somewhere ahead of him and called out again without getting an answer.

He followed the main shaft for a short distance and had just passed a break in the wall marking the first side tunnel when he heard the noise again. This time it was closer, and seemed to come from the tunnel he'd just passed.

He turned and shined his cap light into the side passage when another cap light flashed on, blinding him momentarily. He blinked to clear his eyes and gradually made out the looming form of Lyle Tanner stepping out from the side tunnel.

Tanner held a shotgun leveled at Owen's midsection. Extra shells were clipped to the left-hand pocket of his orange hunting vest. Four sticks of dynamite protruded from the right-hand pocket. But the most disturbing aspect of his outfit was not his vest but his headgear. He was wearing Emily's bright red miner's helmet.

20

Shagging and Ragging

TANNER jerked the double-barreled shotgun toward the mine's dark interior and brought it back to point at Owen's midsection. "Just keep on walking."

Owen took two steps in the direction Tanner had indicated and stopped. "I'll keep walking. Just be careful where you point that thing."

"You're the one needs to be careful. Think I'm some kind of fool? Think I don't know you've been taping me with the cameras in them phony light standards? Think I don't know what your car looks like? Think I didn't see the camera poking out of the neck of that Reds jacket in the back window?"

Owen began walking again, keeping just ahead of the shotgun barrels. "Jesus. I thought you were overreacting when you cut down my mall cameras. This is way over the edge."

"Overreacting?" Tanner's voice sounded genuinely puzzled.

Owen felt the hairs on the back of his neck stand on end. He finally figured out what had been nagging at him. "It was your alibi, wasn't it? For when you worked the late shift. You blew Anson's mine. You called in the alarm."

"I couldn't have done those things. I was logging in on my rounds when the shaft blew. You can check the records."

"No. You rigged a box to bring your baton in contact with the check-in chip behind Rexall Drug's water meter while you were off calling in the alarm."

Owen stopped walking. Tanner's cap light cast his shadow along the rails leading deep into the mine. The security guard prodded Owen in the back with the shotgun. "Just keep moving."

"I'm not the only one who knows," Owen said. "I've been working with Sheriff Thad Reader."

"Bullshit. If the sheriff knew anything, I'd be in jail already, and you wouldn't still be trying to videotape my check-ins."

"We needed positive proof for a trial. That's why we planted the camera in the car. It won't do you any good to kill me."

"Kill you? What makes you think I'm going to kill you? You're about to have a tragic mining accident."

"Hard to imagine a mining accident that would leave me filled with buckshot."

"I'm hoping I won't have to use the shotgun. If I do, though, I'll leave you buried under enough rock so they won't try to dig you out. Just put a memorial marker back there at the shaft entrance."

The tunnel walls telescoped in Owen's mind, closing in on him. "What about Emily Kruk?"

Owen could sense the shotgun barrels dipping as Tanner shrugged behind him. "Wrong place, wrong time. Her and Virgil both."

"Where are they?"

"Almost to the end of this here shaft."

Owen dreaded the answer to his next question. "You shotgunned them?"

"No. No need to use the gun if I don't have to. You're right about it being a tip-off. I just put them out and took their cap lights. They won't be going anywhere before the mine blows."

Owen slowed his pace, trying to sense exactly where the shotgun barrels were located. "Is that necessary? They're no threat to you."

"They are now. I couldn't figure out how to get you without getting them too."

"And you wanted to get me because I'd uncovered your little 'time-out tool.'"

"You were about to. Since I saw your camera in the car, I didn't use the box the other night. I figured you already knew too much, though."

"And you used the box to give you an alibi when you blew up Anson's mine."

"That wasn't why I rigged the box. At first, it was just what you said, a 'time-out tool.' That's why I built it, anyhow."

Tanner's voice was calm and reasonable, as if he were giving directions to a slow child. Owen recalled Thad Reader's remarks about criminal imbeciles and reminded himself that the man behind him holding a shotgun had already killed at least three people. He slowed a little more and the shotgun barrels caught him right below his spine.

Tanner prodded him with the barrels. "It's a pretty simple tool, really. Just a box with a timer and a cam that runs the baton up against the chip and back again. I tested it out until it was foolproof."

Owen moved ahead, lengthening the space between his back and the shotgun. They passed a side tunnel. He tried to remember how many side tunnels were mapped on the plans he'd reviewed. Eight tunnels, he thought. Maybe nine. But he wasn't sure whether they'd already passed two or three. He'd been too stunned to notice. He'd have to pay closer attention. At a minimum, they were likely to pass at least five more breaks in the wall before the main shaft ended. Whatever he was going to do, he'd have to act before they reached the end of the shaft, where Tanner probably planned to set off his blast.

"Pretty clever device," Owen said to keep Tanner talking about his time-out tool.

"I thought so. First time I used the tool to give me a real time-out, I left the mall in the middle of my shift and headed for my trailer. Thought I'd surprise Maddie, get in a little home poking."

Owen swung his cap light beam from wall to wall, looking for anything that might distract Tanner. The smooth blank limestone reflected the beam without providing any hope.

"Well, I was the one who got surprised," Tanner continued. I showed up outside the trailer just before two in the morning and found Maddie was already occupied. With Cable Stokes."

"You walked in on them?"

"Hell no. No need to do that. Them trailer walls was pretty thin tin. I could hear right through. There was no doubt what Maddie was doing. Or who she was doing it with."

Empathize, Owen thought. Keep him talking. Keep yourself alive. "My ex-wife was unfaithful with a first-class jerk. It must have been a real shock to you."

"That wasn't the worst of it. Worst of it was, Cable would come to our Friday night poker games, him and me and Virgil Gibbs and some others, and make jokes about Maddie's weight."

Owen recalled Cable's jibe about a double-wide coffin at the memorial service. "That must have really hurt."

"I started noticing it the week after I found out Cable was planking Maddie. He'd start in with some snotty remark just as soon as he pulled up a chair to buy chips. 'Say Lyle,' he'd smirk. 'I hear the NFL wants to use Maddie's panties to measure first downs.' "

"Everybody laughed but me. They must have seen I wasn't taking it very good, 'cause everybody piled on. It got to be a regular part of the game, just like dealer's choice. Cable would always lead off."

Tanner imitated Cable by raising his voice an octave and exaggerating his nasal twang. "Hey Lyle, I hear when Maddie wants to haul ass, she has to make two trips."

"Or, 'Say Lyle, must be tough finding Maddie's pussy in all them folds of fat. What do you do, roll her in flour and aim for the wet spot?' Know what I said to that? I said, 'You should know, Cable.' "

Tanner paused. "Couple of the guys laughed, but they didn't really get it. Stopped Cable cold for a second or so, but then he come back with, 'Know what I'd do to get through them fatty folds? I'd tickle her under her tit till she pees and swim upstream like a salmon.' "

Where Tanner had been self-assured in describing his time-out tool and matter-of-fact in recounting his wife's infidelity, his voice climbed and fell, cracked and broke, as he related Cable's jibes.

"Cable would lead off, but everybody chimed in," Tanner continued, his voice hoarse and choking. "Like, Cable would say, 'Hey, Lyle, is it true Maddie's so big she's got her own zip code?' and Virgil would jump in and say something like, 'Zip code, hell. She's got her own solar system.' "

Tanner sucked in his breath and expelled it in a single snort. "I tell you, I don't mind sending Virgil Gibbs to his maker at all. Not after the way he insulted my Maddie.

"And Cable." Something like a short sob escaped Tanner's lips. "My God, Cable. Here he was shagging my wife during the week and ragging on her Friday nights."

Tanner's voice turned firm. "Well, I decided to put a stop to it. I waited till Riley was out of town, so that them two was the only ones left in the hollow, and blew out Anson Stokes' old mineshaft."

Good God, Owen thought. This is all about Cable's chubby chasing. He tried to keep his voice level. "You risked flooding three counties just to kill two people?"

"Well, there's the beauty part. A flood like that, where the water comes through an underground shaft, is only likely to kill somebody who's right smack dab in its path and close to the mouth of the mine."

"The shaft acts like a firehose nozzle," Owen said.

"Exactly. Reason I know is, there was a flood like that a couple of years back in Martin County, Kentucky, just the other side of the Big Sandy. One of A. T. Massey's dams busted through into an underground shaft. Flooded out two hollows, raised creek levels, and blackened the Big Sandy all the way to the Ohio and beyond, but it didn't kill nobody.

"Kentucky studied the flood and the feds studied it some more. Assigned a blue-ribbon panel that come out with a big thick report. One of the panel members, a geologist from Kansas, told how the size of the mine mouth limited the flow rate. I heard him on the evening news. You get a breakthrough into an underground mine, he said, and you'll get some environmental damage and flood a few backyards, but the chance of losing lots of lives is pretty much zippo."

They passed another side tunnel. Owen counted only four more till the end, and the only plan he had so far was to walk slower. Not a very promising strategy.

Tanner continued to talk about the blue-ribbon panel set up to study the Kentucky flood. "So this guy from Kansas says the only way anybody is likely to die from a mineshaft flood is if they're standing right near the mine mouth.

"But that's the situation I had, don't you see. Anson's old shaft looked right down on Drybone Hollow, and the only two trailers in the hollow was Cable's and ours. If the dam busted through Anson's shaft when Riley was gone, I was pretty sure the only lives lost would be Maddie's and Cable's."

"Except Cable wasn't home," Owen said. "And you had that Tennessee couple crossing the Crawley Creek Bridge."

"I never intended to hurt anybody else. Them honeymooners was just in the wrong place at the wrong time."

"And you caused forty million dollars of property damage."

"I called 911 soon as the blast went off, so's they could get the hole stopped up quicklike. You go look at that creekbed now. It's as clear as it ever was. Hell, I've moved right back in."

"Into a trailer provided by the government."

"They owed me that one. I wasn't greedy like Cable. One trailer was all I needed."

"Must have galled you that Cable wasn't home when the flood hit." Owen felt a shiver of apprehension. "It was you that planted dynamite in his truck."

"I could have got him then, if you and the sheriff hadn't showed up and made him drive those cinderblocks back to where he got them. Screwed up my timing."

"You're lucky the blast didn't kill a few more innocent people."

"Cable's the lucky one. Man's luckier than a double-dicked dog in a breeding kennel. His luck run out, though. I got him eventually. He come to the mall to load up on provisions. Parked way behind the Big Bear like he didn't want to be seen. His car was right near my checkpoint, so I seen it when I was making my rounds."

Jesus, Owen thought. The Big Bear connection. It had been right there in front of him, but he'd been focusing on the other end of the mall, on the drugstore and the check-in chip.

"I hung around till Cable come out with a cart full of groceries. Offered to help him load his trunk. When he was bent over it, I coldcocked him with my baton and finished the job with his own tire iron. Then I loaded him into the trunk." Tanner laughed, a series of short, high-pitched barks. "Helped him load his trunk, just like I promised."

They passed another break marking a side tunnel. Only three more till the end, Owen calculated, and the only thing he could think of to do was to keep Tanner talking. "So you ditched Cable's car and wheelbarrowed his body over the backwoods path to Anson's mine. Hit him once with Anson's wrench for good measure."

"You got that part figured pretty good."

"So does the sheriff."

"That turd don't flush. If the sheriff really had it figured, he wouldn't have charged Anson with Cable's murder."

Owen stopped and turned quickly, shining his caplight directly into Tanner's eyes. "Why'd you pick on Anson?"

Tanner blinked, but the shotgun barrels didn't waver. He brought one hand up to shield his eyes. "Why do you think I picked Anson? Hell, everybody in the county must have heard him threaten to kill Cable at least once."

Tanner stepped backward, taking the shotgun barrels out of Owen's reach. "Besides, I figured Anson owed me. I had a little piece of Cable's share of the Stokes' first dog hole. Won it at poker." He leveled the barrels at Owen's stomach. "Just turn around and keep moving."

Owen turned and plodded deeper into the dark shaft. "That's the share Anson bought out when coal prices tumbled."

"For loose change that wouldn't fill a gnat's navel. Not a patch on what the mine was finally worth."

Owen fought to keep his voice even, to hide his outrage. "When you killed Cable, you know you caused Mary Beth Hobbs' death and damn near did in Riley Stokes as well."

"That's on Cable's head. I didn't know nothing about what he'd done with them two. Another case of wrong place, wrong time."

"Lot of that going around."

"Appears like you may have caught a dose of it yourself."

They came abreast of the next side tunnel. Something skittered in the left-hand shaft. Both men swung their cap lights toward the noise, freezing a huge gray rat in the glare. The rat rose on its haunches, turned, and scampered away down the side shaft.

Owen realized too late that Tanner had swung the shotgun toward the noise at the same time they'd turned their cap lights on the rat. By the time the shift in the shotgun's aim registered on Owen, the barrels were back pointed at his midsection, and he'd missed his chance.

He could feel his heart beating faster. Would he get another chance? Maybe he could make one. There were one or two side tunnels left before the shaft ended. He directed his cap light toward the shaft floor, looking for anything that might distract Tanner, and raised his voice, hoping he could wake up another rat. "Look, Tanner, so far you've only deliberately killed the two people who wronged you. Like you say, a few others happened to be in the wrong place at the wrong time. What you're getting into now, though, is a whole new ball game. Once it starts, it'll never stop."

Tanner raised his voice to respond at the same level. "I thought on that. Don't see any way around it, though."

"There's no need to kill the girl," Owen yelled back. "Or Virgil. They don't know anything."

"Too late now," Tanner shouted. "Virgil's the one told me about your inspection. And the girl seen me conk Virgil."

"The sheriff knows everything I know," Owen said, still shouting. "He'll piece it together. Sooner or later, you'll have to run."

"I'll take that chance," Tanner yelled back.

"Why not run now? Just take off. Tie us up so you'll get a good head start. There's no need for more killing." Owen's words echoed down the empty shaft.

"If I bring enough mountain down on top of you, I may not need to run. Not ever."

Owen could feel his throat getting hoarse. He stopped shouting and said in a level voice, "You're not giving Thad Reader enough credit. Another mine explosion is going to look pretty suspicious. And he knows I was videotaping you."

Tanner lowered his voice to a menacing rasp. "You didn't figure it out for sure until you saw me here with my shotgun. Reader may never figure it out."

Owen's throat hurt and he couldn't think of anything more to say. He played his cap light beam on the tunnel walls and floor. Shards of broken glass and rubble lay between the rails about ten yards ahead of them. He began to slow down, waiting for the shotgun barrels to poke his spine.

Tanner filled the silence with his raspy voice. "I told Maddie some of the worst cracks Cable made about her, hoping it would turn her against him. Like the one about the wet spot in the flour. I told her that one. Told her it come from Cable. Know what she did?"

Owen stopped just before he reached the rubble. "No. What did she do?"

"She just laughed. Didn't get mad or nothing. If I'd have said that, she'd have brained me and locked me out of the bedroom. Cable says it, though, and she just laughs. Said Cable was just jealous." He pitched his voice higher, imitating his wife. "Said, 'Everyone knows fat girls give you more cushion for the pushin'.'"

Owen felt the double barrels in the small of his back.

"Move along, there," Tanner said.

Owen stumbled forward and pitched headfirst into the rubble, breaking his fall with his outstretched hands. A glass shard stung and bloodied his right palm.

"Get on up," Tanner said. "We just got a little ways to go."

Owen pulled himself up onto one knee. He bent forward and placed his hands on the ground like a sprinter to shove himself upright. As he rose, he closed his bloody fist around a handful of pebbles and glass shards.

Tanner prodded him with the shotgun. "Move along there."

Owen shuffled ahead, cradling the shards and pebbles in his right hand just above his belt buckle. As they approached the next pair of side tunnels, he slowed again and lodged his thumb behind the pebbles as if he were going to shoot marbles.

When they came to the break in the wall, Owen flicked the debris as far as he could into the left-hand tunnel, hoping that Tanner would swing his shotgun barrels toward the sound.

The instant the pebbles landed, Owen stepped back and chopped at the barrels with his forearm, knocking them away from his body.

One barrel exploded in a blaze of light, filling the empty tunnel with buckshot.

Owen clamped both hands on the shotgun barrels and yanked, trying to pull the weapon away from Tanner.

Tanner stumbled forward, but he managed to keep his finger in the trigger guard and one hand on the shaft of the gun. He regained his balance and began jerking the gun back and forth, hoping either to wrest it away from Owen or point the muzzle at his body. "Still got one load left for you, Allison."

Owen slipped and slid on the tunnel floor, struggling to keep both hands clamped on the shotgun barrels. He knew he was dead if he released them or allowed Tanner to swing the muzzle toward him.

Tanner jerked the gun toward the tunnel wall and swung it back quickly, trying to point the barrels at Owen's midsection.

Owen gave ground on the backswing, still clinging to the barrels, when his heel caught on a ground rail and he stumbled backward. Some innate survival instinct kicked in perversely, causing him to release the barrels so that he could cushion his fall with his hands. He landed on his tailbone and crabwalked backward, dreading the shotgun blast.

Tanner barked out a single harsh laugh. As he raised the gun to fire, a figure sprang from the darkness of the side tunnel swinging a shovel.

The shovel blade clanged off Tanner's helmet, sending it flying, and the gun barrel exploded.

Pain seared through Owen's right foot.

The second swipe of the shovel caught Tanner flush on his unprotected head. As the security guard crumpled and fell, Owen saw that the shovel wielder was Emily Kruk.

Caught in the glare of Owen's cap light, with her hair wild about her face and her backpack flapping, Emily looked like an avenging angel. She straddled Tanner's prone body and raised the shovel to deliver another blow. When the body didn't move, she hesitated, then plunged the shovel blade into the tunnel floor, retrieved the loose helmet, and stripped Tanner of his utility belt.

She strapped the belt around her waist, connected the battery pack to her helmet, and shined her cap light on Owen. "You all right?"

Owen looked down at his right foot. His boot extended into a circle of buckshot and was pitted with tiny holes. "Could be a lot worse."

"Son of a bitch took Virgil and me by surprise." Emily helped Owen to his feet. "Can you walk?"

Owen's foot felt as if it had been stung by a hive of angry bees. When he tried putting weight on his leg, it buckled.

He hopped on his good leg over to the shovel, uprooted it, and put the blade under his right armpit, using the handle as a crutch. "I can walk enough to get out of here and call for help."

"I'd best see to Virgil. He's out cold just beyond the last tunnel break. That man hit him pretty hard, then clobbered me and left us in the dark. When I came to and couldn't rouse Virgil, I started back along the main wall." Emily nodded toward the side tunnel. "I took to that tunnel when I heard you coming. You two were shouting something fierce."

"I was trying to wake up the rats."

Emily picked up Tanner's shotgun, straddled his body, and rolled him over onto his back. She bent over, took two shotgun shells from the security guard's vest, and reloaded his weapon. Then she rested the loaded shotgun under her arm and stood looking down at Tanner. "Sure seems like he's out." She kicked him once, hard, just below his orange vest with her steel-toed boot. There was no response.

"He ought to be out at least as long as Virgil. Better tie him up, though, just to be sure." Emily bent and took the dynamite sticks from Tanner's vest. "We're just lucky he didn't hit me as hard as he hit the old man. Guess he figured I was the weaker sex."

21

Marxmanship

O WEN's hospital room was small and cramped, with a TV set that jutted out from a wall fixture high in the corner. He used the remote to flip through the available channels. It was too early for base-ball scores, but AMC was featuring a Marx Brothers festival, and he tuned into the beginning of *The Cocoanuts*. Groucho was telling Mar-garet Dumont she reminded him of the Prince of Wales. "I don't mean the present Prince of Wales, one of the old Wales. And believe me, I know a whale when I see one."

Owen tried to imagine Margaret Dumont's husband angry enough to kill Groucho over a few fat jokes. But then, Margaret Dumont always played a widow in the Marx Brothers' movies. Lucky for Groucho.

On the TV screen, Dumont was saying, "I don't think you'd love me if I were poor." Owen mouthed the response aloud along with Groucho. "I might, but I'd keep my mouth shut."

Thad Reader backed through the door carrying a large cardboard box. He set the box down on the bedside stand and looked around the tiny room. "You alone? I thought I heard you talking to someone."

"Just me and Groucho." Owen switched off the TV. "Now it's just me and you."

Reader rapped the cast that covered Owen's right leg from his toes to his kneecap. "This is where I came in. What'd the doctors say?"

"They say the human foot has twenty-six bones. I, however, have thirty-two bone segments."

"Shotgun's a nasty weapon."

"They say the cast can come off in a month."

"When you're young, you heal fast. What about lasting side effects?"

"I won't be running any marathons."

"Ought to *thank* Tanner for that."

"Some good in everything, I guess."

Reader reached into the cardboard box and pulled out a streetlight fixture and a small video camera. "Found your cameras in Lyle Tanner's trailer. Turns out you were right about him."

"I was right about him having something to hide. If I'd known what, I'd still be walking."

"But you'd have no excuse for skipping marathons."

"I'll give you that." Owen slumped back against his pillow. "Any evidence at Lyle's place that he blew Anson's mine?"

The sheriff shook his head. "Nope. Didn't really expect to find any. We're trying to match voice prints with his 911 call."

"Shouldn't be too hard to nail him for the blast. He admitted it to me."

"Right now, he's denying he had anything to do with the mine blast."

"Does he deny spraying my foot with buckshot?"

"Claims he only did that because you were invading his privacy with your cameras."

"Holy Christ."

"He admits everything that happened with you, Virgil, and Emily. It's the Drybone Hollow flood he's denying. I think he's afraid the feds will take back his nice new trailer if they know he's responsible for the flood."

"I'm sure the feds will be glad to provide alternative accommodations."

"There's no chance he'll weasel out of it. We'll have the voice print and your testimony. In addition, we've already got clothing fibers and prints from Cable's car. What's more, it's likely Judge Vereen will hear the case."

"Seems like overkill, but it couldn't happen to a more deserving guy."

Anson Stokes appeared in the doorway, knocked twice on the frame, and entered without waiting for an invitation. "How they hanging, Owen? Gonna let you go home soon?"

"Tomorrow." Owen rapped twice on his cast. "Knock plaster."

Anson acknowledged Thad Reader's presence by nodding and pointing at the box beside the sheriff. "What's in the box? A little crow for you to eat?"

"Sorry for your trouble, Anson," the sheriff said. "You sure fit the profile, though."

Anson waved off the sheriff's apology. "Hell, it was just a matter of time. I would have killed Cable if I'd seen him."

Anson pulled a video camera and its streetlight housing from the cardboard box and examined it. "Looks like you found Owen's cameras."

"It was Tanner cut them down," the sheriff said. "He didn't want Owen recording his job lapses."

Anson returned the camera and light fixture to the box. "Reckon I could repair that trailer rig, then buy it and put it beside my guardhouse permanent. That way you wouldn't be stuck for the cost."

"That'd be a load off my mind and my wallet," Owen said.

"Least I can do. I owe you big time. If you don't flush out Tanner, the sheriff here might have nailed my balls to the wall for something I only wanted to do."

"I had in mind a different sort of payback," Owen said.

"Name it."

"Your nephew Riley needs a home."

Anson frowned. "Thought he was staying with his brother."

"That didn't work out."

Anson scratched his forehead. "Never quite saw myself as a daddy."

"I never quite saw you as a man who could run a mine," Owen said. "Or repair a surveillance fixture."

"Regular pillar of the community," Reader said.

"I wouldn't go that far," Anson said. "What about the boy's mama?"

"She'll take him in, but only if he gets some significant money from those class-action suits Cable signed onto."

Anson screwed his face into a disgusted frown. "Woman's about as useless as a eunuch's condom." He made a sucking noise with his tongue against his teeth. "I'd have to ask Mary Gil."

"What I hear," the sheriff said, "you're the master in that house. What you say goes."

"Don't believe everything you hear." Another, longer, sucking noise came from Anson's mouth. "What the hell, why not? We can do it. I mean, the boy's out of diapers and sleeps through the night. The worst is over, right?"

"Another year, and you can send him off to college," Owen said.

Anson laughed. "Jesus. College. For a Stokes. That'll sure take him above his raising."

"He seems bright enough," Owen said. "And he's got a fastball that could land him a scholarship."

"Hell, I could help out with college expenses," Anson said. "No problem there, now that the mine's reopened. I'd still have to clear it with Mary Gil, though."

"The boy is family, after all," Owen said.

"Don't know that's much of a recommendation," Anson said. "Don't forget, Cable was family too."

After Thad and Anson had gone, Owen reached for the remote to catch up with the Marx Brothers. The phone rang before he could turn on the TV, and he picked up the receiver to hear Judith say, "Your mom called me. Is it the same leg as last time?"

He found he was happy to hear her voice. "Same leg."

"And you're worried about your *mom* repeating herself."

"Did she talk to you about repeating herself?"

"More than once."

"It's not funny. She either denies she's doing it or makes up excuses. Her favorite is that she wanted to make sure I was paying attention."

"Get it diagnosed properly. Then you can either stop worrying or start taking some positive steps."

"From what I hear, all the steps are negative."

When Judith didn't respond immediately, Owen assumed she was going to attack his pessimism and braced to defend himself. Instead she changed the subject, asking, "How are things going with Jeb Stuart?"

"I think it's working out pretty well. We're lining up colleges and scholarships."

"Well, you've always wanted a child."

"That's true."

"Your mom says you've got more than one."

"You mean Riley Stokes. He's only with us until the school year ends."

"No. The child your mom mentioned was female. I believe 'cradle robber' was the term she used."

"Oh, for Christ's sake. That's all in Mom's imagination. The girl is closer to Jeb Stuart's age than mine, and there's nothing going on between us."

"I'm sorry. I had to check. It was working on my mind."

"That's okay. I understand. The thought of you and Dusty Rhodes worked on me for a good while."

"Your mom says Dusty made attorney general."

"Because of something I did. How's that for irony?"

"What you did was put a scoundrel behind bars. That's nothing to be ashamed of. Besides, I keep telling you Dusty's not as bad as you think."

"That's pretty faint praise. The man could be shown to be the bastard son of Satan and still not be as bad as I think."

"You're still after him, then?"

Owen sighed. "Oh, yes. I just don't have the feeling I'm gaining ground."

"I miss you. I even miss your worries and your perpetual pessimism."

"I miss you too." It came out as a reflexive response, but he recognized it as the truth.

"But you're not coming back."

"Not for a while." He tried to explain. "There's Mom, and Jeb Stuart. And I've even found some useful work."

"Good for you." Her clipped voice cut him off.

It was clear she didn't want to hear more, but he went on anyhow. "Staying just feels right for now. It's like I belong here. It's got nothing to do with you."

"That's the whole problem, isn't it? It's got nothing to do with me."

After Judith hung up, Owen stared at the phone. He'd said it all wrong. He considered calling back, but all he could think of were a dozen different ways to say the wrong thing again. He dropped the phone and picked up the remote.

On the TV screen, *The Cocoanuts* had ended, and the Marx Brothers festival was moving on to *Animal Crackers*. The credits for *Animal Crackers* were rolling when Emily showed up, carrying a Blenko glass vase holding a dozen yellow roses.

Owen reached for the remote to turn the TV off, but Emily said, "No. Leave it on for a couple of minutes. Groucho's about to sing 'Hello, I Must Be Going.'"

Owen dropped the remote onto the bedspread. "A woman after my own heart."

Emily surveyed the cramped room. The only level spot for the flowers was the window sill. She rearranged the bouquet so it would fit on the narrow sill and they watched the beginning of *Animal Crackers* while Owen brought her up to date on his doctors' diagnoses. Emily shushed him when Groucho began singing his theme song.

When the song had ended, Owen turned off the TV and asked, "How's Virgil?"

"Seems okay. They examined him for a possible concussion, watched him for four hours to be sure he was all right, and let him go. He had a room just down the hall. Hank Clanton from Johnson, Crane visited him there."

"Guess I'm not surprised Clanton didn't stop in to visit me."

"You were out at the time having your foot fixed. Turns out your mall surveillance cost them their state contract. Clanton said the state issued a stop-work order on their inspections."

"They'll have to give Johnson, Crane thirty days to wrap things up. You could still get some inspection time in."

Emily frowned. "Clanton didn't mention that."

"In any case, the state will put the work out for rebid. The inspections need to be finished."

"Will you bid on the new contract?"

"Oh, yes." Owen looked down at his cast. "I'm not going anywhere. I'm here for the duration." He realized it was the first time he'd admitted it out loud.

Emily smiled. "That's nice to know." She followed Owen's gaze to his cast and her smile disappeared. "If I'd swung on Tanner a little earlier, you wouldn't be here."

Owen reached for her hand. "If you'd swung a little later I wouldn't be here either. And I wouldn't be able to smell those flowers."

Jeb Stuart surged into the room, forcing Emily to drop Owen's hand, and move into the corner by his headboard. The boy was followed by Ruth and then by Riley Stokes, who hung back, barely squeezing into the small space between the door and the foot of the bed.

"Oh, wow," Jeb Stuart said. "Look at that cast."

"Shotgun blast broke six bones in my foot," Owen said.

"I thought I was through with hospitals when I finished chemo," Ruth said. "Can't you be more careful?"

Instead of assuming Ruth was kidding, Emily took her at her word. "It wasn't exactly his fault."

"I understand that, dear," Ruth said. "I gather you were with Owen."

"If she hadn't been there," Owen said, "the buckshot would have hit higher and I'd be wearing a coffin instead of a cast."

"Well, then," Ruth said to Emily, "I suppose I should thank you."

There was an uncomfortable silence, which Owen broke by telling Riley, "I think we've found you a home. Your uncle Anson would like to be your guardian. He just needs to run it by his wife."

Riley pressed his back against the door frame. "I don't know. My dad never liked him."

"Your dad was jealous of his success," Owen said.

"He's family," Ruth said. "That counts for a lot."

"Will I have to move out before the weekend?" Riley asked.

"You just take your time," Ruth said. "There's no hurry."

Riley shifted from foot to foot in the doorway. "It's just . . . well, we had something planned."

"The Reds are starting a new home stand in Cincy this weekend," Jeb Stuart said. "I thought we might go. You, me, and Riley."

"Sounds like a great idea," Owen said. "You drive. I'll finance the trip."

"Is this an all-male jaunt?" Emily asked. "Or are you an equal-opportunity tour guide?"

"You're more than welcome to come, too," Owen said. "It's a brand-new season." He turned to his mother. "What about you, Mom?"

Ruth looked as if her mind had been elsewhere. "What about me?"

"Want to go to Cincinnati? See the Reds?" Jeb Stuart said. "We're all going."

Ruth shook her head. "I don't think so. I had my fill of baseball when Owen and his brother were Little Leaguers. You go, Owen." Ruth looked pointedly at Emily. "Take the youngsters. I'll dog-sit."

A candy striper showed up in the doorway with a tray of food. She stood behind Riley, not sure how to get through the visitors to deliver the tray.

Owen smiled. "This place is as crowded as the Marx Brothers' stateroom."

Jeb Stuart furrowed his brow. "Who are the Marx Brothers?"

His question drew all the eyes in the room to him. "Geeze, dude," Riley said, "Don't you know anything?"

Jeb Stuart endured the stares, then said, "Can't somebody just answer my question?"

Owen eyed the remote. "No. It'll be a lot more fun showing you. In fact, I'm looking forward to it."